San Diego
STOKERCON
2024

Edited by

Cynthia Pelayo

StokerCon® 2024 Souvenir Anthology: San Diego

Print ISBN: 978-1-957918-02-0
First Edition: May 2024

Edited by Cynthia Pelayo
Book Design by Todd Keisling | Dullington Design Co.
Art direction by Cynthia Pelayo & Todd Keisling
StokerCon® 2024 Logo by Gabrielle Faust
Illustrations by Cassie Daley, Red Lagoe, Don Noble, & Chris Panatier

Published by Burial Day Books, LLC.
Chicago, Illinois
www.BurialDay.com

TABLE OF CONTENTS

IN MEMORIAM

RICHARD (DIRRANE) BOWES

FRED DAVIS CHAPELL

JOHN R. (RICHARD) DOUGLAS

DAVID A. (ALLEN) DRAKE

WILLIAM FRIEDKIN

RAY GARTON

HERBERT GOLD

TOM JOHNSON (THOMAS P. JOHNSON)

RICK LAI

BRIAN LUMLEY

L. (LEONARD) H. (HUGH) MAYNARD

DEREK (ELLISTON MICHAEL) MALCOLM

JAMES A. MOORE

WESTON OCHSE

K.M. PEYTON (KATHLEEN WENDY HERALD PEYTON)

MARK (F.) SAMUELS

DAVID J. (JOHN) SKAL

TIM (EDWARD) UNDERWOOD

ABOUT THE HORROR WRITERS ASSOCIATION

The Horror Writers Association (HWA) is a nonprofit organization of writers and publishing professionals around the world, dedicated to promoting dark literature and the interests of those who write it. Founded in the late 1980s, it now has close to 2000 members around the world and is the oldest and most respected professional organization for creators of horror fiction. The HWA encourages public interest in and appreciation of horror and dark fantasy literature and hosts an annual professional conference, StokerCon. HWA is also dedicated to recognizing and promoting diversity in the horror genre and practices a strict anti-harassment policy at all of its events. Please direct any questions regarding these awards to the Vice President of HWA. For more information about the Horror Writers Association, please visit https://horror.org/. For more information about the Bram Stoker Awards® and our other awards, please visit https://www.thebramstokerawards.com.

HWA ANTI-HARASSMENT POLICY

he Horror Writers Association (HWA) is dedicated to providing a harassment-free experience for everyone, regardless of gender, gender identity and expression, sexual orientation, disability, physical appearance, body size, race, age or religion.

We do not tolerate harassment of our members or others in any form, including but not limited to any and all of our events, both in person, and online, and also on our social media platforms.

REPERCUSSIONS

Attendees and users violating these rules may be sanctioned or expelled from the convention or the organization without a refund at the discretion of the chairs and/or Board of Trustees.

REPORTING HARASSMENT

As evidenced by our anti-harassment policy, we at StokerCon take any type of harassment at conventions seriously. To that end we would like to announce the process for reporting harassment.

All of the StokerCon staff and volunteers will be identifiable by their specially-marked badges. Each volunteer will be briefed before the con begins on StokerCon's anti-harassment policy and on how to handle reporting. If anyone sees or experiences an instance of harassment, they can bring their complaint to a volunteer or event staff.

Additionally, we have created an email address specifically for this issue. That address is complaint@stokercon.com. Anyone who sees or experiences harassment can, if they aren't comfortable speaking to someone in person, file their complaint through that email address.

All complaints will be immediately brought to the Convention Chair(s). They will then follow-up with any needed communication or investigation. If they determine that a formal investigation is called for, they will follow the procedure outlined below.

As said, we take this topic very seriously and want to ensure that everyone who attends StokerCon has a great time free from any type of harassment.

FORMAL INVESTIGATION OF COMPLAINTS

Using guidelines set forth by the U.S. Equal Opportunity Employment Commission (at https://www.eeoc.gov/policy/docs/harassment.html) and procedures established for use by other non-profit organizations, HWA/StokerCon's procedure for investigation of harassment complaints is as follows:

1. **REPORT** – Reports of harassment that occurred at one of HWA's StokerCon events should be made to complaint@stokercon.com. The initial report should include the date and location of the incident(s), contact information for any witnesses, and as much detail as possible.

2. **CONFIDENTIALITY AND PROTECTION FROM RETALIATION** – HWA/StokerCon will protect the

confidentiality of harassment allegations to the extent possible. HWA cannot guarantee complete confidentiality, since it cannot conduct an effective investigation without revealing certain information to the alleged harasser (the respondent) and potential witnesses. However, information about the allegation of harassment will be shared only with those who need to know about it. Records relating to harassment complaints will be kept confidential on the same basis. HWA/StokerCon will also work to protect complainants against retaliation.

3. DETERMINING IF AN INVESTIGATION IS NEEDED – As soon as HWA/StokerCon learns about alleged harassment, it will determine whether a detailed fact-finding investigation is necessary. For example, if the alleged harasser does not deny the accusation, there would be no need to interview witnesses, and HWA/StokerCon could immediately determine appropriate corrective action.

4. INVESTIGATION PROCEDURE – If a fact-finding investigation is determined to be necessary, HWA's management or administrator will conduct the investigation as soon as possible. The investigation will objectively gather and consider the relevant facts. When detailed fact-finding is necessary, the investigator(s) will interview the complainant, the alleged harasser, and third parties who could reasonably be expected to have relevant information. Information relating to the personal lives of the parties outside the workplace would be relevant only in unusual circumstances.

5. CONDUCTING INTERVIEWS – The following are examples of questions that may be appropriate to ask the parties and potential witnesses. Any actual investigation must be tailored to the particular facts.

Questions to Ask the Complainant

- Who, what, when, where, and how: Who committed the alleged harassment? What exactly occurred or was said? When did it occur and is it still ongoing? Where did it occur? How often did it occur? How did it affect you?
- How did you react? What response did you make when the incident(s) occurred or afterwards?
- How did the harassment affect you? Has your career been affected in any way?
- Are there any persons who have relevant information? Was anyone present when the alleged harassment occurred? Did you tell anyone about it? Did anyone see you immediately after episodes of alleged harassment?
- Did the person who harassed you harass anyone else? Do you know whether anyone complained about harassment by that person?
- Are there any notes, physical evidence, or other documentation regarding the incident(s)?
- How would you like to see the situation resolved?
- Do you know of any other relevant information?

Questions to Ask the Alleged Harasser

- What is your response to the allegations?
- If the harasser claims that the allegations are false, ask why the complainant might lie.
- Are there any persons who have relevant information?
- Are there any notes, physical evidence, or other documentation regarding the incident(s)?
- Do you know of any other relevant information?

Questions to Ask Third Parties

- What did you see or hear? When did this occur? Describe the alleged harasser's behavior toward the complainant and toward others in the workplace.

- What did the complainant tell you? When did s/he tell you this?
- Do you know of any other relevant information?
- Are there other persons who have relevant information?

6. CREDIBILITY DETERMINATIONS – If there are conflicting versions of relevant events, HWA will have to weigh each party's credibility. Credibility assessments can be critical in determining whether the alleged harassment in fact occurred.

<u>FACTORS TO CONSIDER INCLUDE:</u>

- Inherent plausibility: Is the testimony believable on its face? Does it make sense?
- Demeanor: Did the person seem to be telling the truth or lying?
- Motive to falsify: Did the person have a reason to lie?
- Corroboration: Is there witness testimony (such as testimony by eye-witnesses, people who saw the person soon after the alleged incidents, or people who discussed the incidents with him or her at around the time that they occurred) or physical evidence (such as written documentation) that corroborates the party's testimony?
- Past record: Did the alleged harasser have a history of similar behavior in the past?

7. PREPONDERANCE OF EVIDENCE – In most civil cases/lawsuits as well as administrative hearings, a party must prove its claim or position by a preponderance, defined as a superiority in weight, force, importance, etc. In legal terms, a preponderance of evidence means that a party has shown that its version of facts, causes, damages, or fault is more likely than not the correct version, as in personal injury and breach of contract suits. This standard is the easiest to meet and applies to all civil cases unless otherwise provided by law.

8. REACHING A DETERMINATION – Once all of the evidence is in, interviews are finalized, and credibility issues are resolved, HWA's Board of Trustees will be presented with the evidence, will make a determination as to whether harassment occurred, and determine appropriate action. The parties will be informed of the determination.

9. APPEALING THE DECISION – The complainant or respondent may request a reconsideration of the case in instances where they are dissatisfied with the outcome. The appeal must be made within five (5) calendar days of the date of the written notification of the findings. An appeal must be in writing and specify the basis for the appeal. The original finding is presumed to be reasonable and appropriate based on a preponderance of the evidence. The only grounds for appeal are as follows:

- New information discovered after the investigation that could not have reasonably been available at the time of the investigation and is of a nature that could materially change the outcome;
- Procedural errors within the investigation or resolution process that may have substantially affected the fairness of the process;
- An outcome (findings or sanctions) that was manifestly contrary to the weight of the information presented (i.e., obviously unreasonable and unsupported by the great weight of information).

The HWA Board

CO-CHAIRS MESSAGE

2024 StokerCon Souvenir Book

San Diego conjures images of beaches, palm trees, and surfers. We're famous for everything from fish tacos to craft beer. We are the home base for classic movies like *Top Gun, Anchorman,* and *Attack of the Killer Tomatoes.* While often overshadowed by its glamorous neighbor, Los Angeles, the horror literary scene in San Diego is extensive and accentuated by haunted locales like the Whaley House in Old Town, the historic tallship Star of India in our harbor, and the Hotel Del Coronado with its infamous room 3327.

Few people know that San Diego is also a large hub for biotech, research, academia, and the arts. We were the final home of literary icon Dr. Seuss, and most of his famous works were penned here following World War II. We are a cultural blend unlike any other, nestled in the perfect geographical spot for fabulous weather, artistic endeavors, and of course… magnificent sunsets.

As such, we are thrilled to welcome our horror-minded colleagues to our city for this year's StokerCon. We've heard from many of you that StokerCon is one of your favorite annual cons, and for good reason: there are dealers' tables with books galore, creative films debuting at Final Frame, thought-provoking offerings through Librarian's Day and Ann Radcliffe, deep dives into fascinating topics through Horror University, opportunities to hear from our esteemed Guests of Honor and Lifetime Achievement recipients, and a smorgasbord of panels. And of course, a major highlight of StokerCon is the much-anticipated annual Bram Stoker Awards®, where we gather to celebrate the best of the best in various horror literary forms. There's an opportunity for author readings, book signings, agent pitching, and so much more. This year's conference is also debuting the first annual StokerConcert spearheaded by HWA Executive Director Maxwell Gold.

Speaking of programming, a big thank you to all the attendees for your enthusiasm and creativity in panel suggestions and participation. It was Yeoman's work to squeeze everything into 60+ some panels. We are thrilled with the final program, which we hope showcases the deep diversity, creativity, and passion that makes the horror genre so vibrant and dynamic.

As you can imagine, organizing StokerCon takes many, many people behind the scenes. First, a huge thank you to this year's volunteers for your time and dedication. Extra kudos goes to the many San Diego HWA members who went above and beyond to support StokerCon 2024's preparation: David Agranoff, Brian Asman, Theresa Halvoren, James Jensen, and many others. The extensive support in preparation and planning spanned beyond our city: thank you to Kate Jonez and Brent Kelly for organizing the panels; Kerri-Leigh Grady for the virtual programming; Jonathan Lees for Final Frame; Bridget E. Keown and RJ Joseph for the Ann Radcliffe Academic Conference; Konrad Stump and Ben Rubin for Librarian's Day; Cynthia Pelayo and Todd Keisling for the lovely souvenir book you hold in your hands; our amazing sponsors; and our incredible Guests of Honor, Scholarship recipient and Lifetime Achievement recipients. We are also immensely grateful for the guidance of HWA leadership, including: John Lawson, Lisa Woods, Max Gold, Brian Matthews and Jim Chambers; and last year's chairs, Mike Arnzen, Ben Rubin and Sara Tantlinger. To all else who helped bring this year's StokerCon to life in America's finest city, you have our deepest gratitude.

Last but not least, we want to share a heartfelt thanks to this year's official bookseller, our local independent bookstore Mysterious Galaxy, for being a thriving hub of genre literature in San Diego and a stalwart supporter of horror authors across the country.

There is no other writing community like the horror community. So while Ron Burgundy urges San Diego to "keep it classy," in this community we encourage a little something different. We want you to keep it creepy, keep it weird, and in every way possible, keep it fun.

As you dive into this year's Stokercon, we hope you find inspiration, make new friends, and…

Stay spooky, San Diego!

Your San Diego Co-Chairs,
Dennis K. Crosby, Sarah Faxon, & KC Grifant

STAY CLASSY SAN DIEGO

By James A. Jensen

*W*elcome to "America's Finest City." Just know that only the Chamber of Commerce and tour guides will greet you that way when you visit San Diego. Many of us San Diegans will simply greet you with a short nod and carry on with our day. We're not rude or anything. It's just that we try to take it SOCAL easy and not get all up in anyone's business. So, let's get the nod out of the way and jump into a little background about the city where you will all be haunting for a few days.

Although San Diego is the last city before you hit the border with Mexico, way back in 1542, it was the first place that Europeans set up shop on what would become the West Coast of the US when Juan Rodriguez Cabrillo stabbed a flag in the sand of a fine natural harbor and claimed it for Spain. It got its official moniker several years later when Spanish explorer, Sebastian Vizcaino named the area San Diego de Alcala. This was all news to the native residents of the region, known as the Kumeyaay, who had settled there around 1000 CE However, as colonialism is, men with bigger weapons took over the land and it passed from nation to nation until the United States claimed it under the Treaty of Guadalupe Hidalgo that ended the Mexican-American War in 1848.

OK, enough of dusty history. Let's talk about the San Diego of now. First, nobody here will say that they live in San Diego when talking about where they live. With the San Diego City government listing over 52 individual areas of Community Planning, our city is known by its hundreds of distinct neighborhoods. So, locals are more likely to say they live in Hillcrest, North Park, East Village, OB, PB, South Bay, University City, Mission Valley, La Jolla, El Cajon, etc. Being a port city with great weather, most of us are, like all of the lush greenery you see around town, non-native transplants. However, that's what make us cool, diverse, with some of the best food around. With the San Diego Zoo, Sea World, Balboa Park, LegoLand, surfing, sailing, and shopping, you're going to want to hop on the trolley and spend all of your free time seeing why we locals pay an arm and a leg to live out here.

Thanks to a thriving literary scene, several awesome Indie Bookstores dot those numerous neighborhoods. Indiebound.org lists sixteen Indie bookstores within 50 miles of the center of San Diego. From the nation's oldest, continuously family run Warwick's Books in La Jolla, to the wonderfully quirky mural-covered walls of Verbatim Books or the all things romance selection at Meet Cute Bookshop in North Park, to the area's best Horror selection at Mysterious Galaxy in Point Loma, to the best titles in Latinx, Chicanex, and Indigenous literature at Libelula Books & Co. in Barrio Logan, you would need a separate vacation to be able to hit all of the loaded shelves in San Diego.

Contributing to those bookstore shelves, San Diego has been and still is the home of some of the greatest writers. Raymond Chandler, Theodore Geisel (Dr Seuss), and Anne Rice lived in La Jolla. Frank Baum worked on the *Wizard of Oz* over in Coronado. While staying at the Hotel del Coronado, Richard Matheson typed out what would become "Bid Time Return". Although born across the border in Tijuana, Luis Alberto Urrea grew up and went to school in San Diego and made it the setting of many of his works. If you were hanging out in Tijuana in the Golden Age of Hollywood, you could have rubbed shoulders with Hemingway at the Jai Alai courts. Raymond Feist and Greg Bear are local boys. Tomi Adeyemi, author of the *Children of Blood and Bone* is a San Diego native. And last, but not least, NYT Bestselling author and multi-Bram Stoker Awards® winner, Jonathan Maberry creates mayhem and destruction on the page while staring down at the Pacific Ocean from his perch in Del Mar with his faithful dog, Rosie at his feet.

Although our sun-filled city seems like a paradise, when that blood-red orb dips into the Pacific with one last green flash, dusty spirits rise from the shadows and drift along the warm ocean breezes. Any of you who have watched the numerous Ghost Hunting shows on television have heard of the Whaley House. The 1857 brick structure in Old Town has been featured so many times that its spectral residents should have their own SAG card. Just down the street from there, be careful where you walk when you arrive at the El Campo Santo Historic Cemetery. If you look down on the sidewalk, you may notice the brass markers of those that rest below. Across the bay in Coronado, you'll find the 130-year-old Hotel del Coronado where *Some Like it Hot* was filmed and is said to harbor several resident haunts. Being a harbor town, of course we have ghost ships. The 1863 Star of India sits moored down at the Embarcadero and is said to be home to the spirit of a young stowaway named, John Campbell who fell 100 feet to his death on the wooden deck. Next door is the Berkeley Ferryboat that operated on the San Francisco Bay for 60 years, starting in 1898. It seems it brought some permanent residents along with it when it moved to San Diego.

Our San Diego Chapter of HWA proudly welcomes you to StokerCon 2024. As with all members of the HWA, our local chapter is a mix of veteran writers, newcomers, traditionally published, hybrid and self-published. Whether it's the Weird West stories of KC Grifant, the dark humor of Brian Asman, the Urban Fantasy/Horror of Dennis Crosby, the mind-bending fiction of David Agranoff, the Macabre poetry of Lori R. Lopez, the hilarious zombie lit of Kevin David Anderson, or many of our other talented collection of writers, our vibrant chapter is proud to be a part of the Mothership known as the Horror Writers Association. Along with our sister chapter in LA, the Southern California horror scene is alive/unalive and well. We've got the skills to spread the chills. Yes, it might seem like the sunny Golden State. However, we know where the bodies are buried and about the ones that won't stay buried.

Stay spooky my friends.

J. A. JENSEN has been a member of the San Diego Chapter of the HWA since 2016. He's also a member of the MWA. His work has appeared in such anthologies as, *California Screamin'*, *Sherlock Holmes & the Occult Detectives Vol I*, and *The San Diego Decameron Project*. A bookseller for over 35 years, he is currently working on edits to his debut mystery series, featuring a 4'4" private detective in Northwest Florida. James shares a book-clogged apartment with his patient wife of 30 years, and a rescue Chigi (Corgi/Chihuahua) named Jeeves.

A LETTER FROM THE EXECUTIVE DIRECTOR

By Maxwell I. Gold

*M*any reading this know me as an author and writing colleague, but by the time you read this, I'll have donned a new cap as the Executive Director of the Horror Writers Association. In some form, my role mirrors that of the president, acting as the chief executive and administrator for the organization. I do wear many hats – one of which is acting as a change-agent for the organization.

Change is an inevitability for any organization, and the Horror Writers Association is no stranger to this. I struggled with how to make such an introduction to the membership, but I found more solid footing when I pondered deeper on the idea of the Horror Writers Association. While change itself, in whatever form or action will often force an organization administratively down one path or another, it is the ideas that steer it along a firm course like a ship navigating rough seas.

There is truly no other idea or experiment like the Horror Writers Association, an almost forty-year-old idea to be precise. In a world constantly in flux, an organization founded on the idea of a space dedicated to the horror genre could not be more powerful. To take it one step further, I hope those in attendance at this year's

StokerCon take note that 16% of the current slate of Bram Stoker Award® nominees are international authors. Membership has grown exponentially since 2023, crossing the 2,000-member mark. I hope to see this trend continue. StokerCon itself has also seen a change for the better with stronger partnerships and ties between major educational and nonprofit institutions forged in 2023 as well as increased registrations over the previous years.

All of these indicate that interest in the horror genre is stronger than ever. It is thriving, prepared to haunt bookshelves and rattle brain cells.

This is my first letter as Executive Director, and brevity felt appropriate. I look forward to many more.

And with that said, welcome to StokerCon 2024 San Diego!

WHY?

By L. Marie Wood

hy?

Why do we write?

Why do we get up early and stay up late, go through our day half there and half in a world of our own making where we poke, prod, and noodle over the thing standing quietly in the corner?

Why do we say good morning to this beast, good night as well, and then hello again in the darkness behind our eyelids every night, all the nights, until their story is told?

Why, when we aren't guaranteed that anyone will read it, that if they do, they'll like it, it will resonate, it will impact—why, in the face of all that, do we draft and redraft?

Why, indeed?

Because we have to.

Because the story needs us to, because our characters require it.

Because we have no choice.

Writers write… isn't that what they say? Makes sense, doesn't it? Afterall, what else would we do with the words floating around in our heads, the characters standing in corners, standing behind us, lying beside us, beseeching we flesh them out, craft their worlds, give them life? This isn't a career choice. Indeed, many an author would say that they were compelled to put pen to paper, to type words onto a new page. It's a calling, its importance intrinsic to our very existence – no? Is that grandiose, sweeping, simply too much?

Hmmm…

Consider art in all of its forms – music, canvas, screen, … paper. Does one not listen to music, allow melody and tone to lighten their load, to soothe their souls? Do people not visit with art, spend hours appreciating brushstroke and color for the beauty as much as the honesty? Do movies and television not bring the world to our doorsteps, giving us purview into the joys and pains of life far and away, of life right next door?

So, too, fiction.

Inasmuch as composers, artists, and scriptwriters help to shape our perceptions of the world we share, authors provide similar guidance in the form of embellishment, discussion, and escapism. Authors write their beautiful words, encouraging readers to look at the world differently, commenting on context and challenging constructs, offering new universes to visit—to escape within—when the reality of the tangible world becomes unbearable.

Those who would change the world…that's who we are.

That's what we do.

And we have so many ways to do it, don't we?

Almost 40 subgenres, ranging from the suggestion of the supernatural to in-your-face gore.

Settings so creepy that if one were to happen upon something similar in their real-life travels, they would shy away from it, if not outright bolt.

And then there are the monsters.

Vampire. Zombie. Ghoul. Hag. Kishi. Werehyena. Wendigo. Jorogumo. Antagonists from different cultures, each with powers and properties that make their arcs unique, terrifyingly so. We tell their stories as they may have been told to us at an elder's knee, as they may have come to us in our dreams. We breathe wretched life into them and watch as they worm their way into the psyche of whoever shall read because what other choice do we have?

So, to the question of 'why' I ask, why does a bird fly?

Why does a siren wail?

Why does a great white have to swim all the time, or does an axolotl regenerate its very skin when shorn?

Because it must.

We must.

Because.

L. Marie Wood is a Golden Stake Award-winning author, a MICO Award-winning screenwriter, a two-time Bram Stoker Award® Finalist, a Rhysling nominated poet, and an accomplished essayist. She writes high concept fiction that includes elements of psychological horror, mystery, dark fantasy, thriller, and romance. Wood has won over 50 national and international screenplay and film awards. She is also part of the 2022 Bookfest Book Award winning poetry anthology, *Under Her Skin*. Wood has penned short fiction that has been published in groundbreaking works, including the anthologies *Sycorax's Daughters* and *Slay: Stories of the Vampire Noire*. Her nonfiction has been published in *Nightmare Magazine* and academic textbooks such as the cross-curricular, *Conjuring Worlds: An Afrofuturist Textbook*. Wood is the founder of the Speculative Fiction Academy, an English and Creative Writing professor, a horror scholar, and a frequent contributor to the conversation around the evolution of genre fiction. Learn more about L. Marie Wood at www.lmariewood.com.

THIRD TIME'S THE CHARM!

Hello and goodbye from your StokerCon Souvenir Book Editor

This is the third year I have edited the StokerCon Souvenir Book. It's also my last year editing. I'll still be around, of course. I'll see you at StokerCon next year and the year after that and so on. I've been attending StokerCon since it wasn't even called StokerCon. My first time attending the Bram Stoker Awards® was at the World Horror Convention back in 2011 in Long Island. I was so nervous, but I was invited to sit at the cool kids table way in the back with Douglas Clegg, Sam Weller and Gillian Flynn. I felt so welcomed. I have been a member of the Horror Writers Association since.

I know in creating this souvenir book I'm so swept up in just getting it done, getting the interviews in, the layout, getting it printed and out to the venue, that I have forgotten to enjoy being in the moment. I know one day I'm going to look back and really think fondly about this experience. It's honestly because of this book that I got to meet so many of you and I'm grateful now to call some of you my friend.

We know writing is lonely and isolating. We know as well that the business of writing is unstable at best, chaotic at worst, but we're still here. We are still here writing. Many of us have our stories of failures, rejections, self-doubt, imposter syndrome, more. Many of us wake up, sit at our computer for hours, and it's just us and the page, no one else. This is what we do. This is who we are. Even when life is stressful and difficult, we still turn to the page. We still enjoy being in that moment, in the writing.

If no one has told you lately, I'm proud of you, dear writer. I'm especially grateful that you found us, the Horror Writers Association. Maybe it will help a little to know that you're not alone. Look around you this weekend. You will see your fellow colleagues and many of them are feeling those same feelings that you are feeling. We all understand the life of a writer. We all understand the sacrifices made to live the writer life. Take a deep breath, because again, you're not alone. When you wake up before the sun rises, and you sit at your computer and start tapping at keys know that some of us are doing that very same thing at that same time with you. When you are struggling with the responsibilities outside of your writer life, of being human, know that we understand too. We understand working day jobs, managing kids, and pets, sick family members, job losses, new jobs, transitioning to writing full-time, illnesses, financial struggle, strain, pressures of success and maintaining it and more.

We understand.

We understand why you write horror.

We understand why you're so in love and excited about this genre. And we understand that you're looking forward to seeing where the genre goes in the future.

So thank you for being here. Thank you for letting me be a part of StokerCon for three years in a row editing this book. It's been so hectic and wild, but so much fun! I will remember these moments forever.

Finally, thank you for being a part of HWA.

Eternally grateful for you,
Cynthia "Cina" Pelayo

STOKERCON 2024
GUEST OF HONORS

Justina Ireland

Jonathan Maberry

Rob Savage

Nisi Shawl

Paul Tremblay

JUSTINA IRELAND

JUSTINA IRELAND is the *New York Times* bestselling author of numerous books including *Dread Nation* and its sequel *Deathless Divide, Rust in the Root*, the middle-grade novel *Ophie's Ghosts*, which won the Scott O'Dell award for historical fiction, and a number of Star Wars books including *Lando's Luck, Spark of the Resistance, A Test of Courage, Out of the Shadows*, and *Mission to Disaster*. She is one of the primary story architects of the *Star Wars: The High Republic* multimedia initiative and has also written a number of Marvel comics. In the screenwriting arena, Justina recently co-wrote episode three of Netflix's *The Fall of the House of Usher* and has staffed a number of other TV writers' rooms. She is a former editor in chief of FIYAH Literary Magazine of Black Speculative Fiction, for which she won a World Fantasy Award. She has been shortlisted for the Hugo, Nebula, and Bram Stoker Awards® and she won the Locus award for *Dread Nation*. She holds a BA in History from Georgia Southern and an MFA in Creative Writing from Hamline University. You can find Justina on Instagram as @justina.ireland, at her website <u>justinaireland.com</u>, and you can find her work wherever great books are sold.

JONATHAN MABERRY

JONATHAN MABERRY is a *New York Times* best-seller, five-time Bram Stoker Award®-winner, anthology editor, comic book writer, executive producer, magazine feature writer, playwright, and writing teacher/lecturer. He is the editor of *Weird Tales Magazine* and president of the International Association of Media Tie-in Writers. He is the recipient of the Inkpot Award, three Scribe Awards, and was named one of the *Today's* Top Ten Horror Writers. His books have been sold to more than thirty countries. He writes in several genres including thriller, horror, science fiction, epic fantasy, and mystery; and he writes for adults, middle grade, and young adult. https://www.jonathanmaberry.com/

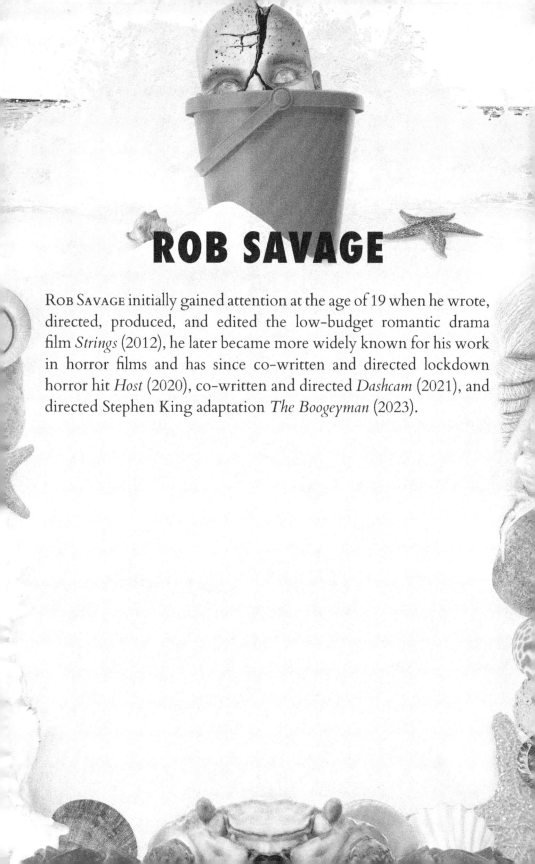

ROB SAVAGE

ROB SAVAGE initially gained attention at the age of 19 when he wrote, directed, produced, and edited the low-budget romantic drama film *Strings* (2012), he later became more widely known for his work in horror films and has since co-written and directed lockdown horror hit *Host* (2020), co-written and directed *Dashcam* (2021), and directed Stephen King adaptation *The Boogeyman* (2023).

NISI SHAWL

NISI SHAWL is the multiple award-winning author, co-author, and editor of over a dozen books of speculative fiction and related nonfiction, including the standard text on diverse representation in literature, *Writing the Other: A Practical Approach*; the Nebula Award finalist novel *Everfair*; the first two volumes of the *New Suns* anthology series; and the short story collection *Filter House*. They've taught and lectured at Duke University, Spelman College, Stanford University, Sarah Lawrence College, and many other learning institutions. Recent titles include a new, horror-adjacent story collection, *Our Fruiting Bodies*; the Middle Grade historical fantasy novel *Speculation*; and *Kinning*, their book-length sequel to *Everfair*, an excerpt of which is available on the Tor/Forge blog. "Sun River" and three other short story sequels to *Everfair* are appearing on the Tor.com site in 2023 and 2024. Their Beat era novella *The Day and Night Books of Mardou Fox* is forthcoming in Fall 2024. http://www.nisishawl.com/

STOKERCON 2024
SAN DIEGO

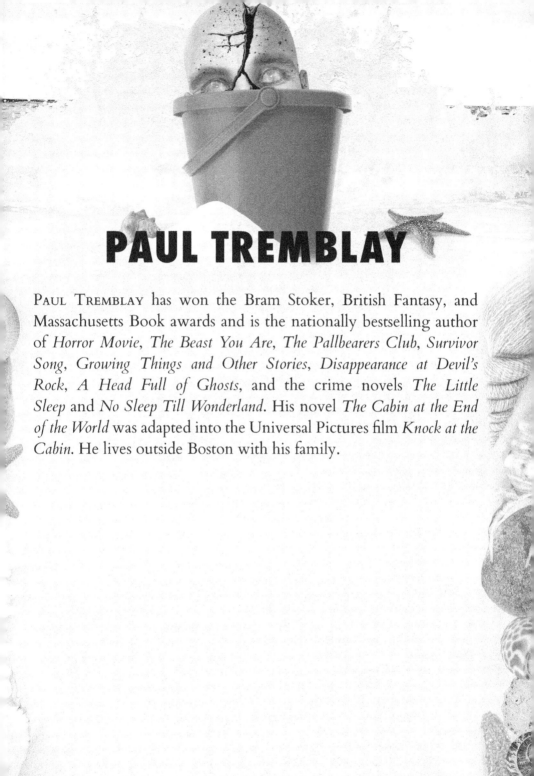

PAUL TREMBLAY

PAUL TREMBLAY has won the Bram Stoker, British Fantasy, and Massachusetts Book awards and is the nationally bestselling author of *Horror Movie*, *The Beast You Are*, *The Pallbearers Club*, *Survivor Song*, *Growing Things and Other Stories*, *Disappearance at Devil's Rock*, *A Head Full of Ghosts*, and the crime novels *The Little Sleep* and *No Sleep Till Wonderland*. His novel *The Cabin at the End of the World* was adapted into the Universal Pictures film *Knock at the Cabin*. He lives outside Boston with his family.

DREAD SOUTH

by Justina Ireland

To the editor of the Savannah Morning News. This letter is in response to your editorial of February 1, 1876, entitled "The Women of the South Have No Need of Self-Defense Arts." In your article you state that the nearly thirteen years since the Undead Rising at the tragic Battle of Gettysburg have led to unprecedented stability and that the Northern system of engaging Negro girl Attendants as protectors should be adopted here in the South. You go on to say that to encourage womenfolk to take up the defense arts would only lead to destabilized families and an increase in spinsters. This, sir, is wrong.

You have neglected fundamental aspects of the system. Many unfortunate families cannot afford to contract Attendants for their daughters. What of these poor girls, endangered by their poverty? Shall we let them be devoured by the undead? And how can the women of the South depend on Negroes to keep us safe? We are not Northerners. We know better the childlike temperament of the colored. Every Southerner knows that Negroes do not have the capacity to reasonably protect themselves or anyone else.... Louisa Aiken, 1876

It was five miles into the city proper from Landsfall, the Aiken family plantation, and Louisa felt every single one of them drag by as she sat in the rider's compartment of the pony with her mother.

Once, they would've traveled to town in a finely appointed carriage, with coachmen and a matched set of four horses. But that was before the restless dead stalked the woods and flatlands, hungry for flesh. Horses were a beacon for the undead creatures and rarely survived the encounter, so instead people traveled in ponies, carriages pulled along by a smoke-belching, steam-powered engine compartment. In the winter, Louisa loved traveling in the pony, when the rider's compartment wasn't nearly so stuffy and insufferable from the Georgia heat. But today her mother generated enough hot air that even August would've been hard pressed to compete.

"Mrs. Helmsley told me that Bradley Winterbrook has already come to call on Rebecca three times. Three! She'll be matched by the end of March, mark my words. Why, I'm sure if you'd just declare your intent for Ashley Ellis, he would've come to call and you'd have a betrothal by now."

Louisa schooled her expression to blankness. Mrs. Aiken had been the most beautiful debutante in her year, way back in 1856, her blond curls and blue eyes and perfect pearlescent skin peerless throughout the Low Country. Now the bloom of her youth and her beauty had faded into something dull and unbelievably sad, like an overblown rose with only a few petals clinging. Louisa shared her mother's looks, a fact her mother frequently brought up whenever Louisa wore a color her mother deemed "unflattering."

At seventeen, Louisa knew her own mind well enough, and her mother's criticisms always put her in a bit of a snit. The only reason Louisa had agreed to accompany her mother into town was the letter to the editor of the local newspaper tucked into her bodice, a letter that Louisa needed to post without her mother's knowledge.

Louisa pulled her attention back to the conversation within the pony. "Mother, the Ellis family's property is nothing but salt marsh. I do not want to live on a salt marsh." It was easier than pointing out the fact that Ashley Ellis had buckteeth and was overfond of groping the servant girls. The last thing she wanted was a husband who was going to put a babe in every colored girl he met.

"Well, what about Everett Hayes? He danced with you twice at the Christmas Cotillion. And he has called on your father about courting you."

"He has?" Louisa fell silent as she thought about Everett. He was the most eligible bachelor in all of Chatham County, and handsome to boot. A few years older than Louisa, he had dark wavy hair, blue eyes, and pale skin that bore the kiss of sunshine. He hadn't just danced twice with her. He'd asked her to step outside with him for a glass of punch, and while they'd been alone he'd told her she was the most beautiful girl at the entire cotillion. The admiration in his eyes had made her heart grow wings.

He hadn't kissed her, of course. That would've been entirely too forward. Even if she was reasonably sure she would have kissed him back.

That being said his attentions hadn't stopped him from dancing with Sophie Parker, a fact that Louisa had been trying to forget even as she nurtured a secret hope that she would see Everett again. It was understandable that she hadn't, though. Travel was dangerous, and as the only son of a shipping magnate, Everett's family preferred he stay inside the safety of the city walls. Those in the city rarely traveled outside of them for fear of the undead.

The pony came to a screeching halt. Louisa fumbled for a handle while her mother yelped in dismay. "Why are we stopping?"

The window between the driver's compartment and the passenger area slid open. A dark face appeared in the space. Herman, the family coachman. "There's a pack of shamblers in the road, ma'am. I'm waiting for them to clear."

"Well, can't you just ram them?" Mrs. Aiken demanded, a quaver in her voice. The undead were a reminder of the trials and travails of the war and the failed attempt at secession. Neither was a subject Louisa's mother liked to think about. The war years had been hard on their family, leaving Mrs. Aiken's brother Louis, for whom Louisa was named, a feral, mindless monster.

Herman shook his head. "There's too many, I'm like to get the wheels mucked up with shambler if I do. Sorry, Miss Alicia. If we're lucky they'll wander off." He slid the window closed, effectively ending the conversation.

Mrs. Aiken flushed and began adjusting the button closures on her gloves. "These damned undead," she swore as she slammed back in her seat. Louisa bit back a smile. On any other occasion her mother would've corrected the help, told them forcefully what to do. But not when the restless dead were involved.

Louisa scooted closer to the window to get a glimpse of the figures moving just beyond the tiny barred window. Louisa could see movement, but it was too far off to discern whether she'd known them or not. It was always quite a scandal when a family got turned. Some part of Louisa secretly hoped she'd see dark-haired Sophie Parker out there, dragging along in her familiar emerald green.

There were a few far-off pops, and the window to the driver's compartment slid open once more. "Looks like the patrol is clearing them out, ma'am. We should be moving in a bit."

"There are Federal troops out there?" Louisa asked.

"No, Miss Louisa, it's the Negro patrol. Well, here we go." The carriage lurched, and they were on their way once more.

Louisa sat back in her seat and grimaced. Negro patrols. No wonder they had had to wait so long. Federal troops would've made sure that the undead never made it to the main road to begin with. But the Federal troops were gone, headed back north thanks to President Rutherford B. Hayes and his Corrupt Bargain.

"This is why you need an Attendant, Louisa," Mrs. Aiken said, fidgeting in her seat. "We both need Attendants. I've heard no self-respecting woman in New York leaves her house without her Attendant. Can you imagine, your own Negro girl to protect you? I'm not sure why the fashion hasn't caught on here. We have more than enough Negroes milling about, shiftless as all get-out."

Louisa's lips twisted, but she said nothing. She shifted in her seat, the letter containing her thoughts crinkling as she moved.

A Negro girl to keep her safe from the undead.

Not if she had any say in the matter.

By the time they pulled into Ellis Square, Louisa was ready to be finished with the whole day, and her mother besides. After a quick stop at the health inspector's to show that they were healthy and untouched by the Undead Plague, the carriage was admitted through the city gate. As soon as the pony stopped, Louisa hurried out as quickly as she could without looking unladylike, which wasn't nearly as fast as she would've liked.

"Louisa, where are you going?" her mother called as Louisa headed down the sidewalk to the post box. Louisa ignored her.

"Louisa!" Mrs. Aiken shrieked, several feet to the rear and not at all ladylike.

Louisa turned toward her mother's call without slowing her pace, which was a mistake. One that sent her hurtling headlong into the arms of Everett Hayes.

"Miss Aiken," he said in surprise, his voice rumbling delightfully as he caught her. A spate of goose bumps sprang up under the sleeves of Louisa's dress, emanating from his hands on her arms, and her breath floundered.

"Mr. Hayes. I am so sorry. Please forgive my clumsiness."

"Already done," he said with a smile, and Louisa's mouth went hopelessly dry. The Hayes family owned a shipping business, and Everett was a skilled sailor in addition to being a gentlemen. He certainly seemed steady on his feet as he gently helped Louisa regain her balance.

"Louisa! You mustn't go rushing off like that—Mr. Hayes! How lovely to see you here in the square."

Louisa stepped back, putting some distance between her pounding heart and Everett's gentle smile. He tipped his hat at Louisa's mother, even though his eyes were still on Louisa.

"It's a welcome surprise," he said.

"What are you about, Mr. Hayes?" Louisa asked, regaining her composure.

"Well, a couple of the boys down at the shipyard got bit and had to be put down, sad to say. So I'm heading over to the market to hire some help."

The market in Ellis Square was well known throughout Georgia. When Louisa was very little, Daddy had taken her to see the Negroes brought in for sale. She didn't remember much about the trip except for the dark faces, their expressions stoic, and the sugar candy her daddy had bought her for being a good girl. But that was long ago, before the War of Northern Aggression and the dead walking, before a single bite could turn a man feral.

Negroes were no longer sold in the market. The Great Concession had ended both slavery and the Confederacy, in exchange for the assistance of Federal troops. So now the market was the place to hire extra help, both colored and white. It was said by some that the labor contracts offered to the whites looking for work were better than the wages offered Negroes, but everyone knew that Negroes were naturally inferior, so no one who mattered made much of a fuss.

Mrs. Aiken smiled and clapped her hands together. "Well, isn't this a happy coincidence. Louisa and I were headed there as well. Perhaps you'd be so kind as to accompany us?" A calculating look gleamed in her mother's eye, and Louisa thought back to the luncheon and Mrs. Aiken's hushed discussion with Mrs. Helmsley.

Louisa's mother was scheming.

Mr. Ellis gave them a smooth bow. "It would be my pleasure, Mrs. Aiken."

Everett held out an arm to each of the ladies and they took them, the trio gliding across the square to a low-slung building with a fresh coat of paint. Mrs. Aiken kept up a lively chatter about the weather while Louisa fumed. She'd been ensnared in one of her mother's plots.

It was a short stroll to the market. Employment agents called out to passersby looking to hire help, creating a cacophony of sound.

"You need a cook? Then you must taste the preparations of Miss Jessie, best cook in the city!"

"Strong men! You need them, and aye! I've got them."

"Don't go anywhere, fine ladies, without an Attendant to see to your safety! Gentlemen, don't you want your womenfolk protected? A faithful Attendant is the thing for you! And here they are, from the finest school in all the states, Miss Preston's School of Combat for Negro Girls, in Baltimore, Maryland!"

Mrs. Aiken stopped suddenly in front of a platform, bringing Everett and Louisa to a halt as well. A short man with a florid face and a frayed stovepipe hat stood in the street, imploring passersby to look at the girls on the platform, to see their prowess and loyalty. The girls didn't look any different than the other Negro girls Louisa had seen, except for the fact that they wore incredibly sharp-looking knives and swords strapped to their bodies. Their eyes were hooded, their hair braided tight to their scalp, and they radiated an air of supreme disinterest in the whole of the goings-on in the square.

"Good sir," Mrs. Aiken called to the small man. "Your girls, they are Attendants?"

The man scuttled over, a wide smile on his face. "Oh, yes'm. Best in all of Georgia, my girls are. More dead have been harvested by these girls than all of the Federal patrols combined! And a fair price too. For one hundred dollars, you can employ one of my girls for a six-month contract."

"A hundred dollars!" Mrs. Aiken exclaimed, her gloved hands fluttering to her face like startled doves. "What exactly does one get for a hundred dollars?" she asked, trying to cover her shock.

"Why, protection, ma'am. What is that worth in these dark times?"

Mrs. Aiken and the small man went back and forth for a moment, but Louisa tuned them out. She was studying the girls, and her gaze was drawn toward one in the back. She didn't wear a dress over pantalets like most of the other Attendants on the platform. Instead, she was dressed like a man: trousers, shirt, waistcoat in a jaunty blue paisley pattern. She wore a belt, low slung on her hips, that looked as though it should carry revolvers but instead carried a pair of short swords, their edges glinting wickedly sharp in the sunlight. The girl's hair was braided in even rows, the braids ending at her shoulder blades.

Louisa's eyes met those of the girl. She tilted her head to the side, openly appraising Louisa. Louisa blinked, taken aback slightly at the colored girl's naked assessment, and when the dark-skinned girl grinned and winked, Louisa gasped audibly, loud enough to distract her mother from her conversation.

"Louisa, what is it, dear?"

"Nothing, Mother."

Louisa busied herself adjusting the ties on her coat to cover the heat rushing to her cheeks. What an impudent Negro! No wonder they were hard pressed to secure employment.

"Personally, I think the idea of Attendants is a good one," Everett interjected, interrupting whatever Louisa's mother had been saying to the barker. "There is nothing quite so important as the safety and security of our womenfolk. Especially our most precious blossoms." He looked straight at Louisa as he said this, and she felt herself flush again.

Everett cleared his throat and turned back to the small man. "Which is why I'm going to give Miss Aiken the gift of an Attendant."

Shock radiated through Louisa's body. "Mr. Hayes ... ," she said, trailing off. Words failed her. The gift of an Attendant? It was much too generous.

Everett took Louisa's hands and smiled down at her. "It isn't jewels or dresses, but your safety is the most precious gift I can give you. If I'm going to court you, the world needs to know that I am going to cherish and protect you."

Something in Louisa's chest shifted, and she felt faint. It was happening so fast, and Mr. Hayes! She'd lain in bed at night and imagined what it would like to be courted by him, but none of her imaginings had included an Attendant. It was strange … and yet perfectly right.

"Mr. Hayes, this is the most generous gift I have ever received."

Everett smiled wide. "Excellent." He moved off with the small man to finalize the paperwork.

"Well, that was fortuitous," Mrs. Aiken said, her finger tapping her chin as she stared off, deep in thought. Louisa glanced over at her mother.

"Why do I suspect that you had something to do with this, Mother?"

"Well, I may have mentioned to Mr. Hayes, when he came to visit your father, how you were in need of an Attendant. Louisa! You realize you're the first woman in Savannah to have one? Hildy Brenner is going to be absolutely flush with jealousy."

Uncertainty settled heavily into Louisa's middle, and suddenly her gift seemed less generous. "You talked Everett into getting me an Attendant?"

"Nonsense, darling! I did no such thing. I made a suggestion, and the boy was bright enough to pick up on it. Trust me, the ability to take a hint is a fine trait in a husband."

The men were returning, a signed document in Everett's hand and a wide smile on the face of the barker. Everett handed the paper to Louisa, while the small man whistled up to the dais. Louisa clutched the paper to her chest. "Mr. Hayes, I'm still not sure how to express my thanks."

"How about by calling me Everett?"

"Of course, and you must call me Louisa."

"Here she is," the small man said, interrupting the moment between Louisa and Everett. Louisa turned. The girl in the trousers was only a few feet away.

"Her?" Louisa said, all of the warmth and happiness from Everett's generosity melting away into irritation. "No, I don't want her. She's highly inappropriate."

The small man laughed nervously. "Oh, you can't judge a package by its wrapper, Miss. Juliet's my best girl and well-mannered despite her odd attire. Your beau there said he wanted my best, and here she is."

Juliet hadn't said a word, but there was an expression on her face like she found this all to be incredibly amusing. She swept into a deep curtsy, her movements fluid like a dancer's. It would've been impressive in a dress but looked strange in trousers. "I'm pleased to make your acquaintance, miss."

Louisa's mother clapped her hands and laughed. "Well, isn't she just a hoot? Louisa darling, you are going to be the talk of the town."

The barker grinned a gap-toothed smile and rubbed his hands together. "Looks like we're all settled."

Louisa looked from Everett's apologetic smile to her mother's satisfied expression to Juliet's smirk and realized with a sinking heart that things were, in fact, quite settled.

It wasn't until they were heading back to the pony, Juliet and Mrs. Aiken's parcels in tow, that Louisa realized that she'd never even mailed her letter.

The girl was completely incorrigible.

It wasn't that she was loud or headstrong or sullen, issues Louisa knew how to handle in Negroes. It was that Juliet was perfectly well behaved, quick to follow a request or to anticipate a need, so that Louisa could find no fault with the girl. But Louisa got the sense Juliet was playing at being the loyal servant, rather than serving loyally. It made Louisa nervous, so much that she tried to avoid the girl.

And the girl was everywhere.

No matter what Louisa was about, there was Juliet, a silent shadow, dogging her steps and watching with that half-lidded, slightly bemused expression.

The only upside to Juliet's constant presence was Everett. He stopped by once a week, sometimes twice if the roads were passable. The undead were always out and about, but as the weather warmed to spring, the creatures became even more prevalent, cluttering roads and making travel nigh on impossible. Everett's visits were chaperoned by Mrs. Aiken and Juliet, although Louisa wanted nothing more than to be alone with Everett—a completely scandalous thought, and one she did not share with anyone.

The first week in April, Everett came to call upon Louisa while Mrs. Aiken was away visiting friends. He walked in carrying a large wicker basket and wearing a smile that had Louisa setting aside her needlepoint and climbing to her feet.

"Louisa! Your father said I could find you in here. I was wondering if you'd do me the honor of accompanying me on a picnic?"

"Of course! It would be a pleasure," Louisa said, smiling up at him. Thanks to his frequent visits, Everett looked completely at ease in the Aiken family drawing room, and Louisa realized that their courtship was going quite well. At this rate, she would be married by fall. The thought brought a strange combination of joy and terror. Louisa pushed it down so that she didn't have to examine the emotion too closely.

"You look beautiful," Everett said, offering his free arm to Louisa. She was wearing a pale green silk that she'd felt undecided about, and Everett's compliment settled her mind that it was a good dress.

Louisa took Everett's arm, and the two of them went out to the Aikens' picnic pavilion, located a short distance from the house. Juliet followed along closely behind, saying nothing, and Louisa found herself irritated at the extra company. She'd thought through a hundred different ways to politely tell Everett that after nearly three months of an Attendant, she didn't wish to have the girl around any longer. But no matter how she tried to parse it out, it just sounded ungrateful, and the last thing Louisa wanted was to have her future husband think her petty.

They were nearly to the picnic pavilion, a short walk across the grounds of Landsfall, when a bloodcurdling scream came from the fields. Louisa turned to see Negroes running from the tobacco fields back to the shotgun houses in the rear of the property. She stared openmouthed as Everett grabbed the arm of a colored woman fleeing past them.

"What is going on?" he demanded, and the woman flinched as though he'd hit her.

"Begging your pardon, sir, but there's shamblers in the fields. The back fence has gone down, and shamblers are all over the place."

Juliet stepped up, her half smile replaced by a steely expression. "Where?"

The woman pointed back behind her before hurrying off. Sure enough, undead were lumbering through the fields, their swaying walk distinctive.

Juliet turned to Everett. "Please escort Miss Louisa to the pavilion, Mr. Everett."

Everett nodded. He was whiter than a christening gown, and when he laid a hand on Louisa's arm to guide her to the nearby pavilion, she detected a tremble. Louisa wasn't quite as scared, but most of her experience with the undead was from a safe distance. God only knew what Everett had been through.

Juliet took long strides toward the tobacco fields. The plants were still small, little more than seedlings, really, and Juliet was careful to step between the rows as she moved toward the undead. From her perch in the pavilion Louisa counted ten shamblers, and for a moment she felt a pang of fear for Juliet. How could she possibly take down so many of them? Walter Mattias, an old man who'd fought in the war, often told the story of the day his unit was overwhelmed by the undead. "If your odds are more than five to one, I guarantee those shamblers will be dining on your flesh. Trust me, boys, you see more than three and you're by your lonesome, you'd best turn tail. No shame in knowing when you're outmatched."

But now, here was that fool girl Juliet walking out into a field with ten—no! Eleven, twelve shamblers, all focused on devouring her.

Louisa sighed. Well, at least she would be finally rid of the girl.

Juliet drew the gleaming swords from their holsters. There was a moment of hesitation, and then she sprang into action.

The short sword whistled through the air in an arc, catching sunlight for a moment before it detached the head of the first undead. Louisa gasped. She'd seen shamblers put down, but she'd never seen it happen so quickly, so effectively. She didn't have time to even consider the creature's end before Juliet was on to the next one, those shining swords detaching another head, silencing the moans and groans of another undead. Juliet moved through the pack with deadly efficiency, her movements fluid, the entire act a rapid dance that left Juliet grinning wide and smeared with the black blood of the undead.

Walter Mattias was wrong. Juliet had just put down twelve shamblers in the space of a few heartbeats, and she barely looked fatigued. The girl was more than competent. She was a master.

Next to her, Everett was saying something inane about Juliet being worth her mettle. From the direction of the house came the Aiken family patrol, led by their overseer, Gregory, a blustering white man with a florid complexion and a limp from the war. All of it was secondary to Juliet standing in the tobacco field, a wide grin on her face, an angel of true death with two gleaming swords.

Something fundamental tilted in Louisa, as though she was seeing reality for the first time. This was what it meant to be a woman of the world. To know how to handle oneself and be endlessly prepared. It wasn't a husband Louisa needed; her mother was wrong as usual. It was this, the ability to defend herself against the undead. A skill she'd been denied in her endless trainings to be a good wife. Now she understood. The defense arts were everything she'd wanted.

And the girl Juliet was going to be the one to give them to her.

Once Everett had been sent on his way, a handful of houseboys accompanying him to ensure he got home safely, Louisa found Juliet outside near the well, hauling up buckets of water and dumping them over her head. For a moment Louisa paused, a curious warmth shifting low in her middle. There was something…appealing… about the way Juliet looked soaking wet, water running over her dark skin, the black blood of the undead rinsing away.

Louisa grabbed the feeling and shoved it down violently. She'd heard stories of men, and women, who developed affections for Negroes, and she had no desire to do the same. Down that path lay ruin, and that was not for Louisa. She was respectable.

Mostly.

"I want you to teach me how to do that."

Juliet paused, the bucket waist-high. "Dumping water over your head? I reckon you just pick up the bucket and dump it, miss."

"No, fighting the undead. Killing them."

Juliet laughed, a surprised bark of sound. "You don't want that, miss. Isn't proper."

"I do want that," Louisa said, and something in her voice caused Juliet to pause, to stare at her intently.

"Teaching you how to kill the dead isn't in the contract."

Louisa took a deep breath and let it out slowly. That wasn't a no. "How about I double your contract fee, give you another hundred dollars if you teach me the self-defense arts between now and when your duties are complete."

"Six months isn't enough time. I went to combat school for three years."

Louisa felt that thing, that nameless desire, begin to slip away from her grasp. "But you can teach me something in that time, right?"

Juliet stood, considering. "Yep, surely something. But a hundred dollars' worth of something? The last thing I need is some agent of the court chasing me down because I stole from some white woman. No, miss, I don't need that at all."

"I promise that won't happen."

Juliet's mouth twisted into an ugly smile. Louisa realized Juliet was talking from experience, not a hypothetical. Louisa felt trapped, and she threw up her hands in exasperation. "I'll have my father negotiate a new contract with your agent."

"That man charges me thirty percent of each contract, so make it a hundred thirty dollars, and you got a deal. Now, if you don't mind, miss, I need to finish getting tidied up. And you need to get inside where it's safe."

Louisa nodded and moved away, toward the house. From the nearby fields came the shouts and calls of the Landsfall patrol clearing out the undead Juliet hadn't put down.

Louisa had convinced Juliet to teach her the self-defense arts. Now she just had to convince her father it was a good idea.

Two weeks later, after much cajoling and begging and even the threat of tears, Louisa's father relented and agreed to pay Juliet to train Louisa in defense.

Mrs. Aiken was quite against the idea, but the thought of undead walking Landsfall sent her to bed with a bad case of the vapors every time it was mentioned, so her objections were easily overlooked.

Louisa had not thought much on self-defense arts beyond knowing it was something she didn't have and therefore wanted. The hunger burned deep inside of her, and if it had not been for Juliet's actions the day of the picnic, that need might have gone on slumbering. But watching Juliet move, seeing her confidence, made Louisa acutely aware of her shortcomings.

Deficiencies she was determined to correct.

They worked from sunup until it was time for dinner. Juliet explained how to hold the short swords, and then watched as Louisa swung one sword to and fro. For her part, Louisa didn't complain. She'd fought hard to be allowed to train with Juliet, and she was afraid that if she said anything about her tired arms or the perspiration pooling under her corset, Juliet would stop showing her the finer points of self-defense.

As Louisa worked with Juliet, her arms became stronger and her corset looser, since loosening the ties allowed her to accomplish more of the drills that Juliet assigned. Working so closely with Juliet gave Louisa a new appreciation for her Attendant. And as Juliet taught her how to hold the swords and move with them, Louisa began to ask questions.

"Juliet, where are you from?"

"Juliet, do you have any family?"

"Juliet, where did you learn how to kill the undead?"

Louisa probed until she had the whole of Juliet's life story: born on a small plantation outside Charlotte, then to Baltimore with her mother in search of her father after the war, and eventually a student at Miss Preston's School of Combat for Negro Girls.

"I figured, if the dead were always going to be trying to kill me, I might as well kill them right back," Juliet said, a laugh in her voice. She reached out and moved Louisa's hands on the swords. The brief contact flustered Louisa, but Juliet didn't notice. "Loosen up on the handle, not too tight. You don't want to get tired too quickly. Shamblers are a persistent sort; you want to be able to outlast them."

Louisa adjusted her grip and practiced the swing again, somewhat breathless from both the training and Juliet's touch. "You are completely unlike any other Negro I've met."

Juliet laughed, the sound hollow. "Truth is, I'm just like every single other colored person on this plantation. You just ain't paying attention. Follow through on the motion, don't halt yourself on the back swing," she said, moving past her gentle rebuke so smoothly that it took Louisa a few moments to realize it had even been said.

But the words had been uttered, and Louisa mulled over Juliet's comment that evening and the next day. And every day after that. She started to take closer note of the goings-on around Landsfall, began to notice small things around her. She noticed the dismissive way her father and Everett talked about the Negroes over supper, as though they were lesser just because of an accident of birth. She saw how the colored servants would laugh and smile when they thought whites were not around. She watched how their expressions became guarded whenever Louisa or any of her family entered the room. And she noticed how a couple of the girls smiled at Juliet, a knowing smile that usually followed small touches. It would've been nothing if Louisa hadn't caught Juliet kissing one of the girls passionately before defense practice one morning, a sight that caused Louisa to blush and gave her fevered dreams that left her troubled and out of sorts.

Louisa liked training with Juliet and listening to her talk about her life before Savannah. But it wasn't the only thing she liked.

She began to appreciate entirely too much. Like the way Juliet's arms looked, the muscles straining at the material of her shirt, and how Juliet would smile at her, truly grin, when Louisa managed to complete an especially tricky series of drills. After two months of working with Juliet, Louisa felt like a different person.

A better person.

"I think I'm ready, Juliet," Louisa said one day without preamble as she turned the swords in a move Juliet called "Harvesting wWheat."

"Ready for what?"

"I want to go out and hunt the undead," Louisa said.

A frown crossed Juliet's face, but it was quickly smoothed away. "Louisa, that isn't a good idea."

Louisa let her swords fall to her side. "Why not?"

"Because you're not ready yet. I trained for a year before I even took on my first shambler, and then I still had my teacher watching to make sure I didn't get the fright. The shamblers out there are thick as mosquitoes in July. You go out, untrained and unready, and you won't stand a chance."

"Have you thought maybe I'm just better than you, Juliet?" Louisa harrumphed.

"No, I haven't, Miss Louisa," Juliet said quietly. Louisa sensed that she'd stumbled into something dangerous. It was the first time Juliet had used the honorific in front of her name in months. Her suspicions were confirmed when Juliet said, "I think that's enough for today, Miss Louisa. Mrs. Aiken told me you needed time to prepare for the trip into town."

"What do you mean, a trip into town?"

Juliet shrugged, something Louisa had never seen her do before. "I don't know anything, Miss Louisa. I just do what I'm told."

Louisa stood in the grass, searching for something to say as Juliet took back her swords, checked their edges, holstered them, and went off into the house to attend to her own business.

Louisa wasn't sure why she felt so bad about Juliet's sudden detachment, but she did. She'd done something wrong, something that had upset Juliet. Louisa didn't want her to be cross; she couldn't bear the thought of not seeing Juliet smile down at her. It made her heart clutch painfully to think that something she had done had erased that joy from Juliet's face.

She didn't know how to fix things, and she didn't know why she cared in the first place.

After washing up and donning a fresh dress, Louisa entered the foyer to find Mrs. Aiken barking at the staff as they brought trunks down the stairs. Louisa recognized her own traveling trunk, one that she hadn't used since she was small, sitting among the stacks.

"What's going on?" she asked.

Mrs. Aiken turned around and smiled brightly at Louisa. "This morning Everett came by and asked for your hand in marriage. Engaged before the fall! Oh, Louisa, you will be the envy of all of

Savannah. Less than a year from debut to wedding. Your father has decided we should spend the rest of the summer in town, since it will make the festivities easier. There've been reports of a considerable horde heading our way, so we're going to leave this afternoon."

Louisa tried to take a deep breath, to steady herself. It was all happening so fast. She was to be engaged. And to Everett! But there was a horde coming toward them, and that seemed like a matter of grave consequence. There was also the matter of Landsfall and the staff.

"A horde, Mother? Shouldn't we stay here and secure Landsfall? That many undead doesn't sound good."

Mrs. Aiken waved away Louisa's concern. "That's exactly why we're going to Savannah. We'll be much safer in the city, behind the wall with the patrols." Mrs. Aiken patted Louisa's hand. "Don't worry, we'll have your girl to see to our safety."

Mrs. Aiken moved off and began instructing a few of the men on loading the pony. Louisa tried not to wring her hands in worry, but abandoning Landsfall seemed like a terrible idea. Wouldn't there be more danger from the undead in a closely packed city, regardless of the wall?

Louisa looked over to Juliet, who was talking in a low voice with one of the other colored girls. The girl was visibly upset, and whatever Juliet said calmed her some. Juliet smiled down at the girl and then pulled her in for a hug, and Louisa was surprised by a sharp stab of jealousy. She wanted Juliet to calm her like that, to wrap her strong arms around her and make her feel safe, the same way she had the day the undead broke through the fences of Landsfall.

Juliet released the girl, looking up to meet Louisa's gaze. Juliet raised her eyebrows in question, and it was at that moment Louisa realized she was staring, her hands clenched in fists.

Purposely looking anywhere but at Juliet, Louisa went to prepare herself for the trip to Savannah.

The trip into town was uneventful, despite Louisa's anxiety that the horde would intercept them before they made it into the city. And as the days filled with engagement dinners and wedding planning, Louisa completely forgot about both the rumored horde of undead and her spat with Juliet.

Because there was Everett.

He was solicitous, coming round to the Aiken family townhouse at least twice a day to check on Louisa, to see if there was anything she needed. He brought flowers and a warm smile, and Louisa couldn't help but think she was going to end up married to the best man in the world.

Even so, there was still a niggle of doubt in the back of her mind. It wasn't that she had any other prospects—marrying Everett was really the only acceptable thing she could do with her life. It was that she wanted something more than Everett's perfunctory kisses and gentle touches and a life of wifely duties.

But what?

And every time she asked this question, there was the image of Juliet kissing one of the Landsfall girls out behind the pavilion.

All of these emotions churned through Louisa the day the undead breached the city wall.

It came as a clanging of bells, and at first Louisa thought there was a fire. But the screams and shouts that filtered through the windows from the street quickly made clear that nothing was burning, but the city was in trouble all the same.

Juliet ran to the front door, throwing it wide and looking down the street.

"What is it?" Louisa asked, hurrying to stand next to Juliet.

"Shamblers."

They were everywhere. Men and women ran down the street in wide-eyed panic while the undead lumbered after them, arms reaching out to, more often than not, clutch empty air. The smell was terrible, a sweetly foul rot that overwhelmed and made Louisa gag. A man tripped and fell, the undead swarming him quickly, the echo of his screams fading soon after they fell on him.

But not soon enough.

Juliet closed the door and locked it, moving the huge barricade bar in place. "We need to get you out of the corset, Miss Louisa. You need to be able to breathe if you're going to run."

"What about Mother?" Mrs. Aiken had gone to Mrs. Arsbury's house for a luncheon. She was trapped out there, somewhere.

Juliet shook her head. "Our best bet is to get out of town, head down to Landsfall. Maybe get a boat and double back through one of the marshes... ." Juliet trailed off as she thought, her teeth capturing her full bottom lip and worrying it. Louisa felt a sudden shock as she realized that Juliet was so young, yet so much wiser than she was.

"Why don't you just call me Louisa anymore?" It was a petty thing to bring up at such a time, but she couldn't help it.

Juliet didn't miss a beat, ushering Louisa up the stairs to change. "Because for a moment I forgot you were a white woman, but then you reminded me, and I don't need for that to happen again."

Louisa didn't want to understand what Juliet meant by that, but she did. Training with Juliet had caused her to see Negroes in a different light ... but not nearly enough, it seemed. Louisa knew it wasn't fair for someone as competent as Juliet to be trapped in a position of perpetual servitude, but that was just the way things worked, and it wasn't up to Louisa to change things.

Was it?

Louisa was full of doubts and questions, but it was a terrible time for existential crises. There was a horde quickly overrunning Savannah. It would all have to wait.

Juliet helped Louisa out of her dress and her corset, and helped her dress again in a plainer traveling dress made of cotton. They ran downstairs to find the undead pounding at the door and the windows, the metal bars the only thing keeping out the ravenous creatures. The cook, Dessa, and her two small girls were standing in the foyer, clinging to one another. Juliet went over and whispered something low to Dessa and the girls, who were crying quietly. They settled a bit, nodding at whatever Juliet said.

"Let's hope they haven't found their way down the alley," Juliet said. She paused to hand her swords to Louisa before pulling Mr. Aiken's cavalry sword from the war off the mantel. She tested the edge while Louisa looked.

"What are you doing with Daddy's sword?"

"You need a weapon. Dessa is going to have to mind the girls as we move through town, and you aren't strong enough to take out a shambler with a single-handed weapon. So I get to pretend to be a Confederate for a minute. More's the pity."

Louisa said nothing, and Juliet continued. "I'm taking the lead. Louisa—" Louisa noticed the lack of honorific, and smiled. "You take the rear. We don't put down a shambler unless we have no choice, you hear? The goal is speed, not glory."

"Shouldn't we stay here?" Louisa said, pointing to the undead trying to claw through the windows. "The bars seem to be holding."

"This is the leading edge of the horde, and it's already a hundred deep. Once the bulk of them get here, we'll be trapped. Our chances are better on the move."

Juliet waited, as though she expected Louisa to argue, but Louisa just nodded. "I'm right behind you, then."

Juliet walked toward the back of the townhouse, through the dining room and the kitchen and out into the garden. The yelling, the gunshots, and the rasping growls of the undead filtered in from the front of the house, but the small alley behind the house was quieter and free of undead.

"Shamblers go after noise and movement. There's enough shenanigans on the main road that we should be able to travel for a while," Juliet said.

They navigated the alleys, moving away from the screams and shouts, dashing across the more exposed lanes like frightened rabbits.

Once they burst out of an alley onto a small pod of three bent over a fallen woman, the wet sounds of their feeding loud. Dessa wrapped her arms around the girls while Juliet removed the heads of the undead, sticking the sword through the eye of the fallen woman so that she wouldn't rise again. Louisa watched, swallowing hard when she felt her lunch attempt to come up.

They kept moving, quickly, cautiously, and once they'd gone a few blocks, the sounds faded away to normal city noise. Juliet led the group toward the river and the docks, and once they were in view, it quickly became clear that others had had the same idea.

The docks were in chaos.

People were trying to climb the boats moored to the shore while sailors pushed them away. A few people had jumped into the water to try and swim across the river, heedless of the undead that might be lurking in the depths. A man waded into the river carrying a door, and after placing it on the water he climbed aboard and began to paddle himself across the murky water. People were pushing and yelling, screaming and pleading, and Juliet looked lost as she took in the scene.

"The scare must've started awhile ago," she said, gesturing to the number of people crowding the wharf. "There's no way we'll be able to hitch a ride out of here at this rate."

"Louisa!"

Louisa turned. Everett hurried toward them, his normally healthy skin unnaturally pale. "What are you doing with those swords? Is it true? Is the city lost?"

Louisa nodded. "We need to find a boat out of here, head back to Landsfall. We'll be safe there."

Everett shook his head. "Not likely. The horde came from the south. I'm sorry, Louisa, but Landsfall may be lost."

A calm settled over Louisa. Her childhood home, gone. And what of the people, what of all the men and women and children who worked the plantation, colored and white alike? Were they also gone?

Everett gathered her up in his arms, and Louisa fell into them gratefully. "I'll protect you, my beautiful Louisa. We'll be married and I'll care for you."

"Not if we don't get across that river," Juliet said. "The horde came from the south? Then that explains why everyone is trying to swim across to Carolina. I've got kin there, if you have a boat that can get us to safety."

Everett released Louisa and looked at Juliet, Dessa, and the girls as though he was seeing them for the first time. "Just exactly who do you think you are, speaking to me that way?"

"Everett, Juliet navigated us through a city full of undead. She knows what she's doing," Louisa said, laying a hand on his arm. His face flushed.

"I'm not of the mind to put up with uppity Negroes, regardless of their use. I can protect you now that we're to be married, and these three can be on their way." Everett pushed Louisa behind him and advanced on Juliet, who once again wore the slight smile Louisa had come to know was a self-defense mechanism.

Louisa straightened, anger making her brave. No one was going to treat Juliet poorly. "I'm not going to marry you, Everett."

Everett turned back around. Louisa prepared for an argument.

That was the moment an undead Negro woman launched herself at Everett, tearing into his throat.

Dessa and her girls screamed in unison, a counterpoint to Everett's howls of pain. Louisa watched the spurt of red with wide eyes, her hands going slack and the swords tumbling from her grasp.

Juliet sprang forward, taking off the shambler's head and Everett's as well. She tucked the cavalry sword into one of her holsters and picked up the short swords Louisa had dropped.

"You hear me?" Juliet said, snapping her fingers in front of Louisa's face.

"Yes! I had a shock, I haven't been struck dumb," Louisa snapped. Then she looked down at the ground and her now headless fiancée. Tears filled her eyes. "Oh, poor, stupid Everett. It was probably better this way."

Juliet laughed, and Louisa realized how her words must have sounded. She'd heard that people acted strangely in life or death situations, and she knew that she probably wasn't acting rationally.

But hearing Juliet laugh was such a welcome sound that Louisa found herself reaching out, pulling Juliet close, and planting a kiss right on her smiling lips.

Juliet leaned back in surprise. "Well now, don't start celebrating yet. We've still got to find a way out of town," she said, glancing over her shoulder at Dessa and the girls. None of them were paying attention, since the undead were starting to flood the riverfront.

"We need to run," Juliet said, pointing north along the waterfront. "If the horde came from the south, we might be able to flank them."

They began to run, quickly at first, then more sporadically as the girls developed side cramps. Louisa made the mistake of glancing over her shoulder, only to see people devoured as the horde of undead rushed into them, pinning them between the river and the fallen city. Some people ran north, like them, and others jumped into the river, drowning or swimming for the South Carolina shore.

Once they were out of sight of the undead, Juliet routed them back through the city. It was still madness, but for the most part the horde had skipped the northern part of Savannah, leaving people to evacuate if they could, and flee.

Juliet was unfazed by all of it. Every so often she would cock her head to the side, listening for some far-off sound and then stepping out smartly once again.

They walked for hours, making their way out of the city's north gates, thrown open wide to allow folks to escape, and onto the main road to Charleston with all of the other refugees. After a while on the road, Dessa saw a few of her kin, and a teary reunion stopped all traffic for a moment. She and her girls parted ways with Louisa and Juliet, Dessa taking a penny from around her neck and pressing it into Juliet's hand despite her refusal. In resignation Juliet fastened the penny around her neck, and Louisa watched them go, a hollowness opening up in her middle. Now that the immediate danger was gone, a dark despair settled over her.

Juliet caught sight of Louisa and frowned. "Hey now, what's the matter?"

"I've got no one," Louisa said, the words catching on a sob. "Landsfall is gone. Everett …" Louisa trailed off, Everett's last moments flashing before her eyes. "I'm all alone and wholly unprepared for this."

Juliet sighed and patted Louisa's hand awkwardly. "Aww, let's hush that fuss. You've got me. I'll make sure you get settled up nice in Charleston. And then we'll find a way to see if your family home is still standing."

Louisa hiccuped one last time. "What about California?"

Juliet stopped and crossed her arms. "What about California?"

"I heard you talking about it last week when Dessa asked you what you were planning to do now, once your contract was over." Louisa looked at the other refugees from Savannah walking on either side of the road and lowered her voice. "I want to go with you. I want to be with you." Louisa tried to put all of her feelings into her voice, to express how she hated the idea of being apart from Juliet, no matter whether it was right or not.

Juliet's expression quickly cycled through shock to anger and finally sadness. "You don't deserve to be with me," she said, and continued walking.

Louisa watched her go, her desperation draining away. Juliet was right. Louisa didn't deserve her. Not yet. But that didn't mean she couldn't change.

Running to catch up, Louisa followed after Juliet, down the road to Charleston.

DREAD QUARTER

by Justina Ireland

There was, as everyone knew, nothing of merit beyond the walls of the French Quarter. Hadn't been for a long time, but especially not since the end of the War Between the States.

There were the dead, sure enough. They walked through the Louisiana swamps just like everywhere else, only difference was they tended to bloat a little faster in the bayou. There were also gators and ne'er-do'wells, pick-pockets and slavers and the like, the rough sort that had been cast out of the city or had left on their own accord, chafing against the rules of law and civility. And there were plantations, terrible places where white men lived like kings on the backs of the negroes they owned despite the emancipation. Of course there were things beyond those high, stone walls, beyond the man-made channels and pit traps that the city used to keep out the dead.

Just, nothing worth commenting upon.

Which made it all the more unfortunate that life beyond the walls of the French Quarter was the only thing Katherine Deveraux truly wanted.

"Kate! Stand up straight and let out all of that air. Puffing out your chest like that is only making it harder for Marie to tie that corset. You are fourteen years old. Stop pouting like a child."

"Yes, Maman." Katherine exhaled as much air as she could,

and schooled her expression to blankness to hide the pain of the whalebone and linen digging into her ribs. Maman would never listen to complaints, especially when they came to appearance. Most especially not on the night of the Full Moon Ball. Maman had gotten both her first and her second protector at the Ball. Even though the dead now walked and the world had gone to ruin some things continued unchallenged, and the Full Moon Ball was one of them. An annual event for all those who could afford the entrance fee, it was better known as a place for beautiful light-skinned Negro girls like Katherine to find a protector who would care for them and their family, a white man who wanted a city wife who could occupy him when he came into New Orleans to conduct his business.

Maman had not thought to ask Katherine if she wanted a protector, but Katherine was a good and dutiful daughter and did not argue.

Marie, a sullen Creole girl the same age as Katherine with skin the color of bleached bone, pulled on the lacings once more, cinching them incredibly tight. Katherine saw spots for a moment and placed a shaky hand against the corner of the vanity to steady herself.

She would not complain. She never did.

"That's good enough. Now, where's the dress, Marie?" Maman snapped open her fan and waved it, sending a few of her loose curls to fluttering in the breeze. The windows were open, but the air that came through them was fetid with late September heat and the stink of the far off swamps. Not even a hint of a breeze stirred the air, and Katherine took several shallow breaths until she was steady enough to stand on her own. Her own honey-blond curls were piled on top of her head in a way that made her neck ache, but she tried to ignore it. In a few hours it wouldn't matter. Not the corset, not the ball, not her mother's machinations and definitely not the leering men who would watch her like she was a canape.

None of it mattered because tonight she would finally see what was beyond the walls of the French Quarter.

Tonight was the night she would escape New Orleans.

The music was subpar, the men reeked of sandalwood, and the food was so sparse as to be negligible. Katherine couldn't fit any of it in her belly, anyway. Not with her corset cinched so tight.

But the dancing was absolutely divine.

The floor was larger than any Katherine had ever seen before. The Harvest Ball might be her first real ball, but she'd been to Mardi Gras at San Saint Sebastian, the grand home of the de Talons, the richest Negroes in the Quarter. San Saint Sebastian possessed a lovely parquet dance floor. But the dance floor in the Grand Ballroom here at the Chateau Noir, the finest and most beautiful hotel in all of New Orleans, was at least three times the size of the one at San Saint Sebastian. And no one at the Harvest Ball pretended to decorum like the de Talons had. Here, there were no waltzes or the occasional cakewalk while everyone tittered in delight. Instead, the men and women danced raucous reels, and Katherine found herself lost in the rowdy music, jumping along and laughing, breathless as one man after another asked her to dance.

It nearly made Katherine forget she had somewhere to be at midnight.

"Kate!" Marie called from behind an over large potted palm as Katherine twirled by, propelled by a tall, blond white man with a sparse beard and hands that were overeager.

"Excuse me," Katherine said to her partner, voice low. She flipped open her fan and made a show of waving it. "I'm afraid I need some air."

"Do you mind if I accompany you?" the man said, his hand still fastened tightly to Katherine's. His smile was full and toothsome like a gator. Katherine could see the calculations in the man's eyes, as though even in that moment he was mentally tabulating how much it would cost him to secure her as a plaçee. The thought made her skin crawl, as though spiders had erupted all over her bare arms.

Katherine widened her eyes and gave the man a rueful smile. "Yes. I'm sorry, I simply must find the comfort room."

That gave the man enough pause that he loosened his grip. Katherine deftly disentangled her hand and exited the dance floor, ducking behind the palm and following the whisper of Marie's skirts.

"Over here," Marie called. Katherine turned and ducked down the hall, glancing over her shoulder to ensure she had not been followed. The last thing she needed was an over excited beau as she tried to make her escape.

"Is everything ready?" Katherine asked. It had been Marie who had suggested they leave the Quarter nearly a month ago when they'd discovered Maman was looking to secure a protector for Katherine. Maman had made a good life for herself in plaçage, but it wasn't something that Katherine wanted.

She wanted freedom.

Katherine followed Marie down one corridor and then another, her steps light and her ribs straining against the corset. "Marie, please, slow your pace!"

"It is just around this corner, Kate." Marie kept to her quick steps and Katherine sprinted to keep up, ignoring the darkness eating away at the edges of her vision.

Marie had paused at a set of service doors. They were very far away from the party now, the music inaudible in this part of the hotel. Katherine gasped for air and took in what looked to be an abandoned service entrance.

"Where are we?" she asked, her words breathless. She leaned against the wall and tried to fight against the faint feeling. Her head swam and it was entirely possible that her hasty trek from the ballroom had given her the vapors.

"This entrance backs out onto one of the canals," Marie said. "Just a little further and you'll have your freedom, Kate." There was a tone to Marie's voice that gave Katherine pause.

Marie knocked thrice on the doors and it opened to reveal a couple of rough looking white men. Their beards were unkempt and their eyes gleamed with an unholy light. There was no mistaking these men for anyone respectable.

Katherine took a step back but Marie grabbed her arm and pushed her forward.

The men caught Katherine, clapping a dirty hand over her mouth. She struggled ineffectually while the men exchanged a few words of French with Marie. Finally, whatever argument they'd had ended in them dropping a few golden coins in Marie's hand. She leaned forward with a smile.

"Enjoy your freedom, Kate," she said, before strolling back toward the party.

Despair surged through Katherine. She'd been betrayed.

It was the last thought she had before darkness overwhelmed her.

Katherine woke to a gentle swaying. The world was rocking to and fro, and the motion was enough to make her ill.

She opened her eyes slowly. It was dark out and the only light was a lantern hanging from a prow, marking the way as a man with pale skin slowly applied his pole to the dark water that lay beyond the edges of the boat.

Katherine was outside of the Quarter, but she was also a prisoner.

This revelation alternately shocked and excited her. All of her life she'd listened avidly to stories of the world outside of the Quarter, of stories about far off places like Paris and Philadelphia, impossible places where snow fell and gaslights twinkled.

Here she was, finally free, and she was not free at all.

It was a quandary.

Katherine worked herself into a sitting position and took stock of her surroundings. The boat was wide and flat, the style used in the swamps where the water could be very shallow. She'd thought she was alone in the boat excepting for the oarsman and his co-conspirators. There were three of them, the two men who had bargained with Marie, curse her treachery, and the pole man who piloted the boat through the murky water. But there was also a group of Negro girls next to her, huddled amongst sacks of rice, whispering and crying. Every once in a while they'd cast fearful glances at the knot of men in the prow of the small boat. Only one girl was unafraid. She sat with her back ramrod straight and her bound hands in her lap, her hair a wild halo of curls around her head. Her skin was dark, luminous in the low light, and her eyes glittered when they landed on Katherine.

"Will you cry like these girls?" the girl had a slight accent, as through the English words were unfamiliar on her tongue.

"No," Katherine said. She had been taught to fall back on her manners in times of difficulty, and that was what she did now. "But I cannot see why their tears are so offensive to you."

The girl threw her hands into the air. "Because their tears are wasted. The Laveaus will come for us, and when they do these men will be gutted like fish. This is the Laveaus' swamp, and they don't tolerate slavers," girl said, directing that last bit at the men in the front of the boat.

Katherine frowned. The stories said that Marie Laveau and her daughters had gone missing right after the dead began to walk in 1863. It was rumored that voodoo had numerous spells to animate the dead, and many in the Quarter had blamed the Laveaus and their workings for the undead plague. The Laveaus had fled the city soon after the rumblings turned accusatory and hadn't been heard of since.

"You stupid girl, the Laveaus are a myth," said one of the girls who couldn't stop crying. "You Haitians are so superstitious, believing in your spirits and the like. No one is coming for us. We're doomed."

"If the Laveaus are still alive I'm certain their cursed dead have devoured them by now," said one of the men in the front of the boat, spitting after saying the Laveau name. "Now hush up back there or we'll do it for you."

The girl gave the men a hateful look, but said nothing further. Her split lip indicated that she'd already run afoul of their ready hands and was loathe to do it again.

Katherine scooted over closer to the Haitian girl, since that was the only place there was room. She no longer wore the corset and fine dress she'd donned for the ball, instead it had been switched out for a rough homespun. Katherine felt very naked without the familiar restrictions of the corset, and the Haitian girl must have seen her worried expression, even in the low light.

"Don't worry, they didn't touch you none. I dressed you and got you out of that too tight binding. They wouldn't bother with you anyway, you're worth more to them untouched, especially with your coloring." The girl gave a sidelong look, filled with a familiar envy. "You might even end up a wife, if you're lucky."

"I'd rather end up in the water with the gators," Katherine said, peering over the side of the boat. She was just considering her chances of going over the side and swimming to freedom when the boat lurched.

The girls in the back let out strangled screams, while the men in the boat began to swear in French. The Haitian girl just smiled. "Don't you worry none, it's just the Laveaus."

A hand clamped on the side of the boat and pulled, causing the craft to list to one side. But it wasn't the girl's fabled Laveaus at all.

It was the dead.

The men at the front of the boat sprang into action, grabbing for axes and other bladed weapons, while the creature tried to pull itself into the boat. Katherine threw herself against the opposite side in her panic to get away from the putrid thing. The skin on the hand sloughed off in viscous sheets, and the head that pulled itself above the water line had no eyes, only teeth and dangling gray skin. It made a strange kind of hoarse cry, it's jaw working like it would chew the air if it had to. It struck Katherine that the dead thing was just as sad as it was terrifying.

"Get back, get back," the men shouted, herding the girls toward the high back of the boat. The craft rocked dangerously, and Katherine grabbed for the side in order to steady herself.

A cold, wet, slimy hand locked around her wrist, as another undead creature rose up on the other side of the boat. Katherine couldn't bite back her scream this time, and it shattered the still night.

One of the men backhanded her across the face. The pain shook Katherine free of the terror of the dead, and gave her something else to fear. She managed to pull her wrist free of the dead creature's surprisingly strong grip and scrambled backward to sit with the other girls.

"You stupid girl! You'll bring all of the shamblers in the Pontchartrain down upon us," one of the men said. But it was too late.

The waters around the small boat boiled, the dark mirror of the surface flickering as the dead rose up. Katherine's heart pounded, her pulse thrumming through her ears. She'd never seen the dead, not like this, and as they multiplied, seeming to manifest out of thin air, their attention focused on the boat, fear threatened to swallow her.

She'd wanted freedom, but she'd had no idea what that meant. This, this wasn't anything that anyone could want.

"We need a distraction," one of the men yelled.

The slaver closest to Katherine bent toward her, and Katherine tensed. "No, not that one," the man with the pole said. "She's worth the most."

The slaver took a few steps, reached past Katherine and pulled another Negro girl to her feet.

The girl's eyes went wide. "No, no, please!"

She didn't get a chance to say much more before the slaver

casually pushed her over the side and into the water.

"Oh my god," Katherine said. The horror of watching the girl go over the side of the boat froze her in place, made her dumb and slow. The girl screamed and the dead took her under, but it was Katherine who felt like she was the one drowning, a hundred hands pushing her below black water. She couldn't breathe, and in that moment she wanted to take it all back, to go back to the Quarter and its gilded rot. She would take a protector and squeeze out his babes, hoping like all plaçees did that he would one day marry her and legitimize her. She would grow old in a tiny house, always fearful that she could be tossed to the side with little more than a small payment and a rueful smile. And when she had nowhere else to turn she would work in a brothel, or maybe open her own small parlor. Wasn't that the life her mother wanted for her? Wasn't the life Maman had lived?

Wasn't that life?

"Help me get out of these ropes before we all end up shambler chow," the Haitian girl said, calm and unaffected. A few of the restless dead had moved away from the boat to swarm the panicked girl, her screams now mercifully silenced, but far too many of the creatures were now trying to overtake the boat. Katherine took a deep breath and pushed her fear and terror to the side. She quickly undid the knotted ropes while the slavers tried vainly to fight off the dead, but anyone with a lick of common sense could see that there was no way any of them could survive. The dead numbered in the hundreds, and there was only the three slavers and handful of scared girls.

"Stand back," the Haitian girl murmured, jerking her head toward the other girls, who had huddled in the middle of the boat. Katherine did as she was told. The Haitian girl rolled her neck, then her arms, and then she began to move.

She tested her movements carefully, adjusting for the boat and the way it moved through the water. She lowered her shoulder and elbowed the pole man in the kidneys, sending him over the side with a loud splash, his pole landing in the boat with a loud thwack.

That grabbed the attention of the other two men. The distraction was enough for one of the restless dead to lock their arms around one of the slavers, and he was pulled over, screaming. As he splashed into the inky depths several of the restless dead let go of the boat, moving toward the easier meal thrashing about in the water.

The Haitian girl didn't waste any time. She hooked her foot under the pole, lifting it up into the air and catching it. "Hold on," she said, before using the end to jab the remaining slaver in the mid-section. The man fell backward, setting the boat to rocking, causing several of the girls to whimper in terror. But the Haitian girl used the pole liberally, righting the boat and sending them shooting off into the night.

Some of the dead tried to hang on to the boat, but a few whacks and a liberal use of the pointed end released them for the sidest. The Haitian girl moved the boat forward before turning it to the left, catching a current that pulled them through the swamp and toward goodness knew where.

The girls in the boat now watched the Haitian girl with distrustful looks, a mixture of wariness and hope. Katherine blinked as she tried to process what had just transpired. One moment, she was about to die, now they gently floated through the swamp, while the girl hummed a little under her breath.

"How did you learn to do that?" Katherine asked. The memory of the girl moving through the boat, fluid as a dancer and deadly as a gator, was the only thing she wanted to remember from this night.

The girl looked back at her and grinned. "It's easy enough to learn if you want to. There's schools. Best one is up north, But there's time to think about that later. We need to meet up with the rest of the Laveaus, find you girls somewhere safe to stay."

"Thank you. I'm Katherine by the way," she said, realizing she still didn't know the girl's name.

"Nice to meet you Katherine, I'm Camille. Now, let's get you to freedom."

LETTERS FROM HOME

by Justina Ireland

*S*ue lay in her bed and examined the letter in her hands. She'd swiped it off of Miss Preston's desk earlier in the day on a whim, and now she didn't have a clue what to do with it. She didn't know what it said. She'd never learned to read, and Miss Preston's School of Combat for Negro Girls didn't include reading in the curriculum. Killing the dead? Yes. Learning to set a fine dinner table? Most certainly. But reading?

What Negro girl needed to learn her letters?

But Sue, Big Sue to the rest of the girls at Miss Preston's on account of her size, had seen letters like the one she held. Back when Jane McKeene had been a student she'd always carried letters from home like the one in Sue's hand. Sometimes, she'd read them aloud. Sue liked to listen to Jane read and tell stories about her mama back at Rose Hill. Sue's own mother was long gone, taken by the dead when Sue was too young to remember, and Jane's own mother seemed as good a replacement as any.

Sue was considering asking one of the uppity Northern girls to read the letter for her in the morning when the screaming started.

Sue rolled out of bed of bed, hitting the floor in a low crouch. Her nightshirt tangled around her legs, and the echoing slap of bare feet hitting wood planks filled the room as the rest of the girls did the same as they woke.

"Shamblers," one of them whispered.

"In the school?" another asked with a quaver in her voice.

"Seems like," answered Sue, her voice deep and low. She wasn't known for being chatty, and this really wasn't the time to get into a lengthy dialogue about the likelihood of the dead, known as shamblers because of their lumbering walk, being inside of the combat school. Truth was, Sue knew this was going to happen, sooner or later. The dead always found a way.

When the dead began to walk at the battle of Gettysburg everything had changed, and here on seventeen years later it was the combat schools, decreed by law and enforced by white folks, that were supposed to keep everyone safe. So it was a keen irony indeed that the dead roamed the halls of the very place established to kill them.

Sue was a girl who could appreciate a fine bit of irony.

"What do we do?" asked another girl. Sue didn't know the voice. It was hard to tell what was happening in the gloom of their room, but most of the girls were younger and less experienced than Sue, who was due to graduate any day now.

"We fight," Sue said. "Get dressed, quickly. Boots, bloomers, leggings. Leave off the modesty corset, we ain't got time, and get ready to move. We got to get to the arms room and get our weapons."

The silence erupted in a hurried shuffling as the girls, nearly twenty in all, dressed quickly. Sue ditched her sleep shirt and pulled on a dress and leggings, quickly tying the stays and tucking the letter away for later. The mystery of it pulled at her, and she'd keep it for now.

While the rest of the girls dressed, Sue approached the closed door and pressed her ear to the wood. The mournful howls of the dead grew louder as they drew closer. If the girls didn't move soon there would be no hope of snagging a bladed weapon.

And wasn't a body alive that wanted to face a shambler bare-handed.

Once most of the girls were dressed Sue found the second eldest girl, a light-skinned girl by the name of Sarah. Sarah's people were from up North and Sue didn't much care for her. Sarah was very proud of the fact that her people had been free since the Revolutionary

War, as though that had mattered when it came time to round up Negroes for the combat schools.

"We need to break up into two groups," Sue said.

Sarah sniffed. "You do what you want. I'm going it alone. I'm not going to waste my time trying to herd cats." A look at a couple of the younger girls made her point abundantly clear.

Sue turned back to the other girls, ignoring Sarah. She knew a lost cause when she saw one, and if she had to get everyone to safety herself she would. Folks might think Sue was dumb because she was so big and rarely spoke, but she knew more about fighting the dead than just about anyone else there. She'd learned long ago that the best way to get things done was to just get it done.

"Okay, listen up," she said to the girls huddled up around her. "We need to move fast. Some of those folks out there might be people you know, but you can't let that stop you. You hesitate, you're dead, you hear?" A few of the girls had started to cry, but most of them nodded, their dark faces cast into deep shadow by the light filtering in through the windows.

"Are we going out there?" asked one of the girls.

"Of course we're going out there," Sarah said. "Otherwise we—"

The sound of the dead crashing through the door swallowed the rest of whatever she was about to say and quickly ended the argument.

The undead poured into the room, their anguished moans sending a chill through Sue. For a single heartbeat she was back on her family's farm, hiding in the woods as the dead over ran the house, biting her fist to keep from crying out in fear.

And in the next moment she was reaching for a chair, slamming it into the ground hard enough to pull off the leg. Sue pushed a few of the smaller girls behind her and dashed forward, swinging the club down in a high arc, catching the nearest shambler in the temple. The makeshift weapon staved in the creature's head, and it had barely hit the floor before Sue was on to the next one.

"Stay with me!" Sue yelled as she cleared a path through the dead trying to crowd into the room. Their fingers tangled in Sue's sleeves and her skirt, their grasping hands and gaping mouths desperate for a taste of her.

Sue was determined that they would stay hungry.

"On your left," came a call, and the shambler nearest to Sue fell to the ground, his body cleaved in half diagonally from shoulder to hip by a scythe. The woman holding the weapon drew up short, halting the swing that would've next come for Sue's own neck. "Susan, very good improvisation," the woman said.

"Thank you, Miss Duncan," said Sue. "You got another one of those?"

The woman tossed the scythe to Sue, who caught it easily, dropping the club. "Take this one. There might be another, but we would be hard-pressed to get to the armory. The dead are thick in the building, and Miss Preston is gone, and along with her the keys to the armory. Our best bet is to see if we can get to the weapons shed outdoors. Clear a path for us to work, dear?"

"Yes, ma'am." Sue turned, swinging the scythe and clearing the dead. There was something satisfying about the way a head separated from a body, the skin tearing, the vertebrate parting. Sue was no stranger to killing the dead and it wasn't work that she sought out. But when it did present itself she was of a mind to take pride in the task.

It was something her mama would've wanted.

Sue made her way out of the room and down toward the end of the hall, swinging the scythe in a wide arc. She was tall and her reach was long, and in no time her hands were covered in the black, sticky blood of the dead and the hall was mostly clear.

The girls came out of their sleeping quarters, some sobbing, others looking around warily, and Miss Duncan adjusted her weaponry. "Girls, those of you who have passed your first practicum, come get a weapon." Even though she'd handed Sue the scythe, the handle long and smooth and the curved blade wicked sharp, Miss Duncan still had an arsenal strapped to her body. Sickles, several knives, two six shooters, a rifle, and two swords. Just the sight of her made Sue grin. Things were starting to look up.

"What's the plan, Miss Duncan?" Sarah asked, taking one of the swords.

"Out of the house, head for the city. The rail line will help us navigate our way to Baltimore," Miss Duncan said, handing weapons to the girls strong enough and experienced enough to wield them.

There weren't nearly enough girls or weapons.

"Where's everyone else?" one of the girls, a first year girl Sue didn't recognize, asked.

Miss Duncan cleared her throat. "Let's keep moving. And let's avoid the south end of the building."

It was answer enough. The dead were merciless.

Sue took up the lead without anyone asking. She was eldest, lead girl now that all the others were gone. First Jane McKeene and Katherine Deveraux, gone after getting hired out at the Mayor's house, and now nearly half the school. She should be sad, but the restless dead didn't leave much space for regrets, not when Sue was much more worried about surviving the night.

Their motley crew, most completely unarmed and little more than children, made their way down the hallway and through the kitchen. But when Sue made to open the door, she hesitated. From the other side of the door came a scrabbling and a chorus of moans that seemed like more than the handful of dead that had been in the hallway. The dead on the other side of the door pushed against it, and the wood groaned from their weight.

It wouldn't hold for long.

"Miss Duncan, we got to go back the other way. Through the windows in the sleeping quarters." Sue stood before the door, and a powerful fear took hold of her. She gripped the scythe so hard that her hand ached. This was no usual pack of dead, lost and opportunistic. This was something more, and Sue had a feeling that if they were to open the door, their end would be written in the gnashing of teeth and their lifeblood spilled upon the fine wood of the hallway.

"Understood, Sue. Let's backtrack, ladies. Back toward the

sleeping quarters," Miss Duncan said, turning and ushering girls back the way they'd come.

That should have been the end of it. They should have retraced their steps and headed back to the safety of the bedroom, removing the bars and scampering out to freedom.

But a low, echoing growl came down the hallway. There, blocking their forward progress, was the headmistress, Miss Preston. Miss Preston had been a massive woman in life, and in death she was just as imposing. Her pale skin caught the small bit of light that filtered in from the windows, the moonlight reflecting off of her teeth. The front of the woman's nightshirt was stained with blood, testifying that she, too, had been caught unawares. But beyond being obviously dead there was something fundamentally wrong with Miss Preston. It took Sue a moment to realize what she was seeing, but once she did a powerful revulsion rippled through her, leaving nausea in its wake.

Half of Miss Preston's face was missing, the skull picked clean.

Behind Miss Preston were the girls from the other room down the hall. Sue backpedaled at seeing so many of her friends, their steps uneven and awkward, a shambler's low moan coming out of their mouths.

But there was no time to panic. They were caught between the proverbial rock and a hard place.

"This way," came a small voice, and Sue looked to see Ruthie, the youngest girl at Miss Preston's, waving them toward a side door propped open with just her foot. She held an overly large knife and the thick black blood of the dead coated her nightclothes. "We can go out through the French doors."

"Go," Sue said, waving the girls without weapons toward little Ruthie.

They didn't need to be told twice. The girls scrambled past Ruthie and out the door, which led to the cellar. Sue didn't know how they'd make it out of that room, but there were few people who knew the layout of Miss Preston's better than Ruthie.

Miss Duncan didn't run, instead she moved forward toward the dead, swinging sickles with a patient and practiced arm. There wasn't enough room for more than one person to work in the hallway, so Sue let Miss Duncan get to work while the rest of the girls hurried past Ruthie.

Sarah had just slipped through the doorway, her expression making it clear that she had no intention of helping, when the wood of the kitchen door gave way at the far end of the hallway, letting in a mass of shamblers from the kitchens.

"Miss Duncan, we gotta move," Sue said, swinging the scythe in a wide arc and backing up towards the door. She took off the head of three of the dead with a single swing, lifting the scythe up and around her head and circling it back around for the new shamblers that appeared in their wake. Beyond them were so many dead, more than Sue had ever seen in her life, and for a moment raw panic threatened to overwhelm her.

They couldn't survive against these odds. They had to run.

Sue grabbed the side door and the back of Miss Duncan's dress as the instructor backed up, trying to keep the dead at arm's length.

"We gotta run, Miss Duncan," Sue said, ducking through the door. Miss Duncan followed, as well as a number of the dead, their grasping hands reaching through the space between the door and the jamb. Sue dropped her scythe and put all of her weight behind closing the door, grunting with effort. Miss Duncan cut the hands off of a few of the dead, removing them from the gap so that Sue could fully close the door.

They'd just managed to get the door shut, lodging a chair under the knob so that the dead would have a harder time following, when screams echoed from the far end of the basement, and the room the lay at the top of another set of stairs.

"If we survive this night it will be a miracle, " Miss Duncan said. She pushed back a few loose tendrils of hair, leaving a smear of shambler blood on her forehead.

Sue ignored Miss Duncan and headed toward the sound of the scream. Now that they were out of the cellar and in the room Sue could see that it was what her friend Jane always called the ballroom. Not that there had ever been any balls at Miss Preston's. But sometimes in the winter they did their combat drills inside when it snowed.

"What happened?" Sue asked as she approached. A few of the girls were crying, and even little Ruthie, who clearly had already been through an ordeal, looked shaken.

"Look," Ruthie said, pointing out to the grass beyond the windows.

Moonlight painted the grounds with silvery light. The ballroom windows didn't have curtains and the glass stretched floor to ceiling, so it was impossible to miss what lay just beyond the glass.

The dead. At least a hundred, maybe more, shambling toward the school.

"I thought Baltimore County was free of the dead?" one of the girls whispered, her voice heavy with disbelief.

"Looks like that ain't true," Sue said. For a moment she bitterly wished her friend Jane were there. Jane would know what to do. Jane always had a plan, no matter what.

But Jane wasn't at Miss Preston's, and it was up to Big Sue to find a way out of the school.

"What do we do?" one of the girls whispered.

"We run," Sue said. She reached down and pulled her dress back, and then up and back around, tying the material up so it wouldn't tangle up in her legs. "Everyone, tie up your skirts like so. All of us with weapons will go first, clear as many dead as we can. The rest of you follow, keeping pace. You fall back, you get left."

"Sue is correct," Miss Duncan said, her jaw set. "The longer we wait, the more the horde will build. We'll run out toward the road and set a course away from Baltimore. If there are this many dead here, the city will be surrounded."

A few of the girls sniffled, but the tears from earlier weren't to be found. They could see what was at stake in the weaving, drunken shapes crossing the lawn in the moonlight.

It was time to run for their lives.

"Wedge formation, with the unarmed girls in the center," Miss Duncan said. "Sue, you have the best reach, so you take point. Guide us right to the road. We go quickly, but carefully. Mind your intervals, and remember your training."

A few of the girls nodded, but not much else was said. No one wanted to state the obvious: not all of them would make it across the grass. In fact, none of them might make it across the grass.

The girls tied up their skirts, and once everyone was ready to go Sue turned to Miss Duncan.

"You ready, Miss?"

Miss Duncan nodded. "Lead the way, Sue."

Sue squared her shoulders and held her head high. Then, with much care, she broke the glass and knocked out the loose pieces before vaulting out of the window.

The grass was only a few feet below the sill, so Sue didn't have far to fall. Which was a good thing. The dead scented her immediately, running over, their moans loud and hungry.

Sue didn't give them a chance to reach her.

She began to swing, up and across, trying to separate as many heads from the dead as she could. The key to the scythe was to get the rhythm down. The weapon was meant for clearing, not necessarily killing the dead, although at Sue's height she was able to easily separate heads from bodies.

The dead gathered closer but Sue only focused on the ones directly within her reach, letting the girls to the left and right of her take care of the rest. Sarah was on the left, and Sue saw her swing her sword with ruthless efficacy. Miss Preston's girls were the best at killing the dead, even the hard-headed ones.

For a moment it seemed like things were finally going right, that escaping Miss Preston's would be as easy as just swinging a scythe, but that was before Sarah let out a bloodcurdling scream, and Sue saw her go down.

Later, Sue would remember Sarah's insistence that she wasn't there to herd cats, and that she could get there faster by herself. Sue didn't know what had happened, but one moment Sarah was running along with the rest of the group, and the next she was veering toward the trees, swinging her sword one-handed and abandoning the rest of the girls to the mercy of the dead.

Only, the dead are never so easy to avoid.

Shamblers chased Sarah as she sprinted headlong for the tree line on the edge of the property. The barrier fences there should've kept the dead out, but at some point in the night they'd come down. But it didn't matter.

Halfway to the trees Sarah tripped. And the dead never tolerate such a mistake.

A chorus of dismayed cries went up as the girls watched the dead swarm Sarah, burying her beneath their weight. The sounds of their feeding echoed loudly across the yard, drowning out everything else.

"Keeping swinging," Sue called, her voice rising over all else. There was no time to grieve, to lose heart. They would mourn the loss later. If they survived. "To the road, to the road!"

The other girls took up the call. And inch by inch, foot by foot, they slaughtered the dead, severing necks and clearing the way until they made their way to the edge of the grounds and to the road beyond.

The way was mostly clear, although a few dead stumbled toward them from the direction of Baltimore. Miss Duncan gained the road, little Ruthie behind her. The rest of the girls followed, some of them clinging to knives and revolvers most likely salvaged from the fallen dead.

"Something must have happened in Baltimore," Miss Duncan said in between deep heaving breaths. "We have to stay ahead of the horde. We go South, toward the rail lines. With some luck, there will be a train. Sue, please lead the way. Let's go, girls."

Sue hefted her scythe and made her way to front of the line. As they walked, the letter tucked inside of her shirt crinkled. Sue decided that she quite liked the sound.

It was a good reminder that she was still alive.

HOUSE ON HUMMINGBIRD LANE

By Jonathan Maberry

"When you say 'haunted'…," I began.

The realtor's attempt at a dismissive smile was heroic. A failure, but a valiant try.

"Well," he said, showing a lot of teeth and crinkles at the corners of his eyes, "that's what they say we have to tell people."

"That it's haunted?"

"What? Oh. No, not specifically that, no."

"Then…what?"

He looked past me at the house and then, for no reason, up at the trees. Big oaks that bookended the porch. "It's just that we have to disclose if someone passed here."

"Passed? As in passed away?"

"Yes," he said. The realtor stood there, not looking at me. Fidgeting as if his suit didn't really fit anymore.

"Someone died there?"

"Yes."

"Recently?"

"Not recently, as one might say."

"Which means what? When did someone die here?"

He kept looking anywhere but at me. "Which time?"

"What?"

"Do you mean the one who died last year or the others?"

I stared at him. "Others?"

"It's priced to sell," he said, changing conversational lanes without blinkers. "The comps in the area are two hundred thousand higher."

"How many others?"

"And," he said, leaning close as if we could be overheard by oak trees, crab grass, or untrimmed hedges, "between you and me, I think we can coax the seller down below ask."

"How many people have died in there?" I asked again. I could see his shoulders both tense and slump at the same time. A remarkable feat.

"A few," he said. "Over the years, you understand."

"How many is a few?"

"Since it was built?"

"Yes."

"House was built in 1816."

"Two-hundred and eight years ago," I said. "So, how many people have died here since?"

"Six," he said, and it sounded like that word was pulled from his mouth with pliers.

I stood there, feeling my mouth work but unable to conjure something to say.

"But," said the realtor hastily, "we are talking about an old house. Built in the early 19th century. Times, as you know, have been tough. There have been wars and all that since then."

"In Pennsylvania? Only war that touched this area was the Civil War."

"Well, okay, there's that…but times were still tough. The death toll in the 19th and early 20th centuries was high everywhere. Before modern medicine and all."

I walked past him to the bottom of the short flight of wooden steps that led up to the wide porch. I was surprised he hadn't paid to have the grass trimmed, leaves raked, and shrubs pruned. The place looked abandoned. Not just empty, but literally abandoned—like people fled from it. I put one foot on the first step and glanced over my shoulder at him.

"How did they die?"

"How…?"

"Yes," I said. "Are we talking Manson murders? Old age? Suicide? I mean, what happened to them?"

"All six?"

I'm a moderately nice guy but I wanted to smack him. Not to hurt, just to wake up his neurons and get them firing in some useful way.

"Yes," I said calmly. "All six."

It was entertaining to watch him. It was clear that he regretted ever mentioning the deaths. Realtors in different parts of the country are required to mention if a listing is a death house. They have other names for it, but it's the same thing. People died there. Living people often have issues with that.

I don't, but I was curious as hell. And curious to see how he'd work it out. Telling an ugly truth was a rocky uphill path to making a sale. Especially in today's market.

To make it a bit more of a challenge for him—or a dare to him—I climbed the steps and walked to the front door, forcing him to follow.

He followed.

People walking to the guillotine must have walked like that. I let him catch up while I stood with my hand on the doorknob.

"I have to ask," he said, "but is this a tourist thing?"

"Tourist?"

"Sure. You're not from around here. Where you from? Mexico?"

"Originally Spain," I said. "But that was a pretty long time ago. Been living here in the States for most of my life. Full citizen, not that it should matter. Why? Is it a problem if someone with different skin tone and a bit of an odd accent wants to buy a home around here?"

"Oh, god, no," he said very quickly. "I'm not being racist or anything. No, no, no."

"Okay. Then what…?"

"It's just that we get people who've heard about the house's reputation, and they come sniffing around. That kind of tourist. Rubberneckers. Thrillseekers. Don't know what it is they expect to see. It's not like there are bodies on the floor, but everyone's some kind of amateur ghost hunter. Before we put better locks on all the doors and fixed the window shutters, some teens even broke in and tried to do a frigging séance."

"People are weird," I said.

"And," he said, sighing a bit, "I know that some prospective buyers are chilled off when they know there was a death in a place."

"Deaths," I corrected.

He tried not to give me a hateful look. It looked painful the way he forced his face to remain neutral. He'd need a cream or ointment for that later.

"Deaths," he said. "But, no, I wasn't suggesting you were an illegal immigrant or anything. My cousin's niece married a guy from Mexico."

I only smiled at that.

"So, I gotta ask," he said, eager to repair the conversations. "Are you here because you're legit interested in the property, or because of the ghosts?"

"Bit of both," I admitted.

The realtor stood there, eyes flicking over my face. "Both…?"

"Sure," I said.

"May I ask what that means?"

I kept my hand on the doorknob. In the yard, dark birds huddled among the oak leaves, chattering quietly to each other. Gossiping, the way crows do.

"I am shopping for a house," I said. "I like this area, this neighborhood. The house is the right size. Four bedrooms, three and a half baths. Has a yard. Has a porch here and deck out back. And it's at the end of a cul-de-sac that isn't under active development. No close neighbors. Plenty of quiet for what I do."

"And…what do you do?"

"I write horror stories," I said.

He gave that a three-count. "You're a writer?"

"Yes."

"Ever published anything I would know?"

I named a few of my titles, but there was no recognition on his face. "They're ghost stories?"

"Some of them," I said. "Ghosts, demons, serial killers, vampires. Some mystery and thriller stuff. A bit of everything, really."

People respond to that in a lot of different ways. Some immediately tell me about what they read—Stephen King, Dean Koontz, Mary Shelley. The classics. Most tell me they watch movies more than they read books, but offer some token movie titles as a kind of reach-across-the-aisle bonding thing. Thirty years ago they would name Amityville Horror or Ghost Story or 'Salem's Lot. These days it's American Horror Story or one of the Insidious movies.

He didn't do that.

Instead he asked, "Why?"

"Why what?"

"Why do you write that kind of stuff?"

"Horror?"

"Yeah."

I shrugged. "Better out than in, I suppose."

Around other writers, or dedicated fans of the genre, that answer works. It makes sense. They understand catharsis. Or think they do. They understand personal darkness.

Or think they do.

He didn't know where to go with that, and so switched the topic. "Well, as you mentioned, this is an undeveloped cul-de-sac. Frankly, the reputation of this place scares most people off."

"It spooks them," I said. Weak joke, and it got only a splinter of a smile. Fair enough.

"Point is," he said, "you'll have all the quiet you need or want. Forest behind the yard is state land. Six miles before it even hits a service road. You could set off Fourth of July fireworks and no one would even notice. Closest other house is a quarter mile that way." He jerked a thumb over his shoulder. "And no schools close."

"I don't mind kids," I said.

He nodded. "If you don't mind me asking, are you married? Wife? Kids of your own?"

"No," I said. "I'm a widower."

"Oh. God, I'm so sorry."

"Thanks. It was sudden. And it was a while ago."

The crows in the trees fluttered their wings. I looked at them, and they looked at me. Above us, the sky was a thick dome of gray. It had been raining for days, though not yet today. The sun was only a memory. It was so gloomy you couldn't even cast a shadow. The air smelled of ozone and wet grass and mud.

"You never told me about the people who died here," I said mildly.

From the way his eyes snapped away from mine I knew he had been hoping I'd forgotten.

"There's a website about it," he said. "Local lady who volunteers at the library put it up —god, has to be a zillion years ago now. Mrs. Carmichael. Anne Carmichael. Kind of our unofficial town historian. She knew one of the families who lived here. She knows all the stories. And the legends, I guess. Urban legends. Nothing serious, but kind of creepy-cool around Halloween. I can give you her URL if you want to know all the details. Has everything. Photos. All of that."

"You won't tell me yourself?" I asked.

"I mean, I can, but I don't know all the details. All the dates."

I waited until he realized that he had to give me something.

"The first was way back after the Civil War," he said at last. "Guy named Peter Cabrillo comes home from fighting the Rebs and then staying down south as part of the army overseeing reconstruction. Gets home in 1868 and discovers that while he was away, wifey was having a thing with a local farmer. Cabrillo goes nuts, I guess. Takes his wife and the farmer and chains them in the basement. Does all kind of…well…we don't need to go into that. Like I said, he must have gone batty."

"I seem to recall something about that," I said. "Didn't that guy torture his wife and her lover for weeks? Draining their blood, letting them die from—what's it called? Pernicious anemia?"

He studied me, reappraising everything about our conversation. "Are you messing with me?"

"Pardon?"

"Are you messing with me?" He repeated it, leaning on it. Not loud, not angry, but with evident suspicion. "Are you just here about the stories and all? Is that what this is about? Because if so, I don't appreciate having my time wasted."

"No," I said quickly. "I'm not messing with you."

Rain began to patter on the leaves and the sloped porch roof. It was faint, irregular, and sounded like someone drumming their fingers on a tabletop but without rhythm.

"Then what is this?" he demanded. "I thought you didn't know anything about this place."

"I never said that. You're the one who brought up the haunting and deaths."

"Okay, but then what's all this?" He paused. "Are you doing research for a novel?"

"More or less," I said. "I want to reconnect with the stories, particularly that first one. The wife and the farmer. I read somewhere that the farmer's family did some kind of ritual for him. Cleared the place, I think they call it. Helped the farmer's spirit pass on."

He paused. "There's something like that. They did a ceremony to send them on into the light or some such."

"Not the wife, though," I said, not making it a question. "They did it for the lover but not the cheating wife."

The realtor shook his head. "No. There was no one to do it. The husband skipped town a few steps ahead of a lynch mob."

"Bet they're sorry he slipped away."

"I guess," he said. Then, with barely disguised disgust added, "You're not really looking to buy, are you? You seem more interested in what happened a hundred-and-fifty-some years ago than in the actual house itself."

"Those are not antithetical concepts," I said. "A horror writer buying a haunted house is hardly a newsflash. We all love haunted houses. Haunted ships. Haunted prisons and asylums. Stanley Hotel, Winchester House, Queen Mary, Eastern State Penitentiary. Places like that. A fascination with haunted houses is more or less a professional requirement. Hell, even the trophy they give out for the best horror writing is a haunted house."

He just looked at me.

I said, "This place is remote, quiet, big, pretty, roomy, and haunted. Seriously, what's not to like?"

"Okay…," he said slowly.

"And I would appreciate a tour," I said.

He stood there, debating whether this was a prank or a potential. Then he told me about the other deaths. Inconsequential stuff—consumption, SIDS, old age. Blah blah blah.

Eventually he fished for the keys and let us in.

"I came by yesterday to air the place out," the realtor said as we stepped inside. "Been a while since I showed it."

The foyer was a short run of hallway that opened left into a study lined with empty bookshelves. On the other side of the hall there was a big set of double doors that led to what used to be called a parlor. Enough space for a variety of chairs and sofas, small occasional tables and a piano. It was empty now, with only a faintness of dust caught by whatever cleaning product had been used on the floors.

It smelled old.

I walked across the parlor to the fireplace. It was big; the kind they built in the 19th century to heat a good portion of the downstairs. The hearth was nearly big enough to set up a table and chairs for four-handed whist. Made me wonder if anyone ever played whist anymore. Probably not, at least here in the States. Bridge, poker, gin rummy…hell, even hearts had likely supplanted it.

The mantle was fashioned from a thick eight-by-eight piece of square oak, and I bent to see where screw and nail holes for Christmas stockings had been filled with putty and stained. Faint memories of holidays past. Of joyful times in a death house.

"I wonder if they knew," I murmured.

And I didn't realize I'd said it aloud until the realtor asked, "What's that?"

I half turned, smiling. "The families that lived here. The kids who grew up here. I wonder if they knew what happened here. What happened down in the basement."

"I don't know," he said, and I believed him. "Maybe Mrs. Carmichael would know."

"I look forward to speaking with her," I said. "Maybe she'd like to come for tea."

His expression told me he didn't know if that was a joke or not, or if it meant I was on the hook to buy the place.

He took me on the full tour, sometimes guiding me, sometimes hurrying to catch up when I went my own way. It was a huge old place, built in an age where they had many small rooms instead of an open floor plan. Smarter choices for heat during the long, cold Pennsylvania winters.

When we were finished and standing in the kitchen, he hoisted his hopeful salesman's let's-close-this-deal smile. Lots of teeth. His eyes were a bright blueberry blue, and I wondered how many deals this fellow made in any average year. His car was six years old, his suit jacket showing some pilling, and his shoes needed some quality time with polish and a rag. Having a place like this in his inventory was likely a drag. It had been on the market for years and it carried that bloody reputation.

"I'd like to see the cellar," I said.

His smile flickered but he managed to keep most of it in place. "Nothing much to see. Just a concrete floor and walls."

"Concrete, you say? Place this old I expected hard-packed dirt."

"Oh, they changed that a long time ago. One of the previous owners finished the basement—poured concrete, dry-wall, ceiling leveled and painted. Water heater's pretty new, but there's a guy in town who sells those tankless versions. But right now there's nothing much to see." He paused. "It's a dry cellar, though. No flooding, no leaks, no mold."

"Let's go look at it anyway," I said.

"All that's down there are some tools. Garden rakes, brooms, a rusted old sledgehammer leftover from when they took out the fireplace in the kitchen."

"Just a quick peek."

"Um, sure…"

He produced a key—a heavy Yale—and unlocked the cellar door. The lock was a muscular deadbolt.

"That's a lot of lock for a cellar door," I observed.

"Guess the previous residents didn't want their kids going down there."

"Why not? Rats? Or ghosts?"

His only reply was a fake laugh. He pulled the door open, reached in to flick on the light, and stepped back.

It was clear he did not want to go down first, or maybe at all. I west past him and stood on the top landing. The electric lights bathed the steps in a weak yellow glow. He'd have done better to put in bright LED lights—they make things look clean.

The steps creaked with each footfall, creating a symphony of spooky noises. Cliché haunted house stuff. Some tropes are classics for a reason.

I paused on the bottom step and took a deep breath. He was right, there was no appreciable mold. Just a feeling of old-ness. Not of age, which has a kind of grandeur, but of something that has gotten old and resents it. I've been in a lot of old house, castles, manors, and I've been in church mausoleums, graveyard tombs, and the crypts of kings in various countries. Research for novels is a ticket to experience. Most of my books deal with places where people have died but some memory or energy or residue of them remains.

Then I took that last step down and stood on the concrete floor. It felt so odd.

I had expected dirt. The really packed-in kind that feels like stone but has just the slightest give to it. The concrete was different. Older concrete, like the kind the Romans used, is different. Sure, both old and new versions still have the same basic ingredients—sand, cement, water, and gravel—but the newer stuff lacks…

Life.

That was the word.

The new concrete has about as much life as plastic. It's a substance without any depth. Go stand on concrete poured by the Romans and you can feel the echoes of life. It's like a vibration of sandaled feet marching through time. You can feel the tap and scuff of temple dancers. Sometimes you can all but smell the blood of failed gladiators and Christians dragged off the sandy floor of the coliseum and into the chambers beneath the stands, where they died and were thrown onto carts. Concrete that was, in its way, as alive as the people who poured it, lived upon it, killed and died on it.

Not this.

It was dead. Cold and empty of any kind of energy. I squatted down and ran the pads of my fingers across it in a vague half circle.

Nothing.

"If you're feeling for dampness, you won't find any," said the realtor.

I nodded, not caring to explain what I was feeling for.

I straightened and walked the length of the cellar. It was about a hundred-and-fifty feet long and seventy wide, with a few support pillars. Not stone or brick, but metal ones, added in some recent decade to bear the load of the sagging pile above.

"Empty, like I said."

I nodded. "Except for the tools."

We both looked at them. A dirt rake and a leaf rake stood against the wall. Between them were a maul, a long-handled spade, a sixteen-pound sledgehammer, some lengths of rebar, a few two-by-fours of various lengths, and a push broom. On the floor was a Craftsman claw-hammer than was pitted with rust, and pair of flathead screw drivers. All of them were covered with dust.

"If you want the place," said the realtor, "you can keep that stuff. Some of it's in good shape. Or I can have it hauled out of here."

I ignored the realtor and walked in silence along the east wall, trailing my fingers over the surface of cheap faux walnut paneling. It was securely nailed to the drywall, though one or two panels sagged out at little at the corners. I studied the corners and saw the marks of flat screw drivers or chisels.

"What happened here?" I asked.

"Oh, it wasn't because of a leak in the wall," he said hastily. When he did not elaborate, I prompted for an explanation. With great reluctance, he said, "That was some local kids. They heard that there was some kind of magical symbols on the wall. Satan stuff, but Mrs. Carmichael says it's not."

"Symbols? Are they still there?"

"I…," he began.

"Or did they just cover it over?"

"Doesn't matter," he said quickly. "You can make it a requirement of purchase to have the walls scraped and repainted. Or sealed, which makes more sense. Then the paneling can be fixed and…"

I waved him off. "It's fine."

I took hold of the loose corner of one panel and with a quick pull tore the entire sheet off the wall. There was a groan of distressed wood and some small puffs of dust.

"Whoa!" cried the realtor. "What are you doing?"

The panel fell onto the floor with a soft whumpf. We stood there, staring at the symbol that had been painted on the wall a very long time ago. It was not a pentagram or anything like that. Nothing Christian, either. No crude sketches of a horned devil, no Satan or Baphomet.

Instead it was a piece of art that was quite exotic, especially for a basement of a rural Pennsylvania house built in the 1800s. It was a stylized work, showing a humanoid figure dressed as a hummingbird, with feathers on his head and left leg. He wore a green hummingbird helmet and held a blue snake in one hands and a shield in the other.

"And people think that's some kind of satanic image?" I asked.

"What else could it be?"

"Well, first," I said, "it's not a Christian symbol. Not Jewish or Islamic, either."

"Mrs. Carmichael said it was some kind of Mexican thing, but that's just her. She's a good person, a nice lady, but she's always going on about immigrants and all that."

"That image is a bit older than the troubles at the U.S.-Mexican border," I said.

"You say that like you know what it is?"

"I do. It's a representation of Huītzilōpōchtli."

"Of who?"

"Huītzilōpōchtli was an Aztec god," I said. "God of war and patron god of Mexico."

"Oh," he said with vast disinterest. "Really?"

"Really," I said. "Lots of stories about him. Warriors who died bravely in battle and women who died in childbirth become a part of his retinue. If the ghosts of those warriors served him well, they would be reborn as hummingbirds."

"We have a lot of hummingbirds in these woods," he said. "You saw the crows outside. We get a lot of bats, too. And that's a good thing because they eat mosquitoes."

"Children of Camazotz," I said.

"Who?"

"Camazotz. A bat god in Mesoamerica. Part of the Aztec cosmology, as well as that of other cultures in that region."

"Okay. Weird, but cool." He cocked his head to one side. "This horror novel you're writing, is it about haunted houses or some historical stuff? Mexican stuff…or, I guess, Aztec?"

"Bit of all of that," I admitted.

"So, you did research down in Mexico?"

"I was there, sure."

"Learn anything cool for your book?"

"I did, in fact," I said. "Here's a creepy-cool bit of trivia. Every 52 years, the Nahua people—"

"The who?"

"Nahua. They're a group of the indigenous people of Mexico, El Salvador, Guatemala, Honduras, Nicaragua, and Costa Rica," I explained. "They believed that every fifty-two years the world would end. That's what their legends and prophecies predicted. In order to prevent that apocalypse, the people prayed and performed various blood rituals to give strength to Huītzilōpōchtli. If he received enough blood he would be powerful enough to postpone the end of the world for another fifty-two years. It's an important belief for some. Not for many, but some. Even after all this time."

"That's wild. Would make a cool movie. Or novel I guess." He laughed as if that was funny. I peeled off a small smile. Then he said, "Are you a historian, too?"

"Amateur one," I said, pacing up and down the long cellar. I stopped by the row of tools and picked up the shovel, weighing it in my hands. "If you live long enough you learn all sorts of things."

"Must be more miles than years," said the realtor. "We're about the same age, I think, but I've never been farther away than Philadelphia. Always meant to travel, never really got around to it. But I guess it's not too late."

"Maybe it is," I said, and hit him with the shovel.

He was out for a while.

When he woke, he stood there, shaking his head, lips rubbery, eyes glazed and confused.

"Wh-what…?" he mumbled.

Then he tried to touch his face and his hand jerked to a stop inches away. That was as far as the shackles allowed.

His eyes snapped open and a lot of things became very clear to him all at once.

He was standing.

He was naked.

He was chained to the wall.

I was also naked.

All of that was in the first round of things he noticed.

Then he saw the hole in the floor. The maul, sledgehammer, and shovel lay against the mound of dirt I'd excavated. In the hole was a collection of very old bones. A female skeleton laid out in new and orderly precision. The clothing had all rotted away or been eaten by insects.

The realtor screamed.

I let him.

When he paused for breath, I reminded him that there were no close neighbors. It was a quiet neighborhood. Nicely quiet. Very private.

"What the fuck are you doing?"

"Well," I said, "for what it's worth, I really am a novelist. Written— oh, god, it must be eight or nine hundred novels over the years. Only the last twenty are under my current name. Used a bunch of pen-names, too. Heinrich August Ossenfelder, Gottfried August Bürger, Johann Wolfgang von Goethe, Robert Southey, Sheridan la Fanu, John Polidori. Bunch of others. Not Bram Stoker, though. Ha! I wish."

"But…but…"

"I was once known as Peter Cabrillo. Pedro, really, but my folks called me Peter to blend in a bit when they moved from Mexico to this part of America."

He stared at me with huge eyes. "Peter…Cabrillo?"

"Uh huh."

"Are…are you descended from the guy who…who…"

"The guy who killed his wife here? No. Not descended from." I smiled, and let him sort out the rest.

"So," I said, squatting on the edge of the pit, "here's the story. Remember what I told you about the end of the world? About how the Nahua believed that it was going to end every fifty-two years and Huītzilōpōchtli used blood sacrifices to postpone it another fifty-two years? Well, that wasn't bullshit. That wasn't just an old folk tale. You might say it's been my life story. For…oh, hard to give it a reliable number. Call it four thousand years and change. Long enough. The fifty-two-year thing is a pain in the ass, but someone has to do it. My mother was Coatlicue, Aztec Earth mother who was both creator and destroyer. The conquistadors and their priests desecrated all of her shrines and temples, and that cast her adrift. She faded, leaving only a curse behind. It was Mom who laid that fifty-two-year thing on the world. She saw that her people were being destroyed. Exterminated by the Spaniards. That apocalypse was her revenge."

The realtor kept staring. Tears ran down his face.

"I realized that her dying curse wasn't necessary. Even though the colonizers wiped out my people, our blood survived. If you know what to look for, you can see the Aztec shadow in the eyes of millions of people in Mexico and elsewhere. We didn't die out and I sure as hell don't want our people to die out. That would mean I'd vanish, too. And, just between you and me, friend, I dig being alive. There's soooo much fun to have in this world. Wars, civil unrest, terrorism. Lots of blood spilled and no one's really checking to see what gets done with it."

"You're a…a…a…"

"It begins with a V and rhymes with glampire."

He just gaped at me.

"I know your head hurts but do the math," I said. "House was built in 1816. My wife and her lover died in 1868. It's simple division. 1816 was two-hundred-and-eight years ago. 1868 was one-hundred-fifty-six years ago. This is 2024. Multiples of fifty-two, and the powers that be—the powers invoked by my mother's curse—need their blood sacrifice. And to be frank, I'm a bit peckish, too."

A sob broke from his chest. I kind of felt bad for him. Kind of.

"If it helps any," I said, picking up one of the screw drivers I'd sharpened while he slept, "you get to help save the world. That's pretty cool for a guy who never got further from home than Philadelphia."

He began to scream then.

Didn't help.

No one could hear him.

No one knew.

And the world did not end.

PANATTER

FILMOGRAPHY

By Rob Savage

FEATURE FILMS

Strings
Host
Dashcam
The Boogeyman

SHORT FILMS

Sex Scene
Act
Sit in Silence
Polaroid
Touching from a Distance
Sticks and Stones
Assessment
I Am
Who Killed the Bear?
Valentine
Healey's House
Absence
Dawn of the Deaf
Salt

TELEVISION

True Horror
Britannia
Soulmates

CRUEL SISTAH

By Nisi Shawl

"Y ou and Neville goin out again?"

"I think so. He asked could he call me Thursday after class."

Calliope looked down at her sister's long, straight, silky hair. It fanned out over Calliope's knees and fell almost to the floor, a black river drying up just short of its destined end. "Why don't you let me wash this for you?"

"It takes too long to dry. Just braid it up like you said, okay?"

"Your head all fulla dandruff," Calliope lied. "And ain't you ever heard of a hair dryer? Mary Lockett lent me her portable."

"Mama says those things bad for your hair." Dory shifted uncomfortably on the sofa cushion laid on the hardwood floor where she sat. Dory (short for Dorcas) was the darker-skinned of the two girls, darker by far than their mama or their daddy. "Some kinda throwback," the aunts called her.

Mama doted on Dory's hair, though, acting sometimes as if it was her own. Not too surprising, seeing how good it was. Also, a nervous breakdown eight years back had made Mama completely bald. Alopecia was the doctor's word for it, and there was no cure. So Mama made sure both her daughters took care of their crowning glories. But especially Dory.

"All right, no dryer," Calliope conceded. "We can go out in the back garden and let the sun help dry it. Cause in fact, I was gonna rinse it with rainwater. Save us haulin it inside."

Daddy had installed a flexible hose on the kitchen sink. Calliope wet her sister's hair down with warm jets of water, then massaged in sweet-smelling shampoo. White suds covered the gleaming black masses, gathering out of nowhere like clouds.

Dory stretched her neck and sighed. "That feels nice."

"Nice as when Neville kisses you back there?"

"Ow!"

"Or over here?"

"OW! Callie, what you doin?"

"Sorry. My fingers slipped. Need to trim my nails, hunh? Let's go rinse off."

Blood from the cuts on her neck and ear streaked the shampoo clouds with pink stains. Unaware of this, Dory let her sister lead her across the red and white linoleum to the back porch and the creaky wooden steps down to the garden. She sat on the curved cement bench by the cistern, gingerly at first. It was surprisingly warm for spring. The sun shone, standing well clear of the box elders crowding against the retaining wall at the back of the lot. A silver jet flew high overhead, bound for Seatac. The low grumble of its engines lagged behind it, obscuring Calliope's words.

"What?"

"I said, 'Quit sittin pretty and help me move this lid.'"

The cistern's cover came off with a hollow, grating sound. A slice of water, a crescent like the waning moon, reflected the sun's brightness. Ripples of light ran up the damp stone walls. Most of the water lay in darkness, though. Cold smells seeped up from it: mud, moss. Mystery.

As children, Dory, Calliope, and their cousins had been fascinated by the cistern. Daddy and Mama had forbidden them to play there, of course, which only increased their interest. When their parents opened it to haul up water for the garden, the girls hovered close by, snatching glimpses inside.

"Goddam if that no-good Byron ain't lost the bucket!" Calliope cursed the empty end of the rope she'd retrieved from her side of the cistern. It was still curled where it had been tied to the handle of the beige plastic bucket.

Byron, their fourteen year old cousin, liked to soak sticks and strips of wood in water to use in his craft projects. He only lived a block away, so he was always in and out of the basement workshop. "You think he took it home again?" Dory asked.

"No, I remember now I saw it downstairs, fulla some trash a his, tree branches or somethin."

"Yeah? Well, that's all right, we don't wanna—"

"I'll go get it and wipe it out good. Wait for me behind the garage."

"Oh, but he's always so upset when you mess with his stuff!"

"It ain't his anyhow, is it?" Calliope took the porch steps two at a time. She was a heavy girl, but light on her feet. Never grew out of her baby fat. Still, she could hold her own in a fight.

The basement stairs, narrow and uneven, slowed her down a bit. Daddy had run a string from the bare-bulb fixture at their bottom, looping it along the wooden wall of the stairwell. She pulled, and the chain at its other end slithered obediently against porcelain, clicked and snapped back. Brightness flooded the lowering floor joists.

Calliope ignored the beige bucket full of soaking willow wands. Daddy's tool bench,

that's where she'd find what she wanted. Nothing too heavy, though. She had to be able to lift it. And not too sharp. She didn't want to have to clean up a whole lot of blood.

Hammer? Pipe wrench? What if Mama got home early and found Calliope carrying one of those out of the house? What would she think?

It came to her with the same sort of slide and snap that had turned the light on. Daddy was about to tear out the railroad ties in the retaining wall. They were rotten; they needed replacing. It was this week's project. The new ones were piled up at the end of the driveway.

Smiling, Calliope selected a medium-sized mallet, its handle as long as her forearm. And added a crowbar for show.

Outside, Dory wondered what was taking her sister so long. A clump of shampoo slipped down her forehead and along one eyebrow. She wiped it off, annoyed. She stood up from the weeds where she'd been waiting, then quickly knelt down again at the sound of footsteps on the paving bricks.

"Bend forward." Calliope's voice cracked. Dory began twisting her head to see why. The mallet came down hard on her right temple. It left a black dent in the suds, a hollow. She made a mewing sound, fell forward. Eyes open, but blind. Another blow, well-centered, this time, drove her face into the soft soil. One more. Then Calliope took control of herself.

"You dead," she murmured, satisfied.

A towel over her sister's head disguised the damage. Hoisting her up into a sitting position and leaning her against the garage, Calliope hunkered back to look at her and think. No one was due home within the next couple of hours. For that long, her secret would be safe. Even then she'd be all right as long as they didn't look out the kitchen windows. The retaining wall was visible from there, but if she had one of the new ties tamped in place, and the dirt filled back in...

A moment more she pondered. Fast-moving clouds flickered across the sun, and her skin bumped up. There was no real reason to hang back. Waiting wouldn't change what she'd done.

The first tie came down easily. Giant splinters sprung off as Calliope kicked it to one side. The second one, she had to dig the ends out, and the third was cemented in place its full length by dried clay. Ants boiled out of the hundreds of holes that had been hidden behind it, and the phone rang.

She wasn't going to answer it. But it stopped and started again, and she knew she'd better.

Sweat had made mud of the dirt on her hands. She cradled the pale blue princess phone against one shoulder, trying to rub the mess clean on her shirt as she listened to Mama asking what was in the refrigerator. The cord barely stretched that far. Were they out of eggs? Butter? Lunch meat? Did Calliope think there was enough cornmeal to make hush puppies? Even with Byron coming over? And what were she and Dory up to that it took them so long to answer the phone?

"Dory ain't come home yet. No, I don't know why; she ain't tole me. I was out in back, tearin down the retaining wall."

Her mother's disapproving silence lasted two full seconds. "Why you always wanna act so mannish, Calliope?"

There wasn't any answer to that. She promised to change her clothes for supper.

Outside again, ants crawled on her dead sister's skin.

Dory didn't feel them. She saw them, though, from far off. Far up? What was going on didn't make regular sense. Why couldn't she hear the shovel digging? Whoever was lying there on the ground in Dory's culottes with a towel over her head, it was someone else. Not her.

She headed for the house. She should be hungry. It must be supper time by now. The kitchen windows were suddenly shining through the dusk. And sure enough, Calliope was inside already, cooking.

In the downstairs bathroom, Daddy washed his hands with his sleeves rolled up. She kissed him. She did; on his cheek, she couldn't have missed it.

The food look good, good enough to eat. Fried chicken, the crisp ridges and golden valleys of its skin glowing under the ceiling light. Why didn't she want it? Her plate was empty.

Nobody talked much. Nobody talked to her at all. There were a lot of leftovers. Cousin Byron helped Calliope clear the table. Daddy made phone calls, with Mama listening in on the extension. She could see them both at the same time, in the kitchen and in their bedroom upstairs. She couldn't hear anything.

Then the moon came out. It was bedtime, a school night. Everyone stayed up, though, and the police sat in the living room and moved their mouths till she got tired of watching them. She went in the backyard again, where all this weird stuff had started happening.

The lid was still off the cistern. She looked down inside. The moon's reflection shone up at her, a full circle, uninterrupted by shadow. Not smooth, though. Waves ran through it, long, like swirls actually. Closer, she saw them clearly: hairs. Her hairs, supple and fine.

Suddenly, the world was in daylight again. Instead of the moon's circle, a face covered the water's surface. Her sister's face. Calliope's. Different, and at first Dory couldn't understand why. Then she realized it was her hair, her hair, Dory's own. A thin fringe of it hung around her big sister's face as if it belonged there. But it didn't. Several loose strands fell drifting towards Dory. And again, it was night.

And day. And night. Time didn't stay still. Mostly, it seemed to move in one direction. Mama kept crying; Daddy too. Dory decided she must be dead. But what about heaven? What about the funeral?

Byron moved into Dory's old room. It wasn't spooky; it was better than his mom's house. There, he could never tell who was going to show up for drinks. Or breakfast. He never knew who was going to start yelling and throwing things in the middle of the night: his mom, or some man she had invited over, or someone else she hadn't.

Even before he brought his clothes, Byron had kept his instruments and other projects here. Uncle Marv's workshop was wonderful, and he let him use all his tools.

His thing now was gimbris, elegant North African ancestors of the cigar-box banjos he'd built two years ago when he was just beginning, just a kid. He sat on the retaining wall in the last, lingering light of the autumn afternoon, considering the face, neck, and frame of his latest effort, a variant like a violin, meant to be bowed. He'd pieced it together from the thin trunk of an elder tree blown down in an August storm, sister to the leafless ones still upright behind him.

The basic structure looked good, but it was kind of plain. It needed some sort of decoration. An inlay, ivory or mother of pearl or something. The hide backing was important, obviously, but that could wait; it'd be easier to take care of the inlay first.

Of course, real ivory would be too expensive. Herb David, who let him work in his guitar shop, said people used bone as a substitute. And he knew where some was. Small bits, probably from some dead dog or rabbit. They'd been entangled in the tree roots. He planned to make tuning pegs out of them. There'd be plenty, though.

He stood up, and the world whited out. It had been doing that a lot since he moved here. The school nurse said he had low blood pressure. He just had to stand still a minute and he'd be okay. The singing in his ears, that would stop, too. But it was still going when he got to the stairs.

Stubbornly, he climbed, hanging onto the handrail. Dory's—his—bedroom was at the back of the house, overlooking the garden. His mom kept her dope in an orange juice can hung under the heat vent. He used the same system for his bones. No one knew he had them; so why was he afraid they'd take them away?

He held them in his cupped palms. They were warm, and light. The shimmering whiteness had condensed down to one corner of his vision. Sometimes that meant he was going to get a headache. He hoped not. He wanted to work on this now, while he was alone.

When he left his room, though, he crossed the hall into Calliope's instead of heading downstairs to Uncle Marv's workshop. Without knowing why, he gazed around him. The walls were turquoise, the throw rugs and bedspread pale pink. Nothing in here interested him, except—that poster of Wilt Chamberlain her new boyfriend, Neville, had given her...It was signed, worth maybe one hundred dollars. He stepped closer. He could never get Calliope to let him anywhere near the thing when she was around, but she took terrible care of it. It was taped to the wall all crooked, sort of sagging in the middle.

He touched the slick surface—slick, but not smooth—something soft and lumpy lay between the poster and the wall. What? White light pulsed up around the edges of his vision as he lifted one creased corner.

Something black slithered to the floor. He knelt. With the whiteness, his vision had narrowed, but he could still see it was nothing alive. He picked it up.

A wig! Or at least part of one. Byron tried to laugh. It was funny, wasn't it? Calliope wearing a wig like some old bald lady? Only...only it was so weird. The bones. This—hair. The way Dory had disappeared.

He had to think. This was not the place. He smoothed down the poster's tape, taking the wig with him to the basement.

He put the smallest bone in a clamp. It was about as big around as his middle finger. He sawed it into oblong disks.

The wig hair was long and straight. Like Dory's. It was held together by shriveled-up skin, the way he imagined an Indian's scalp would be.

What if Calliope had killed her little sister? It was crazy, but what if she had? Did that mean she'd kill him if he told on her? Or if she thought he knew?

And if he was wrong, he'd be causing trouble for her, and Uncle Marv, and Aunt Cookie, and he might have to go live at home again.

Gradually, his work absorbed him, as it always did. When Calliope came in, he had a pile of bone disks on the bench, ready for polishing. Beside them, in a sultry heap, lay the wig, which he'd forgotten to put back.

Byron looked up at his cousin, unable to say anything. The musty basement was suddenly too small. She was three years older than him, and at least 30 pounds heavier. And she saw it, she had to see it. After a moment, he managed a sickly smirk, but his mouth stayed shut.

"Whatchoodoon?" She didn't smile back. "You been in my room?"

"I—I didn't—"

She picked it up. "Pretty, ain't it?" She stroked the straight hair, smoothing it out. "You want it?"

No clue in Calliope's bland expression as to what she meant. He tried to formulate an answer just to her words, to what she'd actually said. Did he want the wig. "For the bow I'm makin, yeah, sure, thanks."

"Awright then."

He wished she'd go away. "Neville be here tonight?"

She beamed. It was the right question to ask. "I guess. Don't know what he sees in me, but the boy can't keep away."

Byron didn't know what Neville saw in her either. "Neville's smart," he said diplomatically. It was true.

So was he.

There was more hair than he needed, even if he saved a bunch for restringing. He coiled it up and left it in his juice can. There was no way he could prove it was Dory's. If he dug up the backyard where the tree fell, where he found the bones, would the rest of the skeleton be there?

The police. He should call the police, but he'd seen Dragnet, and Perry Mason. When he accepted the wig, the hair, he'd become an accessory after the fact. Maybe he was one even before that, because of the bones.

It was odd, but really the only time he wasn't worried about all this was when he worked on the gimbri. By Thanksgiving, it was ready to play.

He brought it out to show to Neville after dinner. "That is a seriously fine piece of work," said Neville, cradling the gimbri's round leather back. "Smaller than the other one, isn't it?" His big hands could practically cover a basketball. With one long thumb he caressed the strings. They whispered dryly.

"You play it with this." Byron handed him the bow.

He held it awkwardly. Keyboards, reeds, guitar, drums, flute, even accordion: he'd fooled around with plenty of instruments, but nothing resembling a violin. "You sure you want me to?"

It was half-time on the TV, and dark outside already. Through the living room window, yellow light from a street lamp coated the grainy, grey sidewalk, dissolving at its edges like a pointillist's reverie. A night just like this, he'd first seen how pretty Dory was: the little drops of rain in her hair shining, and it stayed nice as a white girl's.

Not like Calliope's. Hers was as naturally nappy as his, worse between her legs. He sneaked a look at her while Byron was showing him how to position the gimbri upright. She was looking straight back at him, her eyes hot and still. Not as pretty as Dory, no, but she let him do things he would never have dreamed of asking of her little sister.

Mr. Moore stood up from the sofa and called to his wife. "Mama, you wanna come see our resident genius's latest invention in action?"

The gimbri screamed, choked, and sighed. "What on earth?" said Mrs. Moore from the kitchen doorway. She shut her eyes and clamped her lips together as if the awful noise was trying to get in through other ways besides her ears.

Neville hung his head and bit his lower lip. He wasn't sure whether he was trying to keep from laughing or crying.

"It spozed to sound like that, Byron?" asked Calliope.

"No," Neville told her. "My fault." He picked up the bow from his lap, frowning. His older brother had taken him to a Charles Mingus concert once. He searched his memory for an image of the man embracing his big bass and mimicked it the best he could.

A sweeter sound emerged. Sweeter, and so much sadder. One singing note, which he raised and lowered slowly. High and yearning. Soft and questioning. With its voice.

With its words.

"I know you mama, miss me since I'm gone;
I know you mama, miss me since I'm gone;
One more thing before I journey on."

Neville turned his head to see if anyone else heard what he was hearing. His hand slipped, and the gimbri sobbed. He turned back to it.

"Lover man, why won't you be true?
Lover man, why won't you ever be true?
She murdered me, and she just might murder you."

He wanted to stop now, but his hands kept moving. He recognized that voice, that tricky hesitance, the tone smooth as smoke. He'd never expected to hear it again.

"I know you daddy, miss me since I'm gone;
I know you daddy, miss me since I'm gone;
One more thing before I journey on.

"I know you cousin, miss me since I'm gone;
I know you cousin, miss me since I'm gone;
It's cause of you I come to sing this song.

"Cruel, cruel sistah, black and white and red;
Cruel, cruel sistah, black and white and red;
You hated me, you had to see me dead.

"Cruel, cruel sistah, red and white and black;
Cruel, cruel sistah, red and white and black;
You killed me and you buried me out back.

"Cruel, cruel sistah, red and black and white;
Cruel, cruel sistah, red and black and white;
You'll be dead yourself before tomorrow night."

Finally, the song was finished. The bow slithered off the gimbri's strings with a sound like a snake leaving. They all looked at one another warily.

Calliope was the first to speak. "It ain't true," she said. Which meant admitting that something had actually happened.

But they didn't have to believe what the song had said.

Calliope's suicide early the next morning, that they had to believe: her body floating front down in the cistern, her short, rough hair soft as a wet burlap bag. That, and the skeleton the police found behind the retaining wall, with its smashed skull.

It was a double funeral. There was no music.

HORROR MOVIE

(Excerpt)

by Paul Tremblay

Our little movie that couldn't had a crew size that has become fluid in the retelling, magically growing in the years since Valentina up-loaded the screenplay and three photo stills to various online message boards and three brief scenes to YouTube in 2008. Now that I live in Los Angeles (temporarily; please, I'm not a real monster) I can't tell you how many people tell me they know someone or are friends of a friend of a friend who was on-set. Our set.

Like now. I'm having coffee with one of the producers of the Horror Movie remake. Or is it a reboot? I'm not sure of the correct term for what it is they will be doing. Is it a remake if the original film, shot more than thirty years ago, was never screened? "Reboot" is probably the proper term but not with how it's applied around Hollywood.

Producer Guy's name is George. Maybe. I'm pretending to forget his name in retribution for our first meeting six months ago, which was over Zoom. While I was holed up in my small, stuffy apartment, he was outdoors, traipsing around a green space. He apologized for the sunglasses and his bouncing, sun-dappled phone image in that I-can-do-whatever-I-want way and explained he just had to get outside, get his steps in, because he'd been stuck in his office all morning and he would be there all afternoon. Translation: I deign to speak to you, however you're not important enough to interrupt a planned walk. A total power play. I was tempted to hang up on him or pretend my computer screen froze, but I didn't. Yeah, I'm talking tougher than I am. I couldn't afford (in all applications of that word) to throw away any chance, as slim as it might be, to get the movie made. Within the winding course of our one-way discussion in which I was nothing but flotsam in the current of his river, he said he'd been looking for horror projects, as "horror is hot," but because everything happening in the real world was so grim, he and the studios wanted horror that was "uplifting and upbeat." His own raging waters were too loud for him to hear my derisive snort-laugh or see my eye-roll. I didn't think anything would ever come from that chat.

In the past five years I've had countless calls with studio executives and sycophantic producers who claimed to be serious about rebooting Horror Movie and wanting me on board in a variety of non-decision-making, low-pay capacities, which equated to their hoping I wouldn't shit on them or their overtures publicly, as I and my character inexplicably have a small but vociferous, or voracious, fan base. After being subjected to their performative enthusiasm, elevator pitches (Same movie but a horror-comedy! Same movie but with twentysomethings living in L.A. or San Francisco or Atlanta! Same movie but with an alien! Same movie but with time travel! Same movie but with hope!), and promises to work together, I'd never hear from them again.

But I did hear back from this producer guy. I asked my friend Sarah, an impossibly smart (unlike me) East Coast transplant (like me) screenwriter, what she knew about him and his company. She said he had shit taste, but he got movies made. Two for two.

Today, producer-guy George and I are in Culver City comparing the size of our grandes while sitting at an outdoor metal wicker table, the table wobbly because of an uneven leg, which I anchor in place with the toe of one sneakered foot. Now that we're in person, face-to-face, we are on more equal ground, if there is such thing as equality. He's tan, wide-chested, wearing aviator sunglasses, a polo shirt, and comfortable shoes, and younger than I am by more than a decade. I'm dressed in my usual uniform; faded black jeans, a white T-shirt, and a world weariness that is both affect and age-earned.

He talks about the movie in character arcs and other empty buzzword story terms he gleaned from online listicles. Then we dis- cuss what my role might be offscreen, my upcoming meeting with the director, and other stuff that could've been handled in email or a phone/Zoom call, but I had insisted on the in-person. Not sure why beyond the free coffee and to have something to do while I wait for preproduction to start. Maybe I wanted to show George my teeth.

As we're about to part ways, he says, "Hey, get this, I randomly found out that a friend of my cousin—a close cousin; we'd spent two weeks of every summer on Lake Winnipesaukee together from ages eight to eighteen—anyway, this friend of hers worked on Horror Movie with you. Isn't that wild?"

The absurd part is that I'm supposed to go along with his (and everyone else's) faked connection to and remembrance of a movie that has become fabled, become not real, when it was at one time decidedly, quantitatively real, and then the kicker is there's the social expectation that I will acknowledge our new shared bond. I get it. It's all make-believe, the business of make-believe, and it bleeds into the unreality of the entertainment ecosystem. Maybe it should be that way. Who am I to say otherwise? But I refuse to play along. That's my power play.

I ask, "Oh yeah, what's their name?"

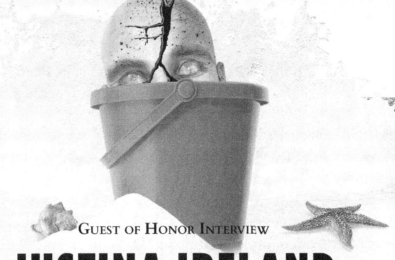

JUSTINA IRELAND

Conducted by Erick Manchilla for Black History Month

ERICK MANCHILLA: What inspired you to start writing?

JUSTINA IRELAND: When I was pregnant with my kiddo I was terrified of losing my identity as a person and being reduced to little more than an incubator for the next generation. So I decided to do something I was afraid of trying to do: writing a book.

EM: What was it about the horror genre that drew you to it?

JI: To be honest, for a long time I resisted the title of being a horror writer, mostly because the genre classification tends to be a little reductive. Also, I'm not a straight white guy. The fact that stories like *Beloved* were never billed as horror (it most definitely is, BTW) kind of cemented my belief that while I was playing in a genre space, horror wasn't for me.

But once I realized that horror wasn't just the stereotypical slashers that everyone identifies with the genre or the problems of middle-aged white men going through a mid-life crisis I realized I'd been writing horror pretty much my entire career. Because I tend to write about the things that scare us. So much of human existence is linked to fear, and fear drives more of our decisions than we tend to admit.

EM: Do you make a conscious effort to include African diaspora characters and themes in your writing and if so, what do you want to portray?

JI: I mean, no, but yes? I write the world that I see around me, the world that existed historically within this country, since I often use history as the basis for my worldbuilding. I don't know of a single time and place since colonization where this country was all one thing or another. It's actually embarrassing when I read a book and the characters are all white, because that in and of itself is a fantasy, and not really one I find believable. It's also a huge tell for those authors, that their life is so monochromatic. How have you managed to create such a sterile existence for yourself, and why would I believe you can successfully convey truths about existence when you're only living a fraction of a life?

So I don't have to work to include Black characters because we exist, like cars and the inevitable disappointment of getting older. And that's all I'm writing about, the truths of existence packaged in a way that hopefully terrifies, delights, and entertains.

EM: What has writing horror taught you about the world and yourself?

JI: I write horror because it's a great way to make the terrifying survivable. If a character can survive the zombie apocalypse then maybe I can survive a Saturday morning at Costco.

EM: How have you seen the horror genre change over the years? And how do you think it will continue to evolve?

JI: I'm really happy that more authors of color and queer authors are being lifted up and bringing us fresh storytelling that doesn't feel like a retread of the same five stories I've been reading since sixth grade. I'm hoping we get more of that. After all, no one knows more about fear and survival than those who are marginalized.

EM: How do you feel the Black community has been represented thus far in the genre and what hopes do you have for representation in the genre going forward?

JI: I mean, terribly. The dead Black character trope exists for a reason. Black characters aren't disposable, but horror sure does make it feel that way.

My hope for the future? All Black everything. That's it, nothing more, nothing less. Black horror doesn't have the depth and breadth it could, but we'll get there.

EM: Who are some of your favorite characters in horror?

JI: Rah Digga's turn in *Thirteen Ghosts* as Maggie Bess will always be my standard for Black characters in horror. She has so few moments on screen but when she is there she's no nonsense and smart. And she actually survives the entire film, so hell yeah.

Just give me smart, capable Black women doing what they need to survive and I'm there for it. It's a shame that's so hard to find.

EM: What is one piece of advice you would give horror authors today?

JI: If the world of your horror story doesn't look like the world we live in you're only writing to a small slice of humanity. Be better than that. It's boring.

JONATHAN MABERRY

Conducted by all of You

JOHN LANGAN: Could you talk about the relationship between your martial arts practice and writing?

JONATHAN MABERRY: Martial arts is the only thing I've been doing longer than writing. I started when I was five. I've logged sixty years since then, predominantly in Japanese jujutsu and kenjutsu. The martial arts helped me cultivate a useful focus of mind and discipline of action. The kind of jujutsu I studied wasn't for sport and it's not particularly pretty, but it's elegant in its technical philosophy –practical, efficient, and true to the structural underpinnings of an understanding of anatomy, physics, physiology, history, psychology, and the law. (All of that study makes it wildly unpopular to the crowd just wanting to wear a black belt!).

That focus and discipline is what keeps me from wasting my own time as a writer. Much as I'd love to spend all day watching 1980s rock videos on YouTube or rescue dog reels on Instagram, but that's not my job. Writing is the job, and discipline acquired through martial arts keeps me on point. The mental focus helps fend off distractions.

And the practical experience of having been a bodyguard

and a bouncer, each for five years, has deepened and clarified my understanding of how to write realistic fight and action scenes. Which is a hell of a lot of fun.

MERCEDES M. YARDLEY: I'm a huge fan of your doggo, Rosie. How often does she make it into your work?

JM: Rosie has only been in one work, and that was Taylor Grant's magnificent adaptation of *Rot & Ruin*, my YA post-apocalyptic novel, which he did for WebToon. That became the WebToon platform's #1 horror comic. A variation of Rosie called 'Bug' was in my novel, Glimpse.

Mostly, though, the dogs in my novels are either combat dogs (like Ghost in the Joe Ledger thrillers) or semi-feral mastiffs in the *Rot & Ruin/Dead of Night* stories.

Bottom line is that I like dogs more than I do most people. No apologies.

DELILAH S. DAWSON: You are so enthusiastic and supportive of other writers and generous with your friendship, help, and opportunities. Which authors helped you when you were on the rise?

JM: When I was in 7th grade, my middle school librarian was the secretary for two different groups of professional authors. One was the Hyborean Legion, a swords-and-sorcery group that met in Philadelphia, at the home of George Scithers. L. Sprague de Camp was a member of that group, and he became a mentor and lifelong friend.

The other group was an unofficial one –a group of bestselling genre writers who would gather at infrequent intervals at a penthouse apartment owned by a publisher. Alas, I can't remember the publisher's name (I was only 12). This was 1970, and if you were a novelist of any note, you went to NY to launch your books.

My librarian brought me along to meet those writers because I had convinced her by then that I wanted to be a professional writer. At the very first of those sessions I met Ray Bradbury and Richard Matheson. I'm embarrassed to say that I had no idea who either was at the time. I learned, however. Ouch.

Over the next three years, the librarian took me from Philly to NYC many times, and I got to see Bradbury and Matheson. Even though neither was based in that city, they were prolific enough to keep coming in for the events. Not every time, but often enough that they took me under their wing and mentored me. They gave me books to read and even provided lessons for how to take an idea and cultivate it into a story plot. Even now, all these years later, I can get teary-eyed thinking about that level of kindness and generosity.

Roll forward a number of years, and my editor was able to secure cover blurbs from them for my first novel, *Ghost Road Blues*. Those quotes are on the 10th anniversary edition of the book. Got very teary-eyed when she told me about the blurbs. I may have ugly cried. Luckily there are no witnesses.

PseudoPod: What is the best part about MC-ing the Stoker Award ceremony? What would surprise people the most about the gig?

JM: I was MC one year (right before Covid), and it was such an honor. The HWA crowd is the most welcoming, down-to-earth, and pleasant group of writers anywhere. I loved hosting that event, though doing it after the hilarious Jeff Strand did it for a while was intimidating. Since then, Kevin Wetmore has crushed it.

As to what would surprise people about the gig is that it's fun and everyone seems to be on your side when you're up there. It's less like giving a speech and more like chatting with friends. Also…people seem happy to buy you drinks afterward. (If I am ever asked to MC again, please remember it's a Bombay Sapphire martini, hint of dry vermouth, straight-up, three olives.)

JONATHAN LEES: I would love to know more about Jonathan's management of time. He does so much in addition to writing that's helpful for writers new and established.

JM: Everyone has a speed they're most comfortable with. I like the fast lane. Always have. I'm happiest when I have ten things to do at once. Less happy when there is only a single project to do. That said, being a high-speed/high-output writer is not only not for everyone; it's not a recommendation. You have to enjoy the pace. I think that this was ignited in me when I was studying journalism at Temple University. Some of those classes were very high-pressure, and there was that news reporter's mantra of "Write it quick and dirty, then fix it in the rewrite."

Journalism also taught me to ignore the mystification of the writing process. I don't wait for the muse to whisper. I don't need to be wearing my luck socks before I write. It's not like that. Sure, writing is an art, but publishing is a business whose main concern is selling copies of art. I learned that early on from Bradbury, Matheson, Harlan Ellison, Avram Davidson, Sprague de Camp, Robert Bloch, and other writers I met when I was a kid.

Time management is the key to all of it. As you do any given project, it's important to observe and assess your process. I always look for things that I do that waste time or squander opportunities. I learn from my colleagues various tricks to amplify output and improve work output. At the same time, I keep a close eye on quality. If my writing speed negatively impacts the quality of my work, then I adjust my speed accordingly.

It's also something that changes over time. It took me three-and-a-half years to write my first novel. Now I'm writing my 51st (since 2006), and I can now write a 160k-word novel in three months, while still giving me time to edit *Weird Tales Magazine*, edit anthologies, write short stories, and do the other tasks necessary to my business (editing, research, outlining, business calls, TV/film pitches, new product pitches, do public appearances, etc.). It's a lot, but it's what makes me happy. Happiness is huge part of my overall business model –if I'm not having fun, then I am definitely doing it wrong.

All that said…it's critically important for a busy writer to take time for health, family, and downtime.

JENDIA GAMMON: Who would win in a battle between Cthulhu and Melkor / Morgoth?

JM: Cthulhu is a pan-dimensional being of godlike power. Even while he sleeps, he is immensely powerful and active in many different dimensions. Morgoth is one of the Valar, and although they are described by Tolkien as being essentially godlike, they seem bound to one reality. Or, at least, to tightly connected realities including Middle Earth and the lands of the Elves. Morgoth has been mentioned as Tolkien's avatar of Satan, and if true, then it is a lesser version of Satan than has appeared in many of the world's religions. It might be a close scrape, but I think the smart money's on Cthulhu. And you know what they say, Nilgh'ri l' vulgtmah throdog r'luhhor." Wise words.

KIERSTEN WHITE: When writing the same character / world over many books, how do you stay creatively engaged?

JM: Series characters are, in a way, like friends in the real world. If a character has become sufficiently real to you (as they should), you keep putting them in situations where you learn new things about them. It's the same in the real world –you go through all kinds of encounters, situations, and adventures with your friends, and in each different situation you see another side of them. Since I base my characters –in whole or part—on people I know/have known, then I can always look at the real-world person for nuance, variation, evolution of opinion, reactions to incidents, and so on. That never gets stale. After all, we writers are natural observers.

Also, with long series, sometimes freshness comes from the antagonist –which is why in my Joe Ledger novels I switch from his first person POV to third person when giving the backstory of the villain. I want that well-developed richness for whomever is going to provide the threat of each book.

And, to that end, freshness can come from supporting characters –fleshing them out, giving them new things to and new story arcs, bringing in new ones, creating interesting incidental characters, and so on.

One more thing…the nature of the threat impacts the way in which characters react, and those varied reactions allow us to deconstruct the personality dimensions of protagonist and supporting character. This allows for all kinds of fresh reactions, responses, damage, healing, etc.

For Joe Ledger, I've so far written 14 novels and 40 short stories about him, and he is a supporting character in books 3 & 4 of the Dead of Night series and books 3-7 of the Rot & Ruin. He's even appeared in my V-Wars novels and comics. He is not the same person he was in book 1, and that reflects how life experiences change everyone.

MATTHEW MERCIER: You're such an inspiration to many in that you started publishing "later" in life. In a culture that worships youthful achievement, what are the benefits of "late" publication? What do you say to a room full of anxious 20-year-olds who are convinced if they don't publish by the time they are (shudder) 30, they are over the hill?

JM: Before I was published as a novelist my friends warned me that I was starting too late, that publishing was a young person's game. I found that to be a bit of unsubstantiated propaganda. Publishing is open to anyone who can shift and change with the evolution of publishing itself. Some folks my age are afraid of social media (or simply haven't bothered to try and understand it). Some writers dug their toes in when eBooks became a thing. Some dislike audiobooks.

Blah blah blah. Publishing changes, and if we want to be active in with and thrive, then we have to embrace it with some sense of joy and optimism.

From a more personal standpoint, I have lived a busy life. It hasn't always been pleasant, but it was never dull. Grew up dirt poor in a low-income neighborhood and with an abusive criminal for a father. I had to break free of my old man's brutality and racism and form my own worldview. I competed in boxing, kickboxing, fencing, and wrestling. I've been a martial artist for sixty years and have been, at various times, a bodyguard, a bouncer in a strip club, a college teacher (14 years at Temple University, teaching Martial Arts History, Women's Self-defense, and Jujutsu), was the expert witness for the Philly D.A.'s office for murder trials involving martial arts, did expert witness work for civil cases, was inducted into the Action Karate International Martial Arts Hall of Fame, used to skydive, hitchhiked across country after high school, was in bands (an Eagles and a Steely Dan cover band), performed in musical theater, worked preparing posters and evidence models for medical malpractice lawsuits, been married, divorced, and married again, adopted and raised a son, gave a Viking funeral once to an old muscle car, and a slew of other things. I mention all of this because living all those years has provided me with experience, some degree of insight, memories both good and bad, a deep well of tellable anecdotes, and –I hope- an understanding of cause and effect deep enough to estimate the worth and merit of things I've done. In short, life teaches. Writers need to have something to draw on and, for good or bad, I have my share.

None of this makes me better or worse, cooler or not than anyone else. We ALL have bigger stories inside us than we'll ever be able to put down on paper. It's just that writers have all that to tap for inspiration. So, in truth, it really is more the miles than the years.

BRENNAN LAFARO: How much, a ballpark, does constantly wearing a Hawaiian shirt improve your outlook?

JM: Hawaiian shirts make me happy. I started wearing them when I was a bodyguard. On cases where we were asked not to dress in the usual faux-Secret Service black suits, white shirts, black ties, a loose and blousy Hawaiian shirt allowed us to carry concealed sidearms without drawing attention to them. And the shirts allowed for easy access. But, after I quit that job, I kept wearing the shirts. Now they represent wearable art. Some are sedate, some are so offensively loud and bright you could get sun poisoning standing next to me. None, however, are crude or obscene; none are too cliché novelty. I have hundreds of them, and have lately been buying exclusively from Big Fun Shirt Company, a mother-and-son mail order outfit in Eureka, California. High quality, vivid prints, and often they'll buy a fabric remnant with a stunning pattern and reach out to me to see if I want a one-of-a-kind exclusive. I wore one of those unique shirts to the Hollywood premier of *Black Panther: Wakanda Forever* (40% of the movie is based on my 2009-10 comic book run). Damon John of Shark Tank, who was at the after-party, complimented the shirt.

Even on dreary mornings when I'm not in a good mood, when I open my closet and see the rows of brightly-colored Hawaiian shirts, I'm immediately happier.

IAN: What brand of coffee do you drink that fuels you to do all the writing and editing you do, and where can I get it?

JM: Funny thing is I have my own coffee brand. Or sub-brand. The good folks at Old Town Roasting Company in Orange County worked with me to create two blends tied to my Joe Ledger novels. One is 'Joe Ledger's Nice Cup of Whoopass' –a nice full-bodied medium blend. And then there's a coffee named after Ledger's best friend, who only drinks decaf –'Rudy Sanchez's Brown Sadness Water Decaf'. That has notes of chocolate, nutmeg, and cinnamon. And I don't just drink them out of loyalty to my own brand –we worked for months to come up with the right mix of beans and flavors.

CYNTHIA PELAYO: You are such a prolific author. You have such an iconic catalogue and range of work, what is next for you?

JM: I have a slew of projects in various stages of development. I recently completed *Burn to Shine*, my 50th novel (and 14th in the Ledger series); and I'm working with Crystal Lake for a Kickstarter for a Joe Ledger graphic novel. I just wrote a Godzilla vs Cthulhu one-shot comic for CMON Games. Here at StokerCon we're launching NecroTek, first in a brand-new series of deep-space/cosmic horror novels for the new *Weird Tales Presents* imprint at Blackstone. The concluding book in my *Kagen the Damned* epic fantasy trilogy drops in August. I also have two short story collections coming out this year –*Midnight Lullabies: Unquiet Stories and Poems,* with a foreword by Joe R. Lansdale, and *Mystic: The Monk Addison Casefiles*, with a foreword by Jim Butcher. And in October, WordFire Press will release *Shadows & Verse: Classic Poems of Darkness with Celebrity Commentary* –an anthology of poems and commentary that will be a fundraiser to provide scholarships for emerging creatives. I'll also be writing the second in the *Sleepers War* science fiction series. The first, Alpha Wave, was co-authored with my dear friend Weston Ochse, but with his tragic passing, I'll be doing the next books in that series alone. Also, I'm editing *Weird Tales. The Stoker Awards* issue debuts at StokerCon, and next up is a monster-themed issue. And I have film in development (*Rot & Ruin*) at Alcon Entertainment, and five different TV projects in various stages of development.

And in my spare time…

ROB SAVAGE

THIS SAVAGE ART

Conducted by Final Frame Director, Jonathan Lees

*A*s director and programmer of Final Frame for the past nine years, I have had the pleasure to witness the formation of a new family. A demented family, yes, but in the best way possible. With the continuing support of Suz Romero and the George A. Romero Foundation, multiple competition finalists returning on-screen, familiar judges' back to mix it up with the new, and our favorite audience ever, the ties are getting stronger.

Rob Savage represents a big part of this new familial identity for Final Frame. A two-time competition finalist for his shorts *Dawn of the Deaf* and *Salt*, we welcome him this year into a starring role as an official Final Frame judge and a StokerCon Guest of Honor.

I had the pleasure of discovering Rob through his work and was thrilled to meet up with him to speak about the art of horror, adaptation, and why he's not done with the short form.

JONATHAN LEES: It's kind of odd to be proud of someone you've never met in person but the second I saw and programmed [your short] *Dawn of the Deaf,* **I knew that you were someone**

that took everything you did very seriously. Usually, the path in filmmaking is to make short films and build up the strength to a feature. You flipped that and your short films came after your first feature, Strings. You said about that project, "every day was a discovery and a humiliation". I think we can all relate to that statement as writers. How do you continually balance both discovery and humiliation?

ROB SAVAGE: Whether you start with a feature or start with shorts, the humiliation is such an integral part of it. You've got to work in the shadows on things that might never see the light of day or get shown on a big screen or a hung blanket in a basement of a bar. You're going to kind of pass through the crucible of bad filmmaking before you can get to halfway decent filmmaking.

I made this first feature when I was seventeen, started working in the industry from like age nineteen, and often I was the youngest person on set. I was directing television in my very early twenties, surrounded by industry veterans. I put a lot of energy into seeming cool and capable and I think my work suffered for it. I had this like brain flip moment where I realized that the way to kind of take myself to the next stage and improve my work was to open myself up to daily humiliation.

Go in and be so energized, open, enthusiastic, and unafraid to say, "I don't know, but maybe this". To get your collaborators in a huddle and say, "Listen, I've got a few ideas, but we're going to solve this together." There's this kind of naive film school mentality of, you know, I'm going to be the next Paul Thomas Anderson, and everything is going to come out fully formed from my brain.

I think people get the most out of filmmaking by building a strong community around them and being open to the kind of broadest collaboration and feeling comfortable to throw in an idea that might be absolute dog shit but might get you an inch closer to what the scene needs to be, to what the film needs to be. Humiliation is key.

JL: What was it about getting that first feature done that helped you refine and define what you wanted to do next?

RS: It helped me clarify everything I didn't want to be, or everything I wasn't qualified to be. At that time, I was a pretentious 17-year-old and I wanted to be the next Lynne Ramsey, my favorite filmmaker. [Strings] was very much an art house movie and my influences have always come from extreme art house, extreme schlock, and everything in between.

So, I made this film and then immediately got these opportunities to pitch the next project. I was shopping around horror ideas, alien invasions, zombie movies, and nobody really knew what to do with it because all I'd shown that I could do was this kind of like very austere art house indie movie in Strings.

Nine times out of ten, when I sit down to watch a movie, my finger will take me to a horror movie. That's where my taste lies at its heart. And that's where I discovered I needed to be.

I realized very early on, around the time of Dawn of the Deaf, by infusing all this arthouse sensibility in something that's geared towards mainstream horror fans, you can do both and audiences really respond to that subversion.

JL: Absolutely. In your short film, Dawn of the Deaf, you have a knack for keeping the real horrors of life grounded while everything that's genre related expands and explodes around them. A deaf girl dealing with a sexual abuse from a father, emotional abuse from bullies, and… zombies. It's just insane. Can you talk about that balance?

RS: Tone is so fundamentally important in horror, and it's something that I really try and pay attention to. It's something that I'm, project to project, learning how to handle better. With Dawn of the Deaf, I wanted to make sure it encapsulated everything that I was interested in, everything that I could do as a filmmaker, both dramatically and in terms of horror.

It was important to me to show just how compelling these characters were. These characters were going to be without any spoken dialogue and on a hair trigger with the tension from just the day-to-day dramatic stories that we were touching on before the horror even arrived.

The intention was to make it so tense and compelling that you forget you're watching a movie called *Dawn of Deaf*. So, when the zombies show up, you're kind of like, "Oh yeah". And that's what I love about horror is you can subvert those moments in a way that feels playful. You're always looking for how you can fuck with the audience.

Giving a character the kind of third act emotional catharsis, that they've been building up their whole lives to say, and then you have their bottom jaw eaten off, you can't really do that in any other genre but horror.

JL: Was Dawn of the Deaf sent out as sort of proof of concept?

RS: The thing that happened with *Dawn of the Deaf* that was so life changing is that it got into Sundance. It started playing a whole bunch of American festivals. I never had any attention from US producers, or from studios, and suddenly all that changed. I visited LA and pitched things around, and I realized that that was the place that I needed to be. I need to be making movies in America because there wasn't an appetite and a bit of a snobbery around genre in the UK. Which I like to think is changing, but very slowly.

JL: What's going on over there? I figured there would be a [horror] onslaught, especially after the UK suffered through the video nasties ban and so many years of censorship.

RS: A lot of the main avenue to getting your movie made, especially your first couple of movies, is through public money, through government money, through the British Film Institute and all these places. A lot of masterpieces get made through those systems, but there is still a snobbery around genre.

When *Host* came out and started to blow up and immediately started to kind of garner all this attention of producers, studios, everyone was clamoring to work with the *Host* team. It took about two weeks for anyone from the UK film industry to email me. And when they did, they would say stuff like, "Um, I haven't watched it yet, but I've heard you've made a short film project on Zoom. Congratulations." Just this condescending, pat on the head bullshit. It just was so evident that it was time to go.

JL: Let's talk about your short film *Salt* a little bit because this is a story purely told in action. It's an exercise in tension at only two minutes. Was this something that you needed to do for train yourself on CGI, creature creation, new ways of blocking and camera movement?

RS: It was. I hadn't done a lot of those things before, the creature design, the dynamic camera movements, but I always had those kind of moves in my head and I always had that sense of this is what my studio horror movie is going to look like. Fox Digital had a bit of money to make two-minute short films for Halloween. I pitched them this idea and they gave us a little bit of money to do it. It was about twice what we made *Dawn of the Deaf* for. I think this was fifteen thousand dollars.

Suddenly we had the attention of studios and companies like Atomic Monster and all these genre filmmakers that I so admired. I was like I'm going to make a short film that feels like it's been plucked from the middle of the best James Wan movie you've ever seen. The storytelling is going to be as clean, and it's going to have that high concept hook that means that you can share it around and you don't need to preempt it with anything. You get it immediately from the first frame. And so, it was really me doubling down on this idea that nobody in the UK wants to make these movies so I'm gonna make it so that Hollywood can't ignore me.

JL: I can see elements [from your short films] in your adaptation of Stephen King's The Boogeyman. There's a through line that I appreciate in your movies. No matter how serious the tone or topic, you love adding pranks. Dawn of the Deaf features a series of online video pranks created for cruelty. The genesis of making Host began as an actual online prank that you involve friends and your future cast in. Dashcam is like a prank on the audience by having us empathize with this contentious cultural and political point of view from the main character. And then in The Boogeyman, the main character has a hard time coming to terms with what her little sister is witnessing until a prank pulled by her classmates forces the horror into their experience. What is it about the art of the prank that you love so much?

RS: I think great horror is kind of like playing a prank on the audience. The thing that I love more than anything is sitting at the back of a cinema, knowing something is coming, watching the audiences' shoulders rise in tension, and then hearing them scream.

It's like pulling a big prank when you execute a great jump scare or set piece. Jump scares get derided a lot, but I'm a huge fan when they're well-executed. It's knowing that an audience is going to be feeling safe because it's a daytime scene or that I'm going to be directing their attention in one corner of the frame and then doing something else in the other corner that's going to scare them.

The actual pranks in the movies themselves, I think Andrew Dominik said it best regarding his film, The Assassination of Jesse James, that the most potent emotion to put on screen is humiliation. That kind of like, "I want to disappear into a black hole and never have anyone look at me again." It's so relatable, and it's so visceral. It's such a great way to pull the audience in because it's a feeling that all of us have felt. Cinema makes us recognize these very lonely feelings in a communal setting and it's very cathartic.

JL: It creates something memorable. It might be an attitude, or it might be the way someone delivers dialogue, but I feel like if you get them in a position where everyone can relate to them no matter what they're saying or what they look like, you win.

RS: Yeah. One of my favorite horror movies of all time is Brian De Palma's *Carrie*, which is the perfect example of that, the most excruciating scene of public humiliation ever put on film.

JL: Well, speaking of that, here's a quote: "Robert, I'm still thinking about your movie". You know who that's from?

RS: Ha! Mr. King.

JONATHAN LEES: Yes, Stephen King himself, speaking on *The Boogeyman*. You were involved with writing on every project you did prior and now you have this script presented to you. Not only a script, but an adaptation of one of the biggest horror authors ever and a very vintage story. One that's very clean cut, short, and ambiguous. What were your trepidations or excitement about heading into this?

RS: Well, the main excitement was doing something that would have the name Stephen King hovering above the title. I mean, that's legendary. Entering that pantheon of filmmakers is the most exciting thing in the world and the most terrifying. I'd read the short story and I remember it fucking me up as a kid.

I've never really seen myself as a writer. I've kind of written by necessity and then it seems almost a bit silly to talk about the writing process on *Host* and *Dashcam* because they were so heavily improvised by the cast, so we kind of workshopped them on the day.

We would have an outline that Gemma [Hurley], Jed [Shepard], and I would put together. It's very much a communally written movie.

JL: That's something that a lot of writers can learn from directors: their process of editing. Whether you're editing live, on-set, with everyone's opinions flying at you, or you're in the post house finalizing your entire film. Those decisions. It is writing. It is creation.

RS: Doing two improvised movies back-to-back helped me with turning up every day and knowing what the scene ahead of me was about, what the fundamental dynamic of it was and not worrying about the camera moves or the individual lines of dialogue. Instead, being like, what is this scene telling us? What is the experience we want to give the audience? We want the audience to be watching through their fingers. We want them to feel moved.

JL: When you're in the editing room, what have you learned about yourself that makes it easier for you to get rid of things that you loved on set?

RS: Strangely, for somebody who's made two fully improvised movies, I don't like them. There is a tendency in those movies to put in too much material because they can't bear to part with some of it. I've got a healthy ego, but I'm also deeply driven by fear of humiliation and fear of failure and fear of not connecting to an audience. It's also why my movies are so short. If a moment doesn't absolutely earn its place, it's on the cutting room floor. There's so much great stuff that ends up there, but I don't take my audience's attention for granted.

It's all about sitting in that cinema and feeling the rise and fall of the audience's attention and how involved they are emotionally. I love the test screening process, which I know is scary for a lot of people. On *The Boogeyman*, we got the studio to allow me to bring in two strangers who had to sign NDAs and watch the cut wherever it was. Anyone who's ever seen a rough cut of a movie before knows how embarrassing that is. But every week I quizzed them on what was working and what wasn't, and it really helped me understand, even though I love this moment, it's not doing anything for them and this is the bit where they're shifting in their seat or checking their phone, and I've really let that kind of like lead the way with how I put a movie together, especially in the edit.

JL: The Boogeyman is a very short story, and your sense of pacing is propulsive throughout the film. It can't be easy to extend a universe that an author has created.

RS: No, no. I'd love to take credit for the way that that short story was extrapolated, but the hard part had been done by [Scott] Beck and [Bryan] Woods. They figured out a way to take the short story and expand it into a feature by making the short story the first act. I immediately saw the great work that Beck and Woods had done but the direction that I wanted to take it in which was a much more propulsive popcorn movie. The reference that I gave to the studio was Ordinary People meets Poltergeist. I brought on this writer, Mark Heyman (*Black Swan*) who I worked with for maybe six months, and we reshaped it.

We came up with the idea of these two sisters as the main protagonists. I thought that I was going to be warring with the studio. I thought that I was going to be screwed over at every turn because that's what we kind of envision studio filmmaking as. It's incredible how I was given complete autonomy over where the movie was going, and everyone agreed on what the movie should be. As long as I was delivering that movie, I got supported from the studio and from 21 Laps, the producers who also made *Stranger Things* and *Arrival*. They're great producers and fucking smart collaborators and it felt like an extension of the process that had begun on Host of not being afraid to incorporate ideas, from all avenues, so long as they're good.

JL: It feels like a natural extension of what you've shown us in the past with Dawn of the Deaf and Salt. It's a morbid drama on grief with hard horror elements. You could have pulled the rug out from under the audience and made The Boogeyman more metaphorical. What was that ultimately your decision? Or was that part of the script from the beginning to have an actual creature?

RS: It was something I always wanted to do. You quite rightly pointed out there's a lot of similarity in the style in the creature between The Boogeyman and Salt. It's a bit both corporeal and wispy and ghostly, but [The Boogeyman] has got that kind of physicality to it. I always wanted to make a kind of monster movie with this very real, very physical creature that runs and falls and stumbles and feels things. It's there in the world and not just, like you say, an idea that's haunting these characters. And, you know, one of the references that I gave the animators very early on was Ghostface from Scream. I love the way that they interpret it. There's a lot of animation in The Boogeyman where the creature is running after on the stairs, but it oversteps, and it bangs into the wall and there's a lot of kind of like slipping and sliding and kind of messy pratfalls that come from the Scream movies. I always wanted to have that physicality to it, and I also just wanted to show that I wasn't fucking around. The idea of killing a child right at the beginning was a way of saying like, "This movie's PG-13, but it's gonna go hard.

JL: Well, I'm glad you did that. I mean, even King's line [in the short story], "The child was white as flour, except for where the blood had sunk." I mean, give me a break, you can't get more gruesome and I love that you kept in that level of dread. Can you describe the euphoria of watching words on a page transform into something that's eventually shared with everyone?

RS: It's an amazing thing to see something that can be interpreted six hundred different ways on a page, start to form into a singular vision. There's something that exists within the shapeless form and the first joy is seeing the fire lighting up in the eyes of your team and they realize how the scene is going to come together and what the dynamic of it is and how effective it's going to be. Then to go through the body-breaking process of making a movie and the hundred or so compromises you have to make every day while trying to hold on to what this thing is, ultimately needs to be for the experience of the audience, which is so central. Even though you could have done with an extra two hours to shoot a scene, even though the lighting isn't quite how you wanted it, even though you wanted one more take to get that performance, to feel that it works allays all those concerns, and it almost washes the movie clean and makes it new again. You're seeing the architecture of it and when you see it with an audience and it works, you get swept up in the energy and that's kind of the best feeling in the world.

JL: I figured with the fracturing of our patience, our time, and the onslaught of online video that the short form, whether the printed word or film, would just become part of our culture in a bigger way, but it hasn't. Can you talk about your love and appreciation of the short form and why you keep coming back to it?

RS: I think stories aren't all meant to be packaged in ninety-five-minute bundles. I'm always advocating for the movie to be the length that it needs to be. Host is fifty-six minutes. And that's exactly the length that it needs to be. *Dashcam* is just a little over an hour. I think sometimes you want to read a novel and you want to be nourished in that way. But sometimes you want to gather around a campfire and be told a ghost story. And a ghost story doesn't want to outstay its welcome.

You want a story that stings in a short amount of time. And this new short that I'm doing, is meant to be a little parable that gets under your skin and stays there. So, it's only five minutes long, but it's going to stick with audiences' way beyond that. It's also a training ground. I'm still learning and I'm still teaching myself. This ghost story that I'm working on is shot in a single take, an unbroken Steadicam shot. And I don't use a lot of Steadicam when I shoot, I tend to prefer tracks and precision. I'm trying to loosen myself up and be even more adventurous in the way that I block things. It's a lower stakes way of opening myself up to fresh humiliation and fresh lessons to learn.

NISI SHAWL

Conducted by Valor Levinson

VALOR LEVINSON: When did you first know that you were a writer?

NISI SHAWL: I can't say when I knew for sure, but it was before I wrote a postapocalyptic short story for my ninth-grade English class. Something about teenagers wandering around a devastated landscape and worshipping the past at the sites of engineering feats. Earlier, I was collaborating with a friend on parodies of the *Wizard of Oz*, comic songs about our teachers, that sort of thing. So maybe then? But it wasn't until my second year in college that I realized I could write professionally. Like, for a living. That was when I read Suzy McKee Charnas's novel Walk to the End of the World. "You can get away with saying things like this? And people will *pay* you to say them?" I didn't understand then how very little that pay could be, of course.

VL: What was the first horror story you ever wrote?

NS: I wrote a flash piece about living next to an annoying neighbor who owned a ghost dog. Just a couple pages typed on my first electric typewriter. It's long lost to time and multiple moves to multiple dwellings. I remember that at the end a massive pack of invisible dogs came pouring down the hallway of the narrator's apartment building.

VL: You've been known to say that writing is far more communal, and less solitary, than most people imagine. Can you unpack what that means?

NS: So many meanings! So many ways that concept is true...from the influence other authors exert on you with their inspirational work, to the feedback you receive from beta readers and critique groups, to the information gathered by researchers and documentarians that you rely on, to the friends you meet virtually or in cafés for co-working sessions, to the publicists and cover artists and editors and all the other contributing members of any given publishing venue, to audiences at public readings, to reviewers—I mean, it just goes on and on and on. Genius is a shared joy. We never work alone.

VL: What other practices inform/enhance/complement your writing (e.g. regular walks through a haunted subdivision; drinking the blood of vegetables; raising eels as pets)?

NS: Nothing so interesting as the examples you've given. I do create altars for every significant writing project: novels, short stories, that kind of thing. I think altar building is a very human activity.

VL: It's well known that Octavia Butler was a friend and mentor of yours. What did she teach you in regards to writing horror?

NS: Octavia was a great proponent of the simple gut punch. She taught me—by showing me—that grimness could be more powerfully depicted via understatement than embellishment.

VL: What's the scariest thing you've ever written?

NS: That's an exercise for the reader. Really, different things are scary (or not) to different people. I will say that after I finished writing "Vulcanization," a short story from the viewpoint of Belgium's Leopold II, I felt coated in nastiness. Such an irredeemably evil man. He left skidmarks on my soul.

VL: What's one of your favorite monsters (fictional or otherwise)?

NS: Chelsea Quinn Yarbro wrote a series of novels about a sexy vampire who lived in France under the assumed name of the Comte Saint Germaine. All swoony and tenderhearted and not terribly realistic—though I didn't focus hard on anything but the tragical romanticism of his plight.

But as a person who is sometimes seen as a monster myself, I have to ask: A monster judged by whose standards?

VL: Your work through *Writing the Other* has been an invaluable resource for many writers who want to represent characters with minority identities in a positive and humanizing light. Why is this work important for the horror genre in particular?

NS: Storytelling in the horror genre has long been a refuge for those bent on enforcing dominant culture's beliefs about what is monstrous. Mary Shelley's sister famously internalized society's view of her as ugly, wretched, beastlike, and some have theorized that Frankenstein's monster is modeled on poor Fanny (women being powerless in that place and time). By "othering" members of the global majority, horror has signed itself up as part of the status quo—and by learning how to fix that with respectful and accurate representation we can switch our allegiance to the forces of change. That's a significant action! Furthermore, have you noticed the growing presence of people of color in this corner of the field? I sure have, and I'm not alone. Let's make it more welcoming and less exclusionary. Reading *Writing the Other: A Practical Approach* is one way of doing that.

VL: What are some horror stories you love that represent minority characters well?

NS: One of my favorites is *The Good House*, by Tananarive Due. Due does a terrific job of representing Black folks, and also of representing adherents of a minority religion, Vodun. Due's most recent novel is *The Reformatory*, another horror novel whose representation of minority characters I just adore. I'm also extremely fond of *Lovecraft Country* by Matt Ruff. The book, I mean, though the series is cool. But Ruff got so much right about his Chicago-South-Side-in-1952 African Americans, my mom, who was a member of that demographic group, felt sure that he belonged to it too. Ruff's white as mayonnaise, so no.

VL: If you could steal the brain of any horror writer, whose would it be?

NS: I really like my own brain, actually. Although it worked faster and more efficiently when I was younger. Wait, maybe if I could take possession of the brain of someone younger and overwrite it with my memories? Cannibalize it? Hmmm. You might be on to something.

PAUL TREMBLAY

EARNING YOUR WAY TO THE CARD TABLE

By John Langan

*P*aul Tremblay is the author of nine novels, five collections of stories, a novella, and a couple of those Amazon-single things. He also co-authored a young-adult novel with Stephen Graham Jones. He's co-edited a couple of anthologies: *Bandersnatch and Phantom*, both with Sean Wallace, and *Creatures: Thirty Years of Monsters*, with yours truly. He's also one of the founders of and driving forces behind the Shirley Jackson Awards.

Although he'd been publishing short fiction since 2001, and novels from 2009, I think it's fair to say that 2015's *A Head Full of Ghosts* was the book that brought him to everyone's attention. His first out and out horror novel, *A Head Full of Ghosts* took the exorcism narrative and pulled it inside out, combining the story of a suburban family whose daughter's strange behavior leads them to seek an exorcism for her—which they agree to have filmed for a reality-TV show—with trenchant observations on the history and problematic nature of the exorcism narrative. Stephen King praising the book on Twitter certainly helped raise its profile, but the fact is, if the book had not been as strong as it was, the effect of King's words would have been temporary at best.

In the decade since that novel, Tremblay has written another five horror novels, each different from the one before, yet all concerned with similar themes: the pressures facing the nuclear family in early-twenty-first-century America; the perils of adolescence; the permutations of the horror narrative; the limitations and failures of the institutions that structure our lives; the places where sense frays and unravels. During this time, he's also published two collections of stories which have further demonstrated the range of his interests and abilities. At this point in his career, he's established a solid, coherent body of work, one that has attracted a dedicated readership. It's led to one film adaptation, M. Night Shyamalan's *Knock At the Cabin* (2023) and the promise of more.

I've known Paul for close to two decades, now. He's not only one of my favorite writers; he's one of my closest friends. We've been through some shit, as the kids say. I'm happy to have had this chance to talk to him and to share the results of our conversation with you.

JOHN LANGAN: First: the inevitable, tell-us-about yourself question. Where and when were you born? What was your life like when you were growing up? What were the formative experiences of your younger life?

PAUL TREMBLAY: I was born in Aurora, CO, while my father was briefly in the Air Force. We moved to Beverly — 20 miles north of Boston — where my dad grew up, when I was less than a year old, so I have no memory of Colorado. As far as when, you'll pry my age from my dead cold hands. Fine, born in 1971.

For the first 4–5 years of my life we lived on the second floor of my grandparents' triple-decker house. My parents eventually bought a small three-bedroom place that has been used/featured one-way-or-another in many of my stories. I have two siblings, my sister is 11 months younger and my brother five years younger. Dad worked at the Parker Brothers factory in Salem, occasionally in a warehouse in Danvers. Mom alternated between staying home and working as a bank teller. We weren't poor, but money was a constant discussion/ concern in the house. Money was probably tightest in my fourth and fifth grade years — or maybe this was when I was first or most aware of it being tight — when my mother's father, Patrick (Grampy Pat) had a major stroke and had to live with us for a few years, and my mother took care of him.

I didn't have many friends growing up (awkward, skinny, not confident) and was instead much closer with my siblings and extended family. Every Sunday we went to my grandparents' house and there would usually be between ten and fifteen people there, including the kid cousins. The adults would play card games all afternoon, usually a game called Donut. You had to earn your way to that card table and the first few times I got to play, I left the table in tears, "sensitive" (how I was described by adults and teachers) child that I was. Those French Canadians took their cards and games seriously. There was also a lot of storytelling done at the table, usually by my gregarious grandfather Gaetan (Grampy Gate) or my father or wildly entertaining Uncle Dennis.

Otherwise, what was life like? I watched a lot of cable TV, listened to records, and shot hoops out back, by myself, for hours.

JL: Do you want to say anything more in the way of formative experiences?

PT: I don't know why I'm resisting the notion of 'formative experiences.' Perhaps it's a kind superstition; having revealed (there's no grand reveal) what I think was formative would then lead to an unraveling. Or, to state the obvious, it was all formative. Sorry, I haven't drunk my uber-caffeinated tea yet.

As a young child I was a devotee of the local weekend program, *Creature Double Feature*, which I do credit for starting me on the path of horror. The horror path! My father and Aunt Mary were also SF/horror film fans and I have vivid memories of them breathlessly detailing their experience of watching *Alien* on the big screen. I was afraid of the dark and slept with a fortress of stuffed animals around my head, despite having my younger brother in the same bedroom as a handy monster sacrifice. Thanks to the much more explicit movies of the 70s/80s on cable TV, my brother Dan became a gore hound, while I would watch those movies with my hands covering my face, if I watched at all. My scoliosis was formative, or anti-formative. It wasn't discovered/diagnosed until I was in high school, and the physical therapy, hard plastic and metal ringed back braces and eventually, spinal fusion surgery, intensified the feeling that my rail-thin, acne ridden body was the enemy.

Lastly (do we stop having formative experiences?), my high school and college summers were spent working on the assembly lines or helping to unload trucks at the Parker Brothers factory. One morning in 1991 management called everyone into the lunchroom, including my father (he was in charge of the mailroom at that point of his twenty-five years at Parkers) to announce Hasbro had completed the purchase of the company and the factory would be closed in three months. In my fiction, I've written explicitly and, um, implicitly about that moment in the lunch room, and the cloud of despair within the factory post-announcement.

JL: That's a great point: maybe if we stop having formative experiences, it means we start to die?

PT: Gah! But yes? Not to put too fine a point on it, teaching, getting married, having children were all formative experiences. Or formative to who I am today, anyway.

JL: As is your recent purchase of a "flying V" electric guitar.

PT: Oh, that is a clear sign of my unraveling.

JL: Which is, if I'm not mistaken, the title of your next book.

PT: So mean. For the interest of posterity, The Unraveling is not the title of my next book. And I'm not telling you what it is. It's a state secret. The State of Paul secret. No one wants to move there because we have shitty health insurance too.

JL: No, I mean My Unraveling. Like Knausgaard. My mockery notwithstanding, this allows me to ask you to talk about the importance of music in your life and work. A Head Full of Ghosts found its title in a Bad Religion song. Survivor Song uses the metaphor of the song to describe its events; while The Pallbearers Club features a protagonist who is involved in the local music scene in and around Providence. Has music always been important to you, or was there a moment something clicked for you? What music continues to speak to you? What relationship do you see between the music you listen to and the fiction you write?

PT: I already wrote that book. It's called The Pallbearers Club and many people find that book as pretentious as I find Knausgaard.

Anyway, music! My parents had all kinds of LP records and vinyl 45 RPM singles, and music, much of it 60s and 70s rock, was ever present. Us kids used to play the 45s of Chicago's "25 or 6 to 4" and "Ride Captain Ride" by Blues Image on the heaviest of rotations. But when Def Leppard put out their single "Photograph" and the record Pyromania in early 1983, that record, and MTV, took over a large portion of my middle school life. Initially the appeal was pure daydream fantasy, as so many of those songs had accompanying videos. I didn't feel that cool but I wanted to be that cool.

Eventually, I branched out to other bands and modes of music but almost all guitar-based, as those distorted strings struck some inner chord in me. Those hours of lying on the dining room floor with the stereo speakers tented over my head was still partially about fantasy and escape, but it was also about giving myself over to the sound and lyrics, to a thing that was outside of me, beyond me, but also inside me somewhere too.

I still follow that ringing inner guitar chord toward the discovery of new bands, or newer bands. Newer to me bands? I've been on a Pile kick for a while, though after seeing mclusky live, I've been listening to their catalogue, plus some new songs, non-stop.

I write by what I would describe as feel most if not all the time: what feels right, or more importantly, what makes me feel or want to feel. Writing is my attempt to pin emotion(s) that can be best described in story or in song. My favorite songs still make me want to pretend/imagine I'm on stage, but they also make me want to feel. Maybe I wasn't really looking to escape through music, but instead, be inspired to engage, to dare to engage more deeply than I thought I ever could.

JL: I'd like to stick with the music question for just a moment longer. To speak personally, I've always associated you with Punk, both in terms of musical taste and aesthetic stance. Is this fair? If so, how do you see yourself as a Punk? How has Punk figured in your writing?

PT: Well, you've certainly always called me a punk. Hey, now...

Definitely fair to say I admire the musical taste/aesthetic, particularly when it's less popular and more outsider art than say a band like Green Day. I do not see myself as a Punk. I haven't earned that moniker with my lifestyle. If I were to make such a claim, Punk writers/friends Nick Mamatas, Liz Hand, Cara Hoffman, and Jim Ruland could and should punch me. Maybe I aspire to it, but also, I don't want to live in a squat or a collective, and sleeping on couches would be murder on my back.

The sort-of-jokes aside, part of what I admire about punk is the idea that you do not have to be from the social/cultural/ class elite to make your art. You don't have to have trained at best the schools.

You don't have to be a wunderkind, or any type of -kind. You learn the basics (maybe), or fake the basics at the very least, and just say fuck it and go and do and do it with self-integrity and maybe it won't be genius but as long as you aren't straight-up lying it'll be yours and maybe if it's good enough it'll be everyone else's too. I don't mean the above as an anti-intellectual call or stance, and there's certainly room for growth in there too (the rigidity of many punk music communities is a fair criticism). Anyway, I guess what I'm trying to say is that if you're going to put a piece of yourself out there, fucking commit to it with as little room for compromise as the real world will allow.

I would never have dared write my first story without that clarion call.

JL: Of course, what punk would call themselves a punk...? Moving on... How about writing? Or maybe I should say, how about narrative? What stories are important to you? I'm thinking in terms of novels and stories, also writers, but I'm also thinking of movies and tv shows.

PT: Some movies and tv shows first, because for my first twenty years of meatbag existence they were how I knew or learned narrative. As a middle schooler and teen I watched *MASH* repeatedly. Hawkeye Pierce quotes (I usually keep those to myself) occur to me nearly as often as Simpsons quotes/ references. Okay, maybe not as often, but definitely it's number 2 on my list. I loved *MASH's* irreverence, particularly in how it was directed toward authority, and the heart-on-sleeve monologues.

Movie-wise, *Jaws* is my most viewed, followed by *The Thing*. Jaws gave me way more nightmares. *American Werewolf in London*, in retrospect, has a similar irreverence to *MASH*, plus a gnarly werewolf. I have fond memories of watching these movies and many more with my Dad and/or my brother. My brother and I will still randomly quote movies or send text send video clips, with our most-often quoted being, "The ice is gonna break," and, "You only moved the headstones. WHY???" If I have to name the movies, then, well, you can't hang out with me and Dan.

While those are surface reflections on those stories, I suppose, it's a sign to me that those narratives are ingrained in me or struck that same inner chord that my favorite songs do, and are a part of my inner language. That those movies are tied to good memories and relationships only makes them the more indelible to me. It has been a joy rewatching these movies with my kids and getting to experience them again through new eyes.

I know, I know, I haven't mentioned a book yet. There are so many writers and books to mention, but a quick timeline, then. "Where Are You Going, Where Have You Been?" by Joyce Carol Oates and Stephen King's *The Stand* turned me in a reader. Clive Barker made me feel unsafe. Peter Straub and Shirley Jackson made me want to be smarter and better. Kurt Vonnegut made me think, 'Hey, maybe I can do something like this.' As an early writer, Jeffrey Thomas's *Punktown*, Aimee Bender's *The Girl in the Flammable Skirt*, and Danielewski's *House of Leaves* were very important to me. Roberto Bolano's *2666* crawls around my head at all hours. Now, I'm lucky enough to be friends or friendly with so many writers that I deeply admire, you included, John. The most recent book that continues to ring like a tuning fork is Marina Enriquez's *Our Share of Night*, which I've read twice.

JL: Your fiction developed from Weird short stories, to offbeat detective novels, to horror novels and stories. I have my own ideas about your development as a writer, but how do you see your progression over the last almost-two decades?

PT: When I first started messing around with stories, I was mimicking my favorites as best I could. I still mimic, but I'm much better at letting my own voice come through. Anyway, yeah, the first stories were all horror and I thought of myself as a horror writer. There was one story called "Cold" that was published on the venerable Gothic.net in 2001, and Mort Castle kindly told me it was a good story and it would've been good even without the horror element. That comment threw me for a loop, a wonderful loop. For my first time, a response to something I'd written wasn't, 'Oh yeah, that was cool because it was creepy and weird,' but that it was a good story. So started thinking of myself not as horror writer, but a writer who wrote horror, which meant that I wouldn't force every story into being a horror story. My interest and leanings would take me in that direction most of the time anyway, so why force a story to be something that it's not?

Novel-wise my first attempts at horror novels were, to quote my UK friends, shite: one King knock-off and another that I got partway through, but it wasn't working. A few years after "Cold" was published I wrote a goofy, plotless comedy novel in Boston. I never sold it, but it did land me my agent (after a two-plus year search). I'm glad the novel isn't out in the world but it did its job. The handful of novels that came after were all darkly comic: *The Little Sleep*, its follow-up *No Sleep Till Wonderland*, and a strange ode to Vonnegut and George Saunders and Thomas's Punktown called *Swallowing a Donkey's Eye*. All the while (the rest of the first decade of the 2000s and the first half of the 2010s) I was still writing horror short stories. It wasn't until A Head Full of Ghosts that I completed a full horror novel, and it felt like something clicked. Not that I'm saying it's great or anything like that, but I better understood (for good, bad, or indifferent) what I wanted a horror novel by me to say, what I wanted it to feel like. I'd still fuck it up of course, but my abiding interests in ambiguity/identity/reality/parenthood now in the age of social media and misinformation seemed like a good match for horror novels rooted in a kind of realism. Not necessarily the literary mode of realism, but that the horror stories would feel real to me. Like they could happen. Or this is as close as I could get to what it might feel like if those horrors were to happen/are happening. And even if there was to be humor, the horror elements would be taken seriously. I wanted and continue to want to take that part seriously.

Um, I don't know if there's a progression in there somewhere. I don't know what the hell I'm doing. I like to think I'm like Buzz Lightyear (but with a much weaker chin): falling with style.

JL: I'd be remiss if I didn't at least mention your connection to the Shirley Jackson Awards.

PT: Back in 2006ish, you and I had heard whispers about the International Horror Guild closing up shop. In a youthful (shh, don't tell the people we weren't that youthful) bout of, um, enthusiasm, we asked Paula Guran if two knuckleheads like us could take over the award and run it. She wisely said no. Undaunted, or somewhat daunted, we began talking about starting another award with friends and colleagues F. Brett Cox, Joanne Cox, and Sarah Langan. I remember the five of us came rather quickly to the idea of naming the award after Shirley Jackson. I believe it was Brett who wrote the agent/lawyer of the Jackson Estate, asking if we could start an award in her name. Or, start an award that would celebrate Jackson's work and influence, while celebrating what was happening in the contemporary horror/dark fiction world even if, especially at the time in 2006/2007, much of horror fiction wasn't being labeled as such by large publishers. Once the estate gave the okay, I remember that as the "oh shit, I guess we have to do this," moment. It was a lot of work and stress (and nothing compared to the amount of work Joann did and continues to do as the administrator) but I'm proud of the award, as we all are. Feel free to correct my memory here, at your bodily peril.

JL: Perish the thought. You've been at this writing thing for a little while now. Any observations about how the horror field has changed over that time?

PT: The best change is that there are so many more women, BIPOC, and queer writers being published, read, translated, and discussed than there were two decades ago. Of course, horror can still do much better in that regard.

Keeping this paragraph to publishing, horror is selling more than it has than at any other point during my career. It was only ten years when my agent and I were trying to sell *A Head Full of Ghosts* and many of the passes we received were, "We love it, but horror doesn't sell." I recently saw a statistic that from '22 to '23 (or maybe '23 to '24) there was a twenty percent increase in the number of horror titles being or to-be published.

The pessimist in me worries that the sales boom (however boom-y it might or might not be) is not sustainable. Maybe it is, but we know that not everyone loves horror. There are plenty of cynical publishers and studios/producers who make decisions based solely on the dollar, which tends not to produce the best works. Especially on the Hollywood side where I've heard many times, "We want horror, but it can't be too grim, and it has to have a happy ending."

The optimist in me (I'm complicated) loves that not everyone loves horror, thinks that horror works best when it prods and pokes at the margins of mainstream culture and makes folks uncomfortable. Optimist-me is very excited by what is being produced by the field and what might come in the future.

JL: Okay, last two questions. First: Math?

PT: It's good for you. Like broccoli. I don't really like broccoli.

JL: Finally: What is Thanksgiving at Stephen King's house like?

PAUL TREMBLAY: Ha! I wouldn't know, John. I imagine I would be seated at the kid's table though.

JL: Sworn to secrecy: gotcha. Thanks, man.

PAUL TREMBLAY: Thank you!

THE 2023 BRAM STOKER AWARDS® FINAL BALLOT

SUPERIOR ACHIEVEMENT IN AN ANTHOLOGY

Aquilone, James – *Shakespeare Unleashed*
(Crystal Lake Publishing, Monstrous Books)

Golden, Christopher, and Keene, Brian – *The Drive-In: Multiplex* (Pandi Press)

Hawk, Shane and Van Alst, Jr., Theodore C. – *Never Whistle at Night: An Indigenous Dark Fiction Anthology* (Vintage)

Peele, Jordan, and Adams, John Joseph – *Out There Screaming* (Random House)

Rowland, Rebecca – *American Cannibal* (Maenad Press)

SUPERIOR ACHIEVEMENT IN A FICTION COLLECTION

Files, Gemma – *Blood from the Air* (Grimscribe Press)

Keisling, Todd – *Cold, Black, & Infinite* (Cemetery Dance)

Malerman, Josh – *Spin A Black Yarn* (Del Rey)

Nogle, Christi – *The Best of Our Past, the Worst of Our Future* (Flame Tree Press)

Read, Sarah – *Root Rot & Other Grim Tales* (Bad Hand Books)

SUPERIOR ACHIEVEMENT IN A FIRST NOVEL

Carmen, Christa – *The Daughters of Block Island* (Thomas & Mercer)

Compton, Johnny – *The Spite House* (Tor Nightfire/Macmillan)

LaRocca, Eric – *Everything the Darkness Eats* (CLASH Books/Titan)
Leede, CJ – *Maeve Fly* (Tor Nightfire/Macmillan/Titan)
Rebelein, Sam – *Edenville* (William Morrow/Titan)

SUPERIOR ACHIEVEMENT IN A GRAPHIC NOVEL

Bunn, Cullen (author) and Leomacs (artist) – *Ghostlore, Vol. 1* (BOOM! Studios)
Cesare, Adam (author) and Stoll, David (artist) – *Dead Mall* (Dark Horse Comics)
Chu, Amy (author) and Lee, Soo (artist) – *Carmilla: The First Vampire* (Dark Horse)
Ito, Junji (author and artist) –*Tombs* (Viz Media)
Tanabe, Gou (author and artist) – *H.P. Lovecraft's The Shadow Over Innsmouth* (Dark Horse Comics)

SUPERIOR ACHIEVEMENT IN LONG FICTION

Due, Tananarive – "Rumpus Room"
(*The Wishing Pool and Other Stories,* Akashic Books)
Jiang, Ai – *Linghun* (Dark Matter INK)
Khaw, Cassandra – *The Salt Grows Heavy* (Tor Nightfire/Macmillan/Titan)
McCarthy, J.A.W. – *Sleep Alone* (Off Limits Press LLC)
Murray, Lee – *Despatches* (PS Publishing)

SUPERIOR ACHIEVEMENT IN LONG NONFICTION

Coleman, Robin R. Means and Harris, Mark H. – *The Black Guy Dies First: Black Horror Cinema from Fodder to Oscar* (Gallery/Saga Press)
Fitzpatrick, Claire (ed.) – *A Vindication of Monsters: Essays on Mary Wollstonecraft and Mary Shelley* (IFWG Publishing International)
Hartmann, Sadie – *101 Horror Books to Read Before You're Murdered* (Page Street Publishing)
Morton, Lisa – *The Art of the Zombie Movie* (Applause Books)
Murray, Lee and Smith, Angela Yuriko (eds.) – *Unquiet Spirits: Essays by Asian Women in Horror* (Black Spot Books)

SUPERIOR ACHIEVEMENT IN A MIDDLE GRADE NOVEL

Henning, Sarah – *Monster Camp* (Margaret K. McElderry Books)
López, Diana – *Los Monstruos: Felice and the Wailing Woman* (Kokila)

Senf, Lora – *The Nighthouse Keeper* (Atheneum Books for Young Readers)
Tuma, Refe – *Frances and the Werewolves of the Black Forest* (HarperCollins)
Young, Suzanne – *What Stays Buried* (HarperCollins)

SUPERIOR ACHIEVEMENT IN A NOVEL

Due, Tananarive – *The Reformatory* (Gallery/Saga Press/Titan)
Hendrix, Grady – *How to Sell a Haunted House* (Berkley/Titan)
Jones, Stephen Graham – *Don't Fear the Reaper* (Gallery/Saga Press/Titan)
LaValle, Victor – *Lone Women* (One World)
Tingle, Chuck – *Camp Damascus* (Tor Nightfire/MacMillan/Titan)
Wendig, Chuck – *Black River Orchard* (Del Rey/Penguin Random House)

SUPERIOR ACHIEVEMENT IN POETRY

Gold, Maxwell Ian – *Bleeding Rainbows and Other Broken Spectrums* (Hex Publishers)
McHugh, Jessica – *The Quiet Ways I Destroy You* (Apokrupha Press)
Pichette, Marisca – *Rivers in Your Skin, Sirens in Your Hair* (Android Press)
Walrath, Holly Lyn – *Numinous Stones* (Aqueduct Press)
Wytovich, Stephanie M. – *On the Subject of Blackberries*
(Raw Dog Screaming Press)

SUPERIOR ACHIEVEMENT IN A SCREENPLAY

Brooker, Charlie – *Black Mirror: Beyond the Sea* (Episode 03:06)
(Zeppotron, Babieka, Banijay Entertainment, Broke and Bones, House of Tomorrow)
Cervera, Michelle Garza and Castillo, Abia – *Huesera: The Bone Woman*
(Disruptiva Films, Machete Producciones, MalignoGorehouse)
Duffield, Brian – *No One Will Save You*
(20th Century Studios, Star Thrower Entertainment)
Rugna, Demián – *When Evil Lurks* (Machaco Films, Aramos Cine, Shudder)
Yamazaki, Takashi – *Godzilla Minus One* (Robot Communications, Toho Studios)

SUPERIOR ACHIEVEMENT IN SHORT FICTION

Daniels, L.E. – "Silk" (*Hush, Don't Wake the Monster: Stories Inspired by Stephen King*, Twisted Wing Productions)

Jones, Rachael K. – "The Sound of Children Screaming" (*Nightmare Magazine*)

Miller, Sam J. – "If Someone You Love Has Become a Vurdalak" (*The Dark*)

O'Quinn, Cindy – "Quondam"

(*The Nightmare Never Ends,* Exploding Head Fiction)

Tabing, Nadine Aurora – "An Inherited Taste"

(*No Trouble at All,* Cursed Morsels Press)

SUPERIOR ACHIEVEMENT IN SHORT NON-FICTION

Bissett, Carina – "Words Wielded by Women" (*Apex Magazine*)

Bulkin, Nadia – "Becoming Ungovernable: Latah, Amok, and Disorder in Indonesia," (*Unquiet Spirits: Essays by Asian Women in Horror,* Black Spot Books)

Kulski, K.P. – "100 Livers"

(*Unquiet Spirits: Essays by Asian Women in Horror,* Black Spot Books)

Murray, Lee – "Displaced Spirits"

(*Unquiet Spirits: Essays by Asian Women in Horror,* Black Spot Books)

Wetmore Jr, Kevin – "A Theatre of Ghosts, A Haunted Cinema: The Japanese Gothic as Theatrical Tradition in Gurozuka"

(*The Wenshan Review of Literature and Culture: Special Issue on Asian Gothic*)

SUPERIOR ACHIEVEMENT IN A YOUNG ADULT NOVEL

Bayron, Kalynn – *You're Not Supposed to Die Tonight* (Bloomsbury YA)

Dimaline, Cherie – *Funeral Songs for Dying Girls* (Tundra Book Group)

Simmons, Kristen – *Find Him Where You Left Him Dead* (Tor Teen)

Smith, Cynthia Leitich – *Harvest House* (Candlewick Press)

Tran, Trang Thanh – *She Is a Haunting* (Bloomsbury YA)

LIFETIME ACHIEVEMENT AWARD

The Lifetime Achievement Award is presented periodically to an individual whose work has substantially influenced the horror genre. While this award is often presented to a writer, it may also be given for influential accomplishments in other creative fields.

The Lifetime Achievement Award is the most prestigious of all awards presented by HWA. It does not merely honor the superior achievement embodied in a single work. Instead, it is an acknowledgment of superior achievement in an entire career.

The recipients of the HWA's Lifetime Achievement Award for 2024 are:

MORT CASTLE

CASSANDRA PETERSON

STEVE RASNIC TEM

MORT CASTLE

A former stage hypnotist, folksinger, and teacher (every level from grade to grad school), MORT CASTLE has been a publishing writer since 1967, with hundreds of stories, articles, comics, and books published in a dozen languages. Castle has won three Bram Stoker Awards®, two Black Quill awards, the Golden Bot (Wired Magazine), and has been nominated for The Audie, The Shirley Jackson award, the International Horror Guild award and the Pushcart Prize. In 2000, the *Chicago Sun-Times News Group* cited him as one of Twenty-One "Leaders in the Arts for the 21st Century in Chicago's Southland." Poland's *Newsweek* magazine listed his *The Strangers* (Obcy) in the "Top Ten Horror / Thriller Novels of 2008" and there will a 40th anniversary edition of the book this year in Spain, Poland, Germany, and the USA. Castle and his wife Jane will celebrate their 53rd wedding anniversary this July. They live in Crete, Illinois.

CASSANDRA PETERSON

From the top of her beehive hairdo to the bottom of her stiletto heels, Elvira, Mistress of the Dark personifies the horror genre in one spooky, sexy, funny package.

As Queen of Halloween, her reign has now spanned 40 years and includes her long-running nationally syndicated television series, Movie Macabre and two feature films: Elvira, Mistress of the Dark and Elvira's Haunted Hills. She has appeared in National ad campaigns for Pepsi and Coors, recorded five record albums and has written a line of young adult novels, a "Coffin Table" photo retrospective, and most recently, her memoir, Yours Cruelly, Elvira from Hachette Book Group.

The worldwide Elvira brand has generated thousands of products, including three pinball machines, four slot machines, eight Funko POP!'s, four comic book series, a line of NECA action figures, a Chia Pet, a Living Dead doll, a Monster High Skullector doll from Mattel, and the best-selling female costume of all time.

Elvira has appeared on hundreds of television shows including Happy Halloween Scooby Doo, Elvira's 40th Anniversary Very Scary, Very Special Special for the Shudder Channel, and the Netflix & Chills Halloween ad campaign.

Played by actress-writer Cassandra Peterson, Elvira, Mistress of the Dark has carved out a niche in popular American culture that is sure to endure for decades to come.

STOKERCON 2024
San Diego

STEVE RASNIC TEM

STEVE RASNIC TEM's writing career spans over 45 years, including more than 500 published short stories, 17 collections, 8 novels, misc. poetry and plays, and a handbook on writing, *Yours to Tell: Dialogues on the Art & Practice of Fiction*, written with his late wife Melanie Tem. His collaborative novella with Melanie, *The Man On The Ceiling,* won the World Fantasy, Bram Stoker, and International Horror Guild awards in 2001. He has also won the Bram Stoker, International Horror Guild, and British Fantasy Awards for his solo work, including *Blood Kin,* winner of 2014's Bram Stoker for novel. Originally from the Appalachian region of Southwest Virginia, he now lives in Centennial Colorado. www.stevetem.com

STEVE RASNIC TEM

Conducted by Kevin Wetmore

KEVIN WETMORE: Thanks for sitting down with me. First and foremost, and apologies for the obvious question – Why horror?

STEVE RASNIC TEM: Well, because I'm a scaredy-cat, I guess [laughs]. I had lots of anxieties as a kid, lots of fears, and although they've mostly gone away through the years I'm still able to tap into them. I think it's always interested me how our fears can tell us a lot about who we are as people – all kinds of things. Kinds of things that get to us; kinds of things that we obsess about. To me, that's always been the key to character. So when I started writing fiction, it took me a while to find the right genre, or the right models, or how to write my kinds of stories. But I knew horror was going to be in the mix.

KW: Well, since you say you're a scaredy-cat. What! What frightens you now? What scares you now? What might lead to future stories?

SRT: I'm still scared of heights, always have been [laughs]. I think most of my fears at this point have to do with aging and illness and death. But maybe more than that is just fear of things happening to my children or other people I love. When you get to be my age you lose people fairly frequently. I'll be 74 this year, and when you get in your seventies you start losing people, seems like every month, especially if you're a writer and you know lots of people.

KW: You have been in the game for quite a while. You've written over five hundred short stories and a dozen and a half novels in that time – quite an output. All I can think of is a lyric from the musical Hamilton: you write like you're running out of time. You just have so many short stories out there. What is the impetus to keep churning out short fiction?

SRT: I've always been obsessed with short stories. I love the form. I've always read a lot of them. I'm also impatient. So I like having the sense of having completed something. The problem with novels is you're putting off that sense of completion for a very long time, sometimes for years–in my case, sometimes for decades. Although my stories take longer for me to finish than they used to, I can still count on having that sense of completion every month or so, and that's what I really find addictive.

KW: Of which works are you most proud, then? Which are the ones that you look at and say, "I nailed it there."

SRT: That's hard to answer for me. I generally like the things I'm working on now more than things I've written in the past. To be honest, I often don't even remember having written them [laughs]. When I see them again, I'm sometimes surprised by certain lines or certain paragraphs, and because I can't imagine myself having written that, sometimes for good and sometimes for ill.

I still like The Man on the Ceiling, the book and the novella I wrote with my late wife Melanie, I think, in part because it started a sea change in my writing. It opened me up to other possibilities in terms of how to structure a story and what stories could be about. I have a certain fondness for that one.

KW: Related/unrelated then: if someone who may not be familiar with your work wanted to dive in, where should they start? What would you recommend?

SRT: I have a collection from Valancourt called Figures Unseen. I picked the two or three best horror stories from each of my collections, things I thought were either the best, or at least pretty representative. So that when now people ask me, "What do you do?", I just point to that book, and suggest they start there. They get a good sense of who I am and what I like to write about.

KW: What writers do you admire? Who are you reading?

SRT: Oh, there's so many. I can just say that among the newer writers I've been reading lately, there's a Chinese-Canadian writer, Ai Jiang. She, I find, is one of the more exciting new writers. There's another young woman, Christi Nogle, who has a couple of collections out from Flame Tree. She's a wonderful writer. Another wonderful woman, Eugen Bacon, an African-Australian writer who writes this really sumptuous, inventive prose, which tends to combine horror with science fiction. I admire her a great deal. One of my favorite writers right now is Claire Keegan, who is not a horror writer, not a fantasy writer. Her portrayals of character are just so right on, just so precise. I read each one of her works carefully. Maryse Meijer is another author whom I admire very much. I just finished reading Simon Strantzas' new collection. He's been a favorite of mine for a long time.

KW: You have an incredible body of work, and you've been active in the field for a long time. How has the field changed since you were on the come up?

SRT: Well. there's more competition, certainly [laughs], which sometimes feels unfortunate when you're trying to get into a table of contents and you know there are hundreds of writers vying for those two or three open slots. The good thing about that, of course, is that as a reader it's an exciting time, at least for me, for finding different kinds of horror fiction. Right now I'm being exposed to different cultures, different points of view. I love the short fictions being produced right now, especially by younger writers. A lot more people are writing horror now than ever before. It's a much, much more diverse genre than it ever was before. On the negative side, I guess, is at the same time the market has shrunk a bit. Anthologies now tend to be put out by small presses instead of the major presses. It's always a bit difficult to sell a horror novel or a horror collection. That's always been true, but maybe even more so now.

KW: What is your writing process? What is the actual process of sitting down to write something?

SRT: Well, it's changed over the years. For the last few years, the average story for me takes about three months to write. About a month to month and a half of that time is just spent thinking about the story, gathering ideas. And then when I actually start writing, I put everything about the story into one Word file. So all my notes, all my research, pieces lifted from the call for submissions, perhaps, anything I know about the themes related to that story. All that goes into one file. So it's basically one giant file of garbage. During the process of writing, some of the research turns into scenes, turns into descriptions, turns into pieces of dialogue, until eventually. with all that material, I start getting a sense of a character who is telling the story, or at least providing their perspective on someone else's story. And at that point I start shifting things around, moving some material upfront, thinking about what might make an interesting opening and it's very much a kind of chaotic process until I find the "heart" of the story, what the story is really about and what it means to the protagonist. Periodically I print out everything I've written, and I sit at a desk, and I cut big swatches out, and I rearrange pieces by hand, and then I edit and start from the beginning again.

KW: Is it similar for a novel?

SRT: For a novel, I will have a separate file for each chapter. It's taken me a while to really figure out a good process for me to write a novel. For a long time I was hung up on research. What, for me is key to writing a novel is narrowing it down and focusing on a specific set of events at a specific time in a character's life. That's been the way I've been able to wrangle that massive amount of material into something that could actually be finished.

KW: In the first collection of yours I read, in the introduction you said something that really struck me. You wrote that you did not try to publish a fiction collection until you had published at least one hundred stories so that way you could select the ones you thought were the best and not have any "filler."

SRT: I think it helps to have a body of stories to choose from. I've noticed a lot of new writers will publish nine or ten stories and want to put out a collection right away. But having dozens of stories to select from made it easier for me to pull together a good collection. It was rather frustrating, because it took a long time for me to get a collection–my first collection came out in 2000–but I knew it was my best work.

KW: I apologize in advance for the triteness of this question, but do you have any advice for early-career writers, folks just starting out?

SRT: I think my biggest advice would be to read a great deal –and read outside the genre as much as possible. One of the things I've noticed about newer writers—the ones who are successful are the ones who bring a literary background from outside the genre to this genre, who have read mainstream literature, who have read a wide range of fiction and are able to apply that to horror fiction. That hasn't always been the case. In the past we had some horror writers who read only horror fiction. I don't think that provides all the answers required to write interesting fiction.

KW: Fair enough. What do you know now that you wish you knew when you were starting?

SRT: How important failure is. In On Writing and Failure Stephen Marche says that the amount of failure in a writer's career is often underestimated or overlooked. If you look at even famous writers like T.S. Eliot or Faulkner, they were very unhappy about their careers in many ways. I think what happens is, as a writer, you have so much of your work rejected and so much of your work has a hard time being marketed. Oftentimes writers find that the things they've written they really care about aren't as popular as some of the other works they've done. I know several very popular writers who had that problem, and they feel dissatisfied with the things that they've actually been able to publish.

KW: What is the best thing about being named a Lifetime Achievement Award recipient?

SRT: Well, I can check that box off now [laughs]. Honestly, I never really anticipated I would get this award but I noticed that the first time I ever got an award was that once I received an award I no longer had to worry about it. When I was starting out, I really thought a lot about, "well, what if I won a World Fantasy Award, or what if I won a Nebula Award?" And there was a real desire and need to win those things. But once I won an award, I was satisfied. It is nice getting the Lifetime Achievement Award, because it's from your peers and it's for a body of work. And so I like to think maybe I haven't wasted my time all these years [laughs], so I am quite honored, and it is totally unexpected.

KW: And my absolute final question: what question did you think I would ask and didn't? And then answer it, please.

SRT: I have a collection of my Appalachian stories coming out later this year from Crossroads Press, entitled Scarecrows, and another probably next year, Everyday Horrors. Other than that, I don't know. "What color underwear?" It's orange, actually– my pumpkin underwear.

KW: [laughs] Me, too! Do you also have Halloween socks, or Jack-o-lantern socks?

SRT: Yes, I do have Halloween socks I get to wear once a year. I have Christmas pajamas, but I seem to wear them most of the year.

KW: Interesting. A lot of horror writers I know have Halloween-themed or horror-themed undergarments and socks. Some wear them only in October, but many go year-round.

SRT: [laughs] Yeah, I've gotten rid of most of that stuff, but I still have a few things like that.

KW: Well, thank you very much for your time, sir. I really appreciate chatting with you and you sharing your wisdom with our readers.

StokerCon 2024
San Diego

MEMORIA

By Steve Rasnic Tem

*D*uring the untold hours, he is all memory and imagination. If he has a body, he is unaware of it. The same was true during certain periods of his life.

What he remembers most about those final years was the fear. They never put it into words, but he could see it in Diane's face, and in his own in the mirror. Now he cannot see his reflection, and it is just as well. He imagines an appearance with no expression, pebble eyes under a film of gray, a mouth fallen open and full of shadow.

He remembers friends and relatives erased, one now and again, then two or three, then entire groups of everyone he knew, gone. The grief that came after. The numbness. He remembers worrying over what an illness actually meant, a weakness in a limb, a headache, an abdominal pain, a lost thought, a missed connection. He remembers her asking, How do you feel? He remembers taking longer and longer to answer. He remembers getting old.

He remembers wanting to ask her, What was the point? After all that effort, he couldn't decide how everything added up. She'd always been the optimist, the one with the comforting answers. What did it all mean? But he didn't ask. He didn't want to hurt her.

He remembers hearing things in the middle of the night. He could never decide if the sounds were new, or the same noises he always heard. There were always sudden drafts. Was a window open? There were always doors opening and closing.

He remembers smelling smoke. He remembers getting out of bed and searching the house but never finding the danger. Diane slept so soundly, it became his job by default. To turn the lights on. To turn the lights off. To walk through the house like a memory, listening, smelling, trying to find a path through the dark.

They gather outside the windows and beat on the glass. He is afraid they will wake her, but she is oblivious. They want him to come out. They no longer require warmth, or shelter, or food, but they do crave companionship. But his love lies here sleeping, and he is reluctant to leave her side.

He wants to close the curtains, so he doesn't have to see their faces, but cannot. Their lack of features is unsettling. He tries to raise his hands to feel his own face but cannot find either his face or his hands.

Diane remains motionless on the couch. He cannot tell if she is sleeping, or resting, meditating, or dead. She has spent most of the past month this way, body covered, eyes closed. He cannot see below her neckline. Her body could be anything, the body of a fish, or a leopard, the body of an aging woman who needs her rest. The clock, ticking, is the only sound in the room. He waits for her to rise, or leap, or swim away.

He watches her through darkness and through day, until she stirs, first her head and then her shoulders, shifting, slipping from the blanket, her face turning toward him, but not seeing, eyes blinking away dead tears. Her mouth stretches into a yawn.

Her cell phone on the coffee table rings and rings, but she doesn't answer. Eventually it dies, becoming yet another useless artifact.

Diane climbs from the couch with the blanket wrapping her

like a shroud. She is smaller than he remembers, thinner, paler. He is beyond all worry, and yet somehow he worries. A few wisps of colorless hair fall across her forehead. She moves with small steps into the bathroom. He waits outside.

He hears the toilet flush, the water running. He follows her from the bathroom into the bedroom. He waits for her to go to the closet, to put something on, but instead she stumbles to the bed and sheds the blanket, and for a moment she is but a figment of flesh before crawling beneath the covers. He watches the sheets rise and fall. Her breath expands to fill the room. He leaves before she gathers him into a dream.

He remembers leaving this house many times but always returning. He remembers wondering if he would ever leave this house again. He can be in two places at once, or even three. So much is possible when you are done.

The house is smaller than he remembers. It seems much dirtier than before, or perhaps he has more time to notice. He feels the walls, ceilings, and floors bleeding dust into the air, the tiny deteriorations of frame and sheathing, furnishings, and flesh.

A fuzziness collects on the edges of things. Time drifts through the rooms, settles into episodes of decay, moves on. He listens to the creatures beneath the wallpaper, the creatures inside the wood, the creatures above and below. These rooms are never completely dead.

During the long night, he gazes from the windows and cannot see the stars. During the endless day, reflections of nothing paint the walls. Outside their house, birds are frozen in midair. The clouds are unmoving.

He watches their neighbors departing their houses, crossing the lawns, moving along the sidewalks. He cannot remember which are living and which are dead. He wonders at the busyness of the living, their preoccupation with appearances, their almost constant disappointment.

He follows the sunlight as it moves through the house, keen for its touch.

Most of his possessions still remain: books and clothing, a few favorite foods, letters, souvenirs, the old dresser from his college years. He doesn't know why she keeps them, or if she will keep them for long.

Diane sits at their modest kitchen table, spooning mac and cheese into her mouth, but he can find no pleasure in her face. He is not sure when was the last time she ate. It may have been days. He resides in the chair across the table, his old spot. She still uses her same chair, leaving his open. But it does not feel like an invitation.

He watches her chew. She has difficulty swallowing. He remembers warning her the bites she took were too large and potentially dangerous. More than once he witnessed the blankness come into her pale eyes as she began to choke.

He has a vague memory of how food tasted, although he recalls the warmth of it better, the heat in his mouth and as it went down. He imagines opening his mouth and tasting the departures, all those moments gone and now irrelevant. Feeling foolish, he stops and tries to keep his mouth closed. He has no idea if he has been successful.

She closes her eyes as if she no longer wants to see. He can imagine much, but he cannot imagine what she must be thinking.

Unable to watch any longer, he turns away and moves into the living room. A novel lies on the coffee table, an overdue bill stuck somewhere in the middle as a bookmark. He'd left it beside the bed, never finished. She has moved it here, by the couch where she sleeps and reads. Does she intend to read it? Will she start from the beginning, or from where he left off?

He studies the cover. The words. He can no longer read.

He spends an age watching the light slip away, the shadows which settle and stay. A distant sound finally arrives. Outside the window, there is a sudden explosion and a flash of brilliance. Everything— what lasts, what does not last—is frozen in silver. The rain outside appears impossible. Why did he never realize this before?

He is drenched in memory. He tries to choose but one to take with him and cannot.

She is crying because he said something that hurt her. He was careless and wishes he could take it back. Now he knows nothing can ever be taken back.

The night of her miscarriage she is lying in the hospital bed, heavily drugged, and he hovers over her. He knows she is alive, but her resemblance to what he imagines death must be thoroughly shakes him. They never try again after that.

The jokes that fell flat because he was trying too hard to make her smile. The jokes he was so proud of because they made her laugh.

That day in a bookstore when they first met. He didn't understand her taste in literature, but he wanted to.

Their first kiss. She kissed him, of course, because he was too shy.

The bright blue dress she bought in Mexico. The spring afternoon they were married in the mountains in front of all their friends. Her parents refused to attend.

That small indentation on the left side of her back.

The many times she forgave him for being a fool.

When they spent hours together in bed.

When they couldn't stop touching.

All these moments gone to light and air and nothing.

His is an instability spreading everywhere.

STOKERCON 2024
San Diego

MORT CASTLE

Conducted by Kevin Wetmore

KEVIN WETMORE: Thanks for sitting down with me. First question: Why horror?

MORT CASTLE: So many, many answers. I first started seriously writing in fourth grade. How did I get hooked? Mrs. Nanberg brought in one of these AV things called a phonograph. And we heard "The Pit and the Pendulum" and "The Tell-Tale Heart." Now, can you imagine fourth graders hearing that today? And how many lawyers would be lined up saying, "He'll be wetting the bed until he's 48-years old!" But I heard it. I got a kick out of it. I started writing, and I said, "This is magic. If I can scare people the way I'm scared, I'm going to do it." So, I had a wonderful teacher. "Okay," the wonderful teacher said. "You don't have to worry about your grammar. You know this stuff. Your handwriting stinks. But you're gonna get a typewriter soon, anyway. And so your English assignment for this year is every week have a story on my desk." And that was my English assignment for fourth grade. Most of those stories were horror, a lot of transformational horror–

with people becoming spiders. I was heavy into spiders then. That was the hook.

KW: It sounds like you had a wonderful elementary school education. Who were some of your influences? Who were you reading? Who were you looking at and saying, "Oh, that's what I want to do!"

MC: Big time: *The Playboy Book of Horror and the Supernatural* – everybody in there. Robert Bloch, Ray Russell, of course Edgar Allen Poe–I've written a number of Poe pastiches. I often feel really guilt because here I am making more money by being Poe than he ever did. So Poe was a profound influence. Ray Bradbury–when I was fourteen and a high school sophomore. I was milking a cold and staying home for close to two weeks off of school and that's when I discovered *Something Wicked This Way Comes.* Magic. It was magic. Do you remember–no, you're too young to remember this. In my day, the anthologies in English class in high school had classical literature, meaning people who are dead for five hundred years, and they had the modern stuff, which was people who were dead for a hundred years.[1] Here comes Bradbury, and I'm saying, "Man, this is literature. Look at this poetic passage!" So Bradbury was the eye-opener and a strong influence. And the influence we were not supposed to mention when we were kids: comic books. I learned to read because of Batman and Little Lulu, so when I was at last able to write a Batman story, I'm saying, "Thanks, Bruce Wayne. Thanks, Robin. Thanks, Alfred. Thanks, crew. You taught me to read, buddies."

KW: What about the old EC comics? Any influence from horror comics in that time?

---

1   Interviewer's note: Sadly, I am not too young to remember this, but thanks for saying it, Mort.

MC: Of course. I can remember being eight-years-old and suddenly those comic books disappeared. I couldn't find them at my barber shop any more. Years later I picked up this anthology of old EC comics and I was hooked.

KW: Shifting gears, let's talk about On Writing Horror, which you edited, I believe, for the HWA. What was the impetus behind that?

MC: There's a story behind that. For those who are thinking about things like networking. Okay, everybody's screaming about networking, which, of course, means schmoozing. Bob Weinberg was the first guy asked to do that book. When Harlan Ellison was in town, we used to call ourselves the Three-man minyan, and you know, hang and schmooze and stuff. So HWA member James Gormley proposes a "how to" created by the organization. HWA and Writer's Digest Books dig it. So Bob Weinberg gets asked to edit. He said, "No. I'm running a business as a bookseller. I'm teaching down in Chicago at Columbia College, and in addition that I'm doing my own writing. But Mort knows this stuff." So the HWA asked me, and I said, "Sure sounds lovely." This was one of those dream projects where absolutely nothing goes wrong. Everybody I asked for something came up with a good something. And if it needed editing, Ramsey Campbell said to me, "Well, of course, edit. You're the editor. Let me know what you're doing. That's all." Harlan Ellison said, "Please make sure about copyrights. So many people, especially with this rising internet nonsense, don't have any respect or idea of copyright." And he was right, of course. But it was a dream project. The book comes out. I'm happy with it. The cover by Brom! I'm happy with it. The second edition comes out. Keep dreaming still. A wonderful project. Granted, the marketing advice is not up to date, but the book has something to say and will still have something to say. I think, in fifty more years, maybe longer than that. One of the books I use for reference is the Writer's

Handbook from 1950, published by the Writer Magazine. It has a whole bunch of interesting articles that now become historical, but nonetheless with something to say to us. Those historical articles mourn the death of dramatic radio because this television thing was really coming on. It mourns the death of the pulp magazines because it predicts maybe paperbacks will replace them.

And here. This advice from 1950 still talks to me. It still talks to me in terms of, "Hey, here's the way we construct a radio show. Can we use this for a comic book? Of course—radio profoundly influenced comic books. Can we use it for film? Of course. So reference books tend to stay referenced, even if the world changes, even if you can't go into your local Waldenbooks and find the Gothic section anymore.

KW: Everything old is new again, though. The pulp's are coming back. Jonathan Maberry is now editing *Weird Tales*. Virtually all of the old radio shows are now available on podcasts. I'm a huge fan of Lights Out.

MC: "Turn out your lights now!" Yeah! "It is later than you think." The folks who made radio drama back then were avid, and the folks making new radio drama now are just as avid.

KW: How has teaching and mentoring influenced you as a writer? How is that shaped your own writing?

MC: It's no longer enough to do what I do. I'd better be able to explain what I do, and how maybe what I do in the process can help you. I also have found that, thank goodness for the classes I've taught in writing comic books. I'm not naturally a visual writer. This forced me to become visual writer, which has a tremendous carryover. is a matter when I really get stuck or stymied, I say, "No, this is not gonna be prose. This is gonna be a comic book script. Forget your beautiful prose, forget your mannered, decorative arabesque phrases, what do you see?" One of the great teachers I've worked with, one of the guys who encouraged me greatly, Lucien Stryk, used to, as a pedagogical process, walk around his classroom asking one question. The question was, "Do you see?" Not, "Do you understand?" Not, "Do you get it?" Or, "What are you thinking here?" He'd ask, "Do you see?" It's helped to define my writing, and it's something I've passed on to writers in every situation. Being a teacher forces me to be a better writer, forces me to break down the process and share it. And I've been a fortunate man, I've worked with some of the best.

KW: What is your writing process?

MC: These days it's slower than it used to be when there was the fire in the belly.

KW: Fair enough.

MC: I mean, when I was beginning–credit hunting like everybody else–something went out every week. Not necessarily a story every time, but certainly an article, or some poetry, or something. Right now, I do what I really want to do. I'm afforded that privilege because I do have something of a rep. And in terms of process, when I'm into it I am ridiculously into it. And now I'm deliberately watching it. It used to be that I would write for twelve, fourteen hours a day then sleep. Currently. I'll work intensely, based on a lot of research. I like that real world grounding. And when–again, I'm stealing this from somebody else: this is Roland Green, who used to write a lot of military science fiction. He said, "If I'm going to write about George Patton, when I know I can walk into George Patton's office and find whatever I need, whether it's his pistol or his cigarette lighter or his number two pencils–what drawer they'll be in– then I know I'm ready to write. I've stolen that from Roland. "Mort, do you see?" "Yes, I do see." "Can you write it?" "Yes,." If I fake it, then I need to do more research because I'm just schmoozing myself trying to get out of actual hard work.

Fortunately, now that I've been around for a while I am doing a number of collaborative things. One with Mark Valadez, who was a producer and a writer on The Queen of the South for three or four seasons. Mark Valadez was also my student when he was fourteen years old, so I know he has some pretty solid background in the biz. I know we can get along. And sure enough, we're working together on a sequel to the novel The Strangers and working on a TV series based on The Strangers. Collaboration helps, man. It's one of the reasons I love comic books. When you're doing a comic book, it's a collaborative effort. If not, and you know this to be true, if it's just you, then after a while it's just you and that spot on the wall where you've been beating your head,

KW: What do you know now that you wish you knew when you were just starting out?

MC: I'll tell you something I'm glad I didn't know. I was still teaching high school full-time.

We had a terrific guidance counselor, very up on psychology, everything else, named Ev Evans. She also claimed to have more than a little Romani blood, and considered herself psychic. She looked at me and she said, I'm reading your aura. You're going to have many readers, but it's going to take a very, very, very long time. I take a look now, and I think, "Lifetime achievement award. Oh, man, that's cool! Overnight success!" My first book came out in 1966 or '67. So I guess she was right. So that's what I didn't know. Had I known the struggles that would be involved in writing, had I known too much, I might have said, "Let's shift to something else." Had music worked out differently, had it been the thing that hit first,

I'd have probably pursued that with the intensity that I did writing. In the sixties, music was a big part of my life. I was in a folk trio, and just when we're hitting it big, we went to Frank Freid, who was a big time guy in Chicago. He said, "You guys are great. I'd sign you tomorrow I'd have a record contract for you. But the

Beatles are coming. Folk music is dead. Goodbye." So I focused on the writing thing. I would sell at least one piece a month. It was a different world. It would be a lower tier market, but that one piece a month was enough to pay the mortgage every month.

KW: Now I have to ask, what instrument do you play?

MC: Name it. If it's if it's got strings, I'll play it. I'm primarily a guitarist: guitar, banjo. mandolin, and I'm a halfway decent harmonica player.

KW: Sounds like you're a one-man trio.

MC: I have been on occasion. You know, every so often I still break it out and perform here and there. We did some big things, but at that point once we got told, "you're not going anywhere," the group broke up. Our bass player went on to lead the New Christy Minstrels for a while. Our lead vocalist went off and got himself a Ph.D. in chemistry. And me? I went off to do whatever it was I did.

KW: For someone who is just encountering your work for the first time, where should they start? What is the first novel or collection they should pick up?

MC: I'm proud of New Moon on the Water. That is a collection of stories that at the time I considered my best. I am no less proud of the collection that followed it, Knowing When to Die. The title comes from a quote from Will Wogers: the secret of being a hero is simple: you have to know when to die. There's all of history in one quick judgment. Bang! Yeah, those 2 books. I have never written a novel that fully satisfies me.

KW: Who are you reading these days? Who excites you?

MC: Oh, that's great. Dan Chaon. Bonnie Jo Campbell, who is probably today's Mark Twain. Absolutely wonderful writer. Eric LaRocca – if people worked at the business the way that guy does with his polished, insightful prose. Those people are always great. I also reread some of the masters. I still wish that James Crumly had written more. I am amazed and delighted that James Lee Burke is still turning out great stuff. Margaret Atwood – always. Always Poe. When I need tranquility, I read Japanese poems translated by Lucien Stryk.

KW: What advice do you have for writers just starting out?

MC: This is gonna sound snide and snarky, but I've said it a lot. It's now helped me earn the title of curmudgeon: Learn to write. Thanks to Mr. Internet, we have people busy worrying about platform. We have people worrying about how do you gain audience? We have people worried about gimmick. We have people who don't know subject, verb, object. It's journalists. It's academics. We have people who do not know. The craft of writing–and writing is a craft–can be learned, it can be taught. You can learn it on your own or you can go someplace, or to someone who knows what it's about. You need to know your craft in the same way a carpenter says, "Yes, I can build a deck. This is my toolbox: hammer, saw, miter box. I know how to use the tools."

Learn to write. How do you learn? You read, read, read and you write, write, write, write, and you hang with those who are helpful. I've talked about networking, but those who are helpful are terrific. I go back to my unofficial mentor, Lucien Stryk, who said he was seventeen when he encountered the first poet who said to him, "No, you're not doing this properly. You have possibility, but you're not there yet." Have people who say no to you, who make you do better. Having those people who said no to me – that was important for me. A Lifetime Achievement Award winner, Jerry "J.N." Williamston helped me once. I was having trouble making a novel work. I saw

Jerry was not that far away from me, geographically speaking. I sent him a letter. I wrote, "Jerry. I don't know what I'm doing. I'm selling short stories all the time, but I can't make a novel happen. Could you give a looksee and tell me if there's something I should tweak?" This is the days before email. I sent him the sixty-page opening of a novel. Two weeks later, Jerry sent me back ten pages of single-spaced commentary. It began, and this is almost direct quote, "Mort, you're a pro. I respect your professionalism. I have to tell you I have seldom seen a bigger bunch of crap coming from a pro." And then in ten pages he sliced, he diced, he dissected, mashed bash and crashed. My reaction was just what, psychologically, anybody's reaction would be. Not, "Thank you, I appreciate it." It was, "You miserable old bastard! What the hell do you know, anyway? Goddamn living in Indianapolis! If you had any sense you'd live somewhere deep. Blah blah blah blah blah." And then I calmed down and looked at what he had written. He wasn't right all the way, he was only right, 90% of the time. So when I could look at it objectively, I realized Jerry was right. That book became *The Strangers*. That's the kind of mentor you want. You need somebody who's not afraid and doesn't worry about your sensitivity.

KW: What about advice for career longevity? Those who have been in the game, you know ten or fifteen years, and it's sort of plateaued. How does one keep going?

MC: With difficulty. How do I get excited? And you have to get excited If it's going to be any good you have to be able to say, I feel something under my breastbone when I'm writing this.

and if you're not...I'm not gonna mention the guy's name because he was very sweet man, but I was at a bar with a longtime writer and we had a drink and he said, "How would you like for your epitaph what I'll have for mine? He wrote 630 novels that no one could remember reading after the last page. If you grind it out like sausage. It is sausage. Okay? This is it. I have to find something that gets me really inspired, really going. Find new stuff that excites you. And if you know your craft you can translate that craft and keep yourself going. Here's the formula. You write it. You make it the best you can. You put it out there and you see what happens. Sometimes it takes forty or fifty years for a book to find an audience, Mort said knowingly.

KW: One final question for you then, sir. What question did you expect me to ask that I did not, and then answer it, please.

MC: How many roads must a man walk down before you call him a man? The answer: I don't know. Go check with Bob Dylan. This has been quite thorough. This has got me thinking in ways I hadn't necessarily anticipated.

THE LAST GOOD COUNTRY

(Excerpt)

By Mort Castle

I. A NATURAL HISTORY OF THE DEAD

*I*n a time not so long ago and far from our time there was a man who wrote as well and as truly as anyone ever did. He wrote about courage and endurance and sadness and war and bullfighting and boxing and men in love and men without women. He wrote about loneliness and wounds that never heal.

And in this same time not so long ago and very much like our time in so many melancholy ways there was a woman who was a sad woman, so sad that she was pronounced "the saddest woman I have ever known" by the author and intellectual Arthur Miller. Arthur Miller wrote plays in which actors pretended to be people but he did not understand this sad woman, though in his intellectual way, he no doubt tried to save her.

What happened was the man died.

The woman died.

These are facts.

In our time there was a man who made houses in which people

lived. The man's name was Frank Lloyd Wright. Though he has no role to play in our drama, he did offer a comment which seems not inappropriate: "The Truth is more important than the Facts."

You see, this is the truth.

II. THE END OF SOMETHING

May 1961
Mayo Clinic
Rochester, Minnesota

In Spring in Africa and in the crazy house there is always much talk but the talk in Africa is stimulated and encouraged and polished by the drinking of beer while the talk in the crazy house is mostly just crazy and with little joy although there is sometimes a sad humor and a sad irony to it.

The old man was thinking something like this or thinking about the green hills of Africa (hyenas and leopards and the House of God) or he thought he was thinking like this—thinking about sometime writing something like this—although writing was now impossible for him—and the doctor was saying, "Let's talk about your suicidal feelings."

The doctor was a doctor of the mind and framed certificates on the wall had been awarded him by other doctors to show that he knew a great deal about the mind.

The old man said, not without irony, "There are times I want to kill myself. How is that?"

"You know what I mean."

"Straight arrow, Chief Big Hem, him know what white eye mean. I know what you mean. Pues y nada. Y pues y nada. That's what you mean."

"What's that?"

"Spanish."

"I know it's Spanish. But what does it mean?"

"Nothing." The old man smiled, not happy, but with the satisfying, though false, superiority one gets from irony. "It means... Well and nothing."

He took off his glasses. He was nor really an old man, not as we now think of old men, he was only 61, but often he thought of himself as an old man and truly, he looked like an old man, although his blood pressure was in control and his diabetes remained borderline. His face had scars. His eyes were sad. He looked like an old man who had been in wars.

He pinched his nose above the bridge. He wondered if he were doing it to look tired and worn. It was hard to know now when he was being himself and when he was being what the world expected him to be. That was how it was when all the world knew you and all the world knows you if you have been in Life and Esquire

"You're really not helping me. You know that."

"Bad on me. I thought I was here for you to help me. My foolishness. Damn the luck."

The doctor had a Waterman pen. He wrote with it a while and smiled as though he had proved something by writing.

"Here is what we will do."

"Yes, tell us what we will do. Pues y nada."

"What we did before, we'll go the way we did before, with electroconvulsive therapy..." The doctor was talking.

"...a series of 12." The doctor was talking.

The old man was thinking about Africa and about a Boer in Africa who was blond and had a blond wife and a 13 year old blond daughter and he was a Boer who talked good sense when he drank beer. It was good to have a daughter, the old Boer said, because in some ways it was like having another wife for whom you were permitted to have true feelings but your daughter was like a wife who was new and you did not know her so well and therefore she did not bore you and you did not bore her and you found a great deal to laugh about.

"… particularly with depression. There are several factors, of course…" The doctor was talking.

The old man thought about blond women and wives and blue water and the truth that comes with first light. He thought about walking in early morning Paris and the dusty flour and heat smell as you walked past that little bakery that fronted the Boulevard Montparnasse and how it made you wish for cafe creme and …

He thought about how much had been lost and how little was left, how he had become a diminished thing.

"… begin tomorrow then." The doctor was talking. "Do you understand?" The doctor was smiling.

"I understand," the old man said. He asked, "Do you speak the same way even when you drink beer?" He winked at the doctor the way you would to a small child or a zoo monkey and it made him look more crazy than sad.

The doctor made a note with his Waterman.

III. I GUESS EVERYTHING REMINDS YOU OF SOMETHING

San Diego is the best city in California and perhaps in the United Stares. The weather is always so near to perfect that you do not think at all about the weather. The youth are golden and smell of sea water and lotions and if you see one of them frowning it is noteworthy. Old cars have no rust, no wrinkles, no dents, nor do old people.

Dos Picos Park is the favorite park of San Diego's residents. The oak trees are majestic as only oaks can be and the shadows cast by their limbs are not frightening. And there are the ducks waiting in the pond. The ducks like visitors.

She tried to tell herself that everything was all right, that she was all right here, squatting at the water's edge, tossing oyster crackers to the appreciative ducks. She should have been in make-up and costume, should have been on the set at Coronado Beach, but she had decided to be difficult (that was it, just my being a spoiled brat!), a star turn and how do you like it, you assholes. She could not stand to be with Mr. Billy Wilder, a certified prick (figuratively speaking) but without the sensitivity of a prick (literally speaking); and she couldn't stand to be with Curtis, who told her, "The script says I kiss you, but kissing you is like kissing Hitler."

Curtis probably would delight in kissing Hitler. The uniform and the leather boots and all. Ooh, and that riding crop…

Curtis definitely thought he could out-beautiful her. Fucking pretty boy would look like a mummified drag queen when he got old.

Oh, God, she was afraid, she was so afraid. The mind was going: Tilt! That's all, Folks! Right into the Mad Mad Monroe Maelstrom.

"It's me, Sugar." That was her part, her only line, for yesterday's scene. "It's me, Sugar." Sugar Kane, ukulele strumming flapper, that is your role, that's who you become this time.

Here is the Reader's Digest "Condensed" version of what she said:

I-i–it's sugar, me.

Sugar me

It is I! Cigar

It's just me, sugar pie.

It's just fucking sugar shit fuck fuck…

It required 37 takes for her to say, "It's me, Sugar," 37 rakes to synch brain with mouth to get out words that Lassie could have managed with one hand cue from trainer Rudd Weatherwax and the promise of two Gaines biscuits.

And there was Billy Wilder, looking like he hadn't had a dump in three weeks and had no hope for the future, and Mr. Tony "I Feel Pretty" Curtis throwing his hands in the air.

She had to get away, had to, had to be alone…

—did not want to be alone, so alone…

Incognito time. Easy, surprisingly easy. Forget Max Factor and Maybelline, slip on the kind of dark glasses that sell three for a dollar at the Texaco station and tie a scarf over the blondness, and a far too big UCLA sweatshirt (Tits? Tits? In this potato sack?) and the kind of shapeless skirt that would embarrass a Jehovah's Witness, and you disappear, you become nobody.

I'm nobody. Who are you?

A line from a poem.

She read poems and wrote them.

And like many poets, I write about death and dying and there are times death is all I want, an ending…

She was out of crackers, nothing more to feed the ducks.

Goddamn it, fuck it, goddamn it, you think you have crackers and you don't have crackers. She had no more crackers for the ducks.

It made her mad and she bit hard into her tongue and tasted blood no it made her sad and she started to cry, digging fingers into the wet earth at the pond's edge, smearing the dirt on her wet face.

And she cries and she cries and she cries and

IV. The Strange Country

There is an old man on a gurney and his belly is big and his legs are splayed and scrawny and a tired line of drool runs down at the left side of his slack mouth. They have just shot lightning through his head. They have tried to blast away whatever has made him sad but something else has happened because his brain is now a flywheel without a catch going clackety-clitch clackety-clitch clackety-clitch and it is always like that gentlemen and now the heavy rifle because the elephant he is a heavy beast and damn all my upper lip stiffy let us go then you and I the hey there Sidney the muleta and of course a daughter always wanted a daughter always wanted a blond daughter and she is calling him she calls because he always calls them daughter and she wants to be a daughter and the lightning you call me mad has gone through his brain and he can leap worlds because no past no tomorrow just now just now just now

Now, daughter, I am come to make it all all right.

Papa? she says.

He knows what she means.

I am come to save you, he tells her. Come daughter.

He takes her hand. Come.

Where, Papa?

The strange country, he tells her. The last good country. It is the good country where nobody ever dies.

Alone, nobody has a bloody chance. But we are not alone. Not us. Not you and me. We are not alone. You gottum me. Me gottum you. We gottum chance.

Papa.

Come daughter.

She takes his hand. She sighs. She hopes.

Ahead, there is a mountain.

It is the House of God.

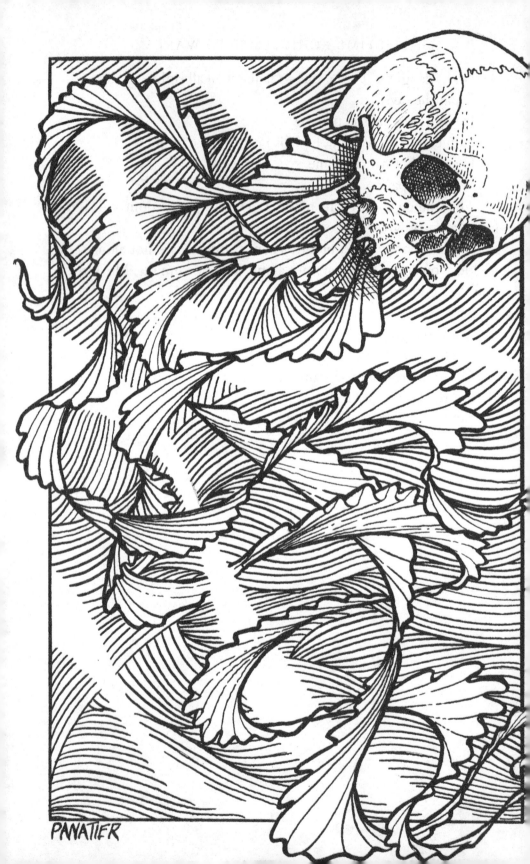

SHORT INTERVIEWS

ERIN E. ADAMS

Why do you write horror?

I write horror as a way to explore what genuinely terrifies me. To take it apart and put it back together in a way that both respects and removes it's power. This way I am not longer restricted by my fears, instead I am liberated by them. Also, it's a genre that invites deep introspection, challenges and specificity without losing a genuine sense of fun.

What are you most excited about in the horror genre today?

I love how horror doesn't to stay in a box. It's always refused to do this, but now horror is louder about refusing to be restrained by conventions or expectations. I'm excited about the ways horror rewards the unexpected. This means that the genre is always pushing itself toward innovation and resisting remaining stagnant. Horror is a genre that every writer can learn from.

What are you most looking forward to seeing in the horror genre in the future?

I'm looking forward to the inclusion of more perspectives and experiences. A part of horror's constant push for innovation must include welcoming writers and storytelling traditions of many different backgrounds. This has been a call to action across all of storytelling, but I feel horror has been uniquely enthusiastic in its embrace.

ERIN E. ADAMS is a first-generation Haitian-American writer and theatre artist. Her debut novel, JACKAL, was named one of the best of the year by Esquire, Vulture, PopSugar, Paste, and Publishers Weekly, and a best horror novel of all time by Cosmopolitan. JACKAL was also a finalist for the Edgar® Award, the Bram Stoker Award®, and the Shirley Jackson Award. Her short fiction was featured in OUT THERE SCREAMING, edited by Jordan Peele. Her sophomore novel ONE OF YOU will be published in 2025.

MEGHAN ARCURI

Why do I write horror?

My answer has multiple parts. First, I was challenged to. To be honest, I hadn't ever planned on writing horror. But at my first Borderlands Boot Camp (where I submitted the lamest, tamest urban fantasy), Richard Payne suggested I write a horror story for Michael Bailey, a young up-start editor, who was accepting submissions for what would become the first in the Chiral Mad series. "Horror?" I said, with what I can only imagine was a look of disgust. "Yes. Horror," Richard said. "You can do it." So I did. And I'm forever thankful to Richard for suggesting it because, in the process of writing that story for Michael, I discovered the second reason why I write horror: It's fun. A lot of fun. Other than acting, where else can you inhabit the mind, body, and soul of a person (or creature) so dark and awful, so evil and twisted, so vastly different than yourself? Basically, it's fun being bad, and writing horror gives me a safe outlet in which to do that. As

SHORT INTERVIEWS

I've grown as a writer, however, I've discovered a third reason: I use horror as a way to grapple with my own fears and demons. I'm still a big fraidy cat, but writing eases the tension for a short while.

What am I most excited about in the horror genre today?

I like the way it has crept into the mainstream. From the more robust horror sections in B&N, to the longer articles about horror in newspapers like the *New York Times*, to the way Jordan Peele has taken Hollywood by giant creepy storm, horror is more easily available to the public. And they're realizing it's not what they thought it was. Even my husband—who's not much of a horror guy—was pleasantly surprised after reading Stephen Graham Jones's *The Only Good Indians* and John Langan's *The Fisherman*.

What am I most looking forward to seeing in the horror genre in the future?

I look forward to the continued and expanding recognition of different voices and perspectives. I took six years of Italian in middle and high schools, and in those six years, I learned more about English than I would've if I hadn't taken a foreign language. When I travel, I learn how people in other places move through the world. Sometimes it's better than my way, and I steal it; other times it's not, and I keep doing what I'm doing. The same is true for literature. When I read books like *Mexican Gothic* by Silvia Moreno-Garcia or *Black Cranes* ed. by Lee Murray & Geneve Flynn, I am exposed to horror through a perspective different than my own, and I learn. I love learning. And when I experience something through another person's eyes, not only do I learn something about them, I learn something about me. And then I grow.

MEGHAN ARCURI is a Bram Stoker Award®-nominated author. Her work can be found in various anthologies, including *Borderlands*

7 (Borderlands Press), *Madhouse* (Dark Regions Press), *Chiral Mad*, and *Chiral Mad 3* (Written Backwards). She served as the Vice President of the Horror Writers Association for over four years and is the recipient of the 2022 Richard Laymon President's Award.

LINDA D. ADDISON

Why do you write horror?

It's not a choice, LOL. When I sit down to write, whether poetry or fiction, it's a very organic process. Even when I write to a theme I don't consciously design the work, it's more like wandering here and there, until I start to see-hear-feel the writing come, and in that emerging work, Shadow often finds its way in. Even if I'm writing in the arena of science-fiction I end up with some twisty edges peeking through the story or characters.

What are you most excited about in the horror genre today?

I'm very excited about the new work coming out each year either by new, emerging writers, anthologies with unique exciting themes. The work in the area of YA, Middle Grade, Graphic Novels is so interesting.

What are you most looking forward to seeing in the horror genre in the future?

I love being surprised. My hope is to continue reading work from other cultures, unexpected themes, etc.

LINDA D. ADDISON is the award- winning author of five collections of prose and poetry, including *The Place of Broken Things* (written with Alessandro Manzetti) and *How to Recognize a Demon Has Become Your Friend*. She is the recipient of the HWA Lifetime Achievement Award and the SFPA Grand Master, and her work appears in *Qualia*

Nous Vol 2; Shakespeare Unleashed; The Drive-In: Multiplex; Black Panther: Tales of Wakanda; and *Predator: Eyes of the Demon.* Online at: LindaAddisonWriter.com.

Nat Cassidy

Why do you write horror?

We're the only animal (as far as we know) who walks around every day, knowing we have to die one day, without any knowledge of what happens next or what it means. I think the horror genre is one of our healthiest ways of incrementally making peace with that dizzying, thrilling, confounding, dreadful fact, and I'm proud to be in the trenches with you all, putting as much entertaining chocolate and/or cheese around the sometimes-bitter pills.

What are you most excited about in the horror genre today?

Growing up in the 80s and 90s, I was all too aware of how society looked down its nose at us horror fans. They made the genre feel untoward, maybe even a little embarrassing. (See also being a comics fan or a Star Wars fan.) Now, though, the genre has once again reminded the Higher Ups of its value and that there's a huge, hungry audience for scary stories. The genre feels unapologetic right now, using its mainstream acceptance to push itself into new shapes, new extremes. The conventions are more accepted and the fringes are getting weirder and bolder. (Thanks, Late Stage Capitalism, for this one good thing?)

What are you most looking forward to seeing in the horror genre in the future?

Even more diversity! More voices! More perspectives! More subgenres! More crossovers! More new monsters! More new takes on familiar monsters! More horror! More Horror! More understanding and embracing and celebrating that we're all in this existential mess (see answer 1) together! Then, all we'll need is the movie industry to get braver about adapting all our damn stories and books...

NAT CASSIDY is the author of *Mary: An Awakening of Terror* and *Nestlings*. His books have been featured in best-of lists from Esquire, Harper's Bazaar, NPR, the Chicago Review of Books, the NY Public Library, and more, and he was named one of the "writers shaping horror's next golden age" by Esquire. His award-winning horror plays have been produced throughout NYC and across the country, including at the Kennedy Center. You've also likely seen Nat on your television, playing various Bad Guys of the Week on lots of network TV shows ... but that's a topic for a different bio.

CAROLINA FLÓREZ-CERCHIARO

Why do you write horror?

To me writing horror requires quite a bit of courage. We pull so much from our own experiences; we sometimes dig into places that we don't normally reach for. It's very personal in that it allows me to explore, confront my own demons and hauntings, which in turn makes me vulnerable. And it is certainly scary to put so much of ourselves on the page, to invite the reader to converse with our fears. It also serves as a form of emotional release, not only to the writers but to readers as well. It helps us process situations within a safe space, with the certainty that no matter how scary the situation is, we'll make it out alive. Horror has helped me survive life at its darkest moments, and I think that's beautiful. I think that's why I've always been drawn to it.

What are you most excited about in the horror genre today?

How the horror genre has opened up to stories from all across the world, from diverse perspectives and historically marginalized communities that don't often get a spot in mainstream media. I love seeing marginalized voices at the forefront, and seeing myself as a member of the Latinx community represented in stories that are not only incredible but also wildly successful. The horror genre is spreading its wings and reaching wider audiences by the day. People who would've never picked up a horror book several years ago, are being drawn to the genre today and devouring dozens of stories because of how vast and diverse the genre has become in the past years. Readers can find something for everyone. People are feeling seen, understood, represented, and that makes this era of horror incredibly exciting.

What are you most looking forward to seeing in the horror genre in the future?

The continuous exploration of diverse stories. Selfishly, I'd love more Latinx representation in the genre; I'd die for a haunted literary tour across Latin America. Give me all the Latinx Horror!

CAROLINA FLÓREZ-CERCHIARO is a Colombian journalist, international politics expert, and author of genre bending speculative fiction. Her debut gothic horror novel BOCHICA is coming out in summer 2025 from Primero Sueño Press / Atria Books. Born and raised in Colombia, her writing is heavily inspired by her heritage, her love of history, horror, and the kind of drama that only Latin American telenovelas know how to deliver.

CLAY MCLEOD CHAPMAN

Why do you write horror?

There's a lot to be frightened about. I used to think I liked to write horror because I wanted to try and scare people, but now I realize I'm trying to unscare myself. I'm desperate to connect with other human beings and release these fears and I've found writing is the best way to reach out.

What are you most excited about in the horror genre today?

Reading it, first and foremost. I've been devouring so many books lately and a lot of them are sticking with me. I've got a fair share of traumas and anxieties pent up within me and reading these books tends to offer up a release valve. This year alone has some of the best books Josh Malerman, Rachel Harrison, Eric LaRocca, Ronald Malfi, just to name a few, have to offer...

What are you most looking forward to seeing in the horror genre in the future?

More of it, for starters. I hope the conversations between horror readers and horror writers continues... and maybe expands even further? There are so many larger cultural conversations happening in the world that horror can help out with, and has the very tools to engage with. I've always felt like horror is at its most impactful when it offers up a metaphor — a monster — to the world to help view and process its collective fears. There's a lot to be afraid of in the world right now... Time for new monsters.

CLAY MCLEOD CHAPMAN writes novels, comic books, and children's books, as well as for film and TV. He is the author of the horror novels *The Remaking*, *Whisper Down the Lane*, *Ghost Eaters* and *Wake Up and Open Your Eyes* available January 7, 2025. You can find him at www.claymcleodchapman.com

JOHNNY COMPTON

Why do you write horror?

I've been in love with the genre since I was very young—since I was seven or eight at least, and possibly since I was five years-old—and I am hopelessly fascinated by and devoted to it. There is, for me, just nothing quite like a scary story. At this point I have self-described and self-diagnosed "horror brain": I see the genre in places where many others may not, and even where others may see it as well, I think I dwell on it more than many others might. I think a lot of horror writers are similarly, happily afflicted."

What are you most excited about in the horror genre today?

So, I don't have any insider sales information, I can't pull up numbers to tell the story of how well the genre currently is doing compared to different points in its past, but I do know that there are two horror book stores within easy driving distance of me now. TWO! I've lived here for thirty years and until very, very recently we had zero. As most people reading this likely know already, many book stores didn't even have a horror section for decades. Now we have entire shops devoted to it. If these places existed when I was a kid I would have lived in them, and I'm thrilled that people are able to embrace their love of the genre and share it with others in meaningful, constructive ways.

What are you most looking forward to seeing in the horror genre in the future?

Hopefully a continued expansion regarding the range of stories and representation of writers, characters, and histories, bolstering health of the genre.

JOHNNY COMPTON's short stories have appeared in Pseudopod, Strange Horizons, The No Sleep Podcast, and several other markets.

He is creator and host of the podcast Healthy Fears, and the author of novels *The Spite House*, and *Devils Kill Devils*.

DONYAE COLES

Why do you write horror?

I write horror because I like it. I like building the dread, the slow creep of doubt. I like monsters. I like the honesty of fear. What it tells us about ourselves, what it tells us about the world at large. There's a sort of freedom in horror, a place in all of us that can only be touched when everything else has been stripped away. Which is all very pretentious sounding but at the core, I write horror because it's fun.

What are you most excited about in the horror genre today?

I'm excited about all the new voices! All the new ways we are writing horror and about horror. The genre is evolving (is mutating a better word? It has a better genre feel, doesn't it?) expanding. The boundaries of what horror is are changing and that's wonderful! There should be no boundaries.

What are you most looking forward to seeing in the horror genre in the future?

I'm really looking forward to more twists on classic tropes. New haunted houses, slashers, boogeymen, gothics, etc. Seeing the backbone of the genre reconceptualized, re-envisioned through different experiences, it's going to be great!

DONYAE COLES has had shorts published in a variety of publications and anthologies. Her debut, *Midnight Rooms* is releasing summer of 2024. You can find her socials and other publications at <u>donyaecoles.com</u>.

Tracy Cross

Why do you write horror?

I write horror because I want to leave a legacy behind. Most of my family elders have passed on but their stories of the past, growing up in the South, practicing hoodoo and living in haunted houses, have stuck with me. It's a way to show homage to them and to share my family history-be it horror-with the rest of the world. In each of my works, there is something related to my family and affiliated with horror.

What are you most excited about in the horror genre today?

I'm most excited about the wide variety of horror. When I was growing up, there was no horror written by POC's. There were very few names in horror until Douglas Winter's Prime Evil series came along. I was baptized by the Twilight Zone and raised with Prime Evil. Yet, I never saw myself reflected in nor represented by any of the horror that I read. Now, there's so much horror out there, that I find it thrilling and exciting.

What are you most looking forward to seeing in the horror genre in the future?

I'm looking forward to seeing more of a fusion of horror types. We as humans intermingle with others and this will bring about changes in the stories we know or the stories we were told. These stories and histories of our lives will change and bend into a newer and even more different perspective than we've known. I guess you could say the continuing evolution of horror is what I look forward to seeing the most.

TRACY CROSS has had her stories featured in several podcasts and compilations. Her debut novel, *Rootwork,* was released by Dark Hart Publishing in November 2022. It delves into the power of family and her past experiences with hoodoo. She is now working on the next novel in the series, "A Gathering of Weapons" which will be released in Summer 2024. She resides in Washington, DC and is an active member of the Horror Writers Association. Additionally, she loves disco music and posts updates to her blog: tracycwritesonline.com

Cassie Daley

Why do you write horror?

The horrors of real life can feel very overwhelming, so I've always liked the idea of being able to control the experience of being scared in a safe environment - both as the audience, and as the person inflicting the creepiness via writing or art. I think with writing specifically, it's primarily a way for me to channel a lot of things I've dealt with in my past regarding trauma and abuse - it's often ugly, and that sort of thing doesn't really suit many other genres in a way that provides the catharsis of being able to deal with your demons through storytelling.

What are you most excited about in the horror genre today?

The inclusivity, although I think there are still leaps and bounds to be made in that regard, so I'll also mention that I love seeing boundaries get pushed further and further in regards to what horror is or can be. In the past, it felt easier to categorize books, movies, etc as a specific genre - now, there are so many blends and ways to tell a story that books that involve the wildest, most gruesome gore can also be followed by a romantic subplot, as an example. There are no real rules, something that more and more horror authors have been embracing, which gives us such a variety of stories to read - and I love that!

What are you most looking forward to seeing in the horror genre in the future?

> More inclusivity, always! I love seeing voices that have been underrepresented get boosted alongside or by established horror writers who have enjoyed success and want to pass it along to others, and seeing the success of great books like NEVER WHISTLE AT NIGHT: AN INDIGENOUS DARK FICTION ANTHOLOGY and SPECTRUM: AN AUTISTIC HORROR ANTHOLOGY make me hopeful that I'll continue to see more books like these being put out.

CASSIE DALEY is a writer and illustrator living in Northern California. Her nonfiction has been published by Unnerving Magazine, and her short fiction has appeared in several horror anthologies. Her first YA horror novella, BRUTAL HEARTS, was published in 2022. She is also the creator ROSIE PAINTS WITH GHOSTS, the first book in an illustrated horror series for kids. You can find Cassie on Instagram and Twitter as @ctrlaltcassie, and you can find her portfolio and more at ctrlaltcassie.com.

BRIAN EVENSON

Why do you write horror?

> I think it's the most vibrant and exciting genre out there, and the only genre based on feeling and intensity. I can write things set in the present and they're horror, I can write thing set in a fantastical past and still make them horror. I can write things in space and they can still be horror because of their mood. It's a flexible, intense genre and able, I feel, to make use of just about any setting and situation.

What are you most excited about in the horror genre today?

I love the way that horror has been expanding over the last few years, both welcoming new diverse voices and also (and this is especially relevant to me) questioning the boundary between literature and horror. There's been a renaissance in horror film over the last decade or so, and we're seeing that in horror fiction now as well. There are so many excellent writers writing horror right now, and pushing it in unexpected directions, ranging from Eric LaRocca to Michael Wehunt to Zin E. Rocklyn to Stephen Graham Jones, with all sorts of people within that range.

What are you most looking forward to seeing in the horror genre in the future?

One thing I've really loved recently is horror that pushes against the boundaries of what people think horror can be. I love horror that questions the notion of what is really monstrous, that reconsiders the monster. The future of horror, for me, is really expansive, something that makes us think about the possibilities of horror in a new way. The wonderful thing about horror is that it's still a growing and changing genre, one that, in the hands of its best writers, keeps surprising us.

BRIAN EVENSON is the author of a dozen and a half books of fiction, most recently *None of You Shall Be Spared* (Weird House Press, 2023). His collection *Song for the Unraveling of the World* won a World Fantasy Award and a Shirley Jackson Award, and was a finalist for the Ray Bradbury Prize. Past work has won the International Horror Guild Award, the O. Henry Prize, and the ALA-RUSA Award. He teaches at CalArts and lives in Los Angeles. A new collection, *Good Night, Sleep Tight*, will appear in September 2024.

Anastasia Garcia

Why do you write horror?

Fear is universal. In reading horror, we find the inner strength to conquer the monster. In writing horror, I can probe my characters and monsters for weaknesses: What will make them crack? How will they slay the beast? The monster can be as mundane as an old house or as imaginative as a shapeshifting alien from outer space. And the monster is always changing; it can be a creature of flesh and blood, an unfathomable cosmic entity, a place, a thing, a feeling, or even something hidden within ourselves.

What are you most excited about in the horror genre today?

Horror continues to live on the bleeding edge of culture (blood pun intended). Writers of horror are tackling new fears that plague humans every day and those change all the time. It can be climate change, toxic love, fertility, war, changing roles within the home, disease, technology, human brutality, or a place unexplored. I enjoy when our industry mixes and matches time periods, fresh locales, and those familiar monsters to make wholly original tales.

What are you most looking forward to seeing in the horror genre in the future?

I look forward to reading more translated horror from around the world that provides a glimpse into different cultures and tackles new fears. I believe modern horror readers crave new voices, characters, and stories that diversify their bookshelves and allow them to explore beyond their own personal experiences. And I look forward to more indigenous horror which has carved a special place in my twisted little heart.

Anastasia Garcia is a Mexican–American writer of horror fiction. Anastasia's short fiction appears in online publications, podcasts, and print anthologies. Anastasia's first book, GHOSTLY, GHASTLY

TALES, a collection of horror stories for young readers, will be published in July 2024. Anastasia is a member of the Horror Writers Association. Originally from Texas, Anastasia is a graduate of the University of Texas at Austin and is heavily influenced by the local myths and legends. She now lives in New York City.

RHONDA JACKSON GARCIA

Why do you write horror?

I wrote horror because it's important to me that stories about darkness are seen and engaged with. The world isn't all light without the dark that balances it.

What are you most excited about in the horror genre today?

I'm really excited to see voices that were previously relegated to the fringes of the genre being included in the mainstream conversations about horror and what it means to be horrific.

What are you most looking forward to seeing in the horror genre in the future?

I look forward to seeing a horror genre that really includes everyone, where it's "us with us" and not "us against us".

RHONDA JACKSON GARCIA, aka RJ Joseph, is an award winning, Stoker and Shirley Jackson Awards nominated creative/academic/ editor who hails from Texas.

CHRISTOPHER GOLDEN

Why do you write horror?

When I was young and had just started writing, my mother asked "why can't you write something 'good.'" By "good," she meant nice. I told her that I had written science-fiction stories, fantasy stories, western stories, but somebody always died. So I was just programmed this way. As a kid, I gravitated toward all things horror. Reruns of The Twilight Zone, monster movies on Creature Double Feature, comics like Tomb of Dracula and Werewolf by Night. Then I found scarier movies, and novels by Stephen King, and it just blossomed from there. I think, for me, the answer is that horror is the genre of possibility. Horror looks at the worst and most terrifying things on offer in the real world and in our imaginations, and says, we can fight this. I've worked in other genres, but horror is my home, and the horror people are my people.

What are you most excited about in the horror genre today?

The answer is really two-fold. First, it's the absolute boom we're experiencing in the genre. My first novel came out in 1994, when horror as a viable publishing genre was collapsing into a massive crater. The golden era that really ignited with Stephen King in the 70's and then grew massively popular in the 80's had come to an undignified end. For decades, we hoped for a resurgence but it never came…until at last, it did. Led by folks like Joe Hill and Paul Tremblay, horror is not only back but literally bigger than it's ever been. I keep telling younger writers to enjoy this boom era while it lasts, because it may not. The second thing—and a big reason why we're in such a boom—is the rapidly growing diversity in horror. Once upon a time, horror—like SF and fantasy—was completely dominated by straight, middle-aged, white men. Now you can't go a week without having exciting new releases from a vast array of diverse voices in horror. This diversity is what is fueling the further expansion of and excitement about the genre. I still love the old tropes, but I want fresh perspectives, other mythologies, new monsters, and protagonists whose experiences are new to me. There's never been a better time to be a horror fan.

What are you most looking forward to seeing in the horror genre in the future?

More surprises, more new perspectives, and more support from publishers at every level. Audiences in every medium are looking at horror with fresh eyes. Lots of people will never be interested—and that's okay—but so many who never thought they would like reading horror are discovering for the first time that there are incredible stories to be told in the genre, and so many extremely talented writers to tell them. Beyond that, so many horror fans are now beginning to delve into the genre's past and discovering the work of writers from earlier decades for the first time, and that makes my twisted little heart happier than you can possibly imagine.

CHRISTOPHER GOLDEN is the *New York Times* bestselling author of such novels as The *House of Last Resort*, *All Hallows*, *Road of Bones*, and the Stoker Award-winning *Ararat*, among many others. Golden co-created (with Mike Mignola) the fan favorite comic book series Baltimore and Joe Golem: Occult Detective. He has also written and co-written comic books, video games, screenplays, and the online animated series *Ghosts of Albion* (with Amber Benson). His work has been nominated for the British Fantasy Award, the Eisner Award, and multiple Shirley Jackson Awards. He has been nominated eleven times in eight different categories for the Bram Stoker Award®, and has won twice. In 2023, Golden and Amber Benson co-wrote and co-directed the Audible Original podcast *Slayers: A Buffyverse Story*. Please visit him at http://www.christophergolden.com

Cynthia Gómez

Why do you write horror?

The short answer is that it's so much fun. I get to play with monsters and ghosts and zombies and witches, for hours at a time if I'm lucky. The deeper answer is that horror is, at its heart, about fear, and I'm a very anxious person – I think a lot of us are – who loves to catastrophize about what if this or that or this other horrible thing happened. So I get to channel those parts of myself into something healthy, or at least healthier than catastrophizing. And something that other people can enjoy. It's also really satisfying when I get to take real-life horrors – violence against women, police brutality, child abuse — and rewrite them into the way I wish the story had ended.

What are you most excited about in the horror genre today?

I love how much hunger there is for indigenous horror: look at the incredible reception that Never Whistle at Night got last year. I'm really excited to see more indigenous horror, and I want to see it get the recognition it's often been denied. I also love how much queer horror there is, and in general it's so thrilling to see writers who come from marginalized groups are now taking center stage. Bring me all of it.

What are you most looking forward to seeing in the horror genre in the future?

This is more what I wish for, not so much what I can be sure is coming: I want lots more of everything I just said one question above. I want the editors of NWAN and all the authors in it to be drowning in offers. I want BIPOC writers to keep taking up more space. I want panels and workshops where all of the guests are BIPOC without it being a panel about being BIPOC. There's an anthology called Long Hidden that has speculative historical fiction – I want someone to not only republish that but start a whole series. Yes, that's partly selfish, because I love speculative historical fiction, but so do a lot of people.

CYNTHIA GÓMEZ writes horror and other types of speculative fiction, set primarily in Oakland, where she makes her home. She has a particular love for themes of revenge, retribution, and resistance to oppression, and she loves to write dark and frightening things while cuddling with her shadow, aka her adorable little dog. Her work has appeared in *Fantasy Magazine*, *Strange Horizons, Tree and Stone*, and numerous anthologies. *The Nightmare Box and Other Stories*, her first collection, is out from Cursed Morsels Press in July 2024. You can find more of her work at cynthiasaysboo.wordpress.com.

CAROL GYZANDER

Why do you write horror?

I've read and loved science fiction and fantasy all my life. So often, though, I would picture a strange ending or some other force lying beneath the surface of the narrative. Horror gives me an outlet for those weird twists that my brain always adds to a story. Plus, I have to say that it's a terrific way to explore and dive into the things that really bother us in a way that won't get you arrested.

What are you most excited about in the horror genre today?

I'm thrilled to see so many folks from a variety of backgrounds, locations, and ages doing more in the genre. It's exciting to hear their words, and it helps give me a new way of looking at my own stories … and even my life!

What are you most looking forward to seeing in the horror genre in the future?

Horror has a unique ability to reach others through suspenseful plots, visceral imagery, and ideas that are both creative and provocative. I hope we continue to have works that draw people in with the story while sharing important themes such as social equality, the importance of combating climate change, and the need to oppose violence against women.

Bram Stoker Award® nominee CAROL GYZANDER writes and edits horror, weird fiction, and science fiction with strong women in twisted tales that touch your heart. She co-edited the ghost anthology EVEN IN THE GRAVE and A WOMAN UNBECOMING, the horror anthology inspired by the reversal of Roe v. Wade, which benefits reproductive healthcare services. Her short stories appear in various magazines and anthologies, including UNDER TWIN SUNS, WEIRD TALES 367, WEIRD HOUSE MAGAZINE, TANGLE & FEN, and NEVERMORE. Carol is HWA NY Chapter Co-Chair and co-hosts their monthly Galactic Terrors online reading series. CarolGyzander.com or on social media @ CarolGyzander

RACHEL HARRISON

Why do you write horror?

I write to figure out how I feel about the world, and the world is a scary place. I can exorcise my demons by writing horror. Also, it's just the most fun.

What are you most excited about in the horror genre today?

The range in the genre right now is the best it's ever been. There's so much originality—strong voices, new voices, people telling their stories their way.

What are you most looking forward to seeing in the horror genre in the future?

> Welcoming in new voices. Expanding what we proudly claim as horror. I'm excited to see the genre continue to open up.

RACHEL HARRISON is the national bestselling author of BLACK SHEEP, SUCH SHARP TEETH, CACKLE, and THE RETURN, which was nominated for a Bram Stoker Award® for Superior Achievement in a First Novel. Her short fiction has appeared in Guernica, Electric Literature's Recommended Reading, as an Audible Original, and in her debut story collection BAD DOLLS. She lives in Western New York with her husband and their cat/overlord. Her next novel, SO THIRSTY, is out September 10th from Berkley.

SHANE HAWK

Why do you write horror?

> I write Horror because I love having the ability to bring my ancestors and my people to the page, but representation is only the surface level. Horror writing is therapeutic for me because I've had a troubled past with my dark mind, and it gives me an avenue to bleed those awful things onto paper and shape them around themes that may connect with others. It's an ominous handoff.

What are you most excited about in the horror genre today?

> Within contemporary Horror, I'm so excited to see the genre stretched and folded over like a blood-tinged taffy by emerging writers from heritages and worldviews that have been historically scant in the marketplace. And like that taffy, these burgeoning writers are twisting and blending subgenres and flipping tropes inside and out. It's so refreshing to see.

What are you most looking forward to seeing in the horror genre in the future?

I'm optimistic about the future of Horror. I anticipate the current trajectory of Horror readership to go higher and higher as the new vanguard takes a sledgehammer and splits the genre wide open, inviting a broadened understanding of what exactly constitutes Horror; they will continue to extend the familiar cursory assumption past it being solely carnage and monsters.

SHANE HAWK (enrolled Cheyenne-Arapaho, Hidatsa and Citizen Potawatomi descent) is a history teacher by day and a horror writer by night. Hawk's literary contributions include his debut story collection Anoka, alongside short fiction featured in numerous anthologies. He recently co-edited *Never Whistle at Night*, an internationally bestselling Indigenous dark fiction anthology published by Penguin Random House. Hawk lives in San Diego, California with his beautiful wife. Learn more at shanehawk.com.

LAUREL HIGHTOWER

Why do you write horror?

Primarily it's because horror is my happy place. The joy and anticipation of sitting down to a good ghost story or possession tale is an unparalleled pleasure, and the same is true of settling in to write my own horror. I love how expansive and exciting horror is—it can be anything, as diverse as our fears. The longer I do this, the more muscles I get to flex in learning to work in different mediums and tackle subjects I never thought I would.

What are you most excited about in the horror genre today?

The emergence of so many new and exciting voices. Small

presses dominate this game, in my opinion, and are able to take chances and swings we don't always see. I remember not so long ago being resigned to the idea that the five horror authors on the shelves of book stores and libraries were all there were to read. Now I can barely keep up with the amazing releases, the stories being told in ways I'd never imagined.

What are you most looking forward to seeing in the horror genre in the future?

I'm excited to see how we tackle the changing landscape of marketing and accessibility. There are a lot of reasons to feel depressed about the state of publishing (also the world, but I'm keeping this narrow.) With the reduction of so much of out social media reach, I'm excited by the appearance of multiple types of conventions, bar readings, and creative launches. The ways we adapt and help each other, the way we'll problem solve and champion one another. We can't control many elements of this industry, but we're a resilient bunch. We're not going anywhere.

LAUREL HIGHTOWER is a bourbon loving native of Lexington, Kentucky. She is the Bram Stoker-nominated author of WHISPERS IN THE DARK, CROSSROADS, BELOW, EVERY WOMAN KNOWS THIS, SILENT KEY, and the upcoming THE DAY OF THE DOOR, and has more than a dozen short fiction stories in print.

JAMAL HODGE

Why do you write horror?

I try not to. I merely try to write the dark side of truth and how pain is like oxygen to living things that are slowly being digested within the living stomach called Earth. See? Lol But in all seriousness, pain, loss, sacrifice, and survival are some of the most powerful themes of life, and horror allows us to not only be honest about the inescapable cost of these inevitable happenings but also allows us to show how we as human beings can find the courage and the compassion and humanity to endure them, indeed to transcend them and turn them into strength, beauty, and truth. I write horror because horror tells us the truth about the best and the worst of what we are or could be.

What are you most excited about in the horror genre today?

The intersection of so many diverse voices. And that those voices are not monolithic, such as every black writer in the genre is not approaching, or even defining, blackness in the same fashion. For so long the genre seemed to be Alaska, meaning it seemed to be white AF. But now here, even in the HWA you see people like Tannarive Due, Linda Addison, Jordan Peele, Stephen Gram Jones, Lee Murray, Cynthia Pelayo, Victor Le'valle, and so many more, The landscape has changed, and I'm honored to be coming in now after all the hard work has been done! Shit, all we newbies gotta do now is tell our truths and do the work of writing and promoting. It's nothing compared to the barriers many of the pioneers I've mentioned have had to transcend on top of honing their craft.

What are you most looking forward to seeing in the horror genre in the future?

The implementation of horror storytelling in virtual spaces and its blending effects. So as different cultures overlap as technology continues to allow our cultures and mythologies to blend, monsters such as the Grootslang,

JAMAL HODGE is a multi-award-winning filmmaker, writer, and poet. He is an active member of The HWA and The SFPA, being nominated for a 2021 & 2022 Rhysling Award while his poem "Colony ' placed 2nd in the 2022 Dwarf Stars. His work has been featured in *Quail Nous 2, The Unioverse Stories of The Convergence, Chiral Mad 5, The Year's Best African Speculative Fiction 2022, SPACE AND TIME Magazine, HYBRID: Misfits, Monsters & Other Phenomena, PENUMBRIC Speculative Fiction Magazine, Savage Planets*, and many others. His debut collection *The Dark Between The Twilight* will be released in 2024 by Crystal Lake Publishing. www. writerhodge.com

PEDRO INIGUEZ

Why do you write horror?

Working in the horror genre allows me to examine, explore, and engage with the things that frighten me from a safe distance. To have an internal dialogue with painful or sensitive topics. Sometimes I come away with answers, and other times I come away with more questions. But ultimately, writing horror allows me to make some sense of my fears, accept them, and convey those thoughts with the world through a literary narrative.

What are you most excited about in the horror genre today?

The diversity of voices we're finally getting. So many people from so many walks of life are telling their stories; unique and powerful perspectives that add so much richness and elevate the genre. Everyone benefits from that.

What are you most looking forward to seeing in the horror genre in the future?

I'm looking forward to the successes of those new diverse voices carrying over into all sorts of media: movies, comic books, video games, TV, etc. I think the world is ready for fresh perspectives and new ideas. To be challenged and entertained in new ways from voices that typically don't get heard. And I think we'll be seeing more of that soon.

PEDRO INIGUEZ is a horror and science-fiction writer from Los Angeles, California. He is a Rhysling Award finalist and a Best of the Net and Pushcart Prize nominee. His work has appeared in *Nightmare Magazine, Never Wake: An Anthology of Dream Horror, Shadows Over Main Street Volume 3,* and *Qualia Nous Vol. 2,* among others.

STEPHEN GRAHAM JONES

Why do you write horror?

I like to see the blood on the wall, and I like to make the reader squirm, and feel things, and maybe leave their lights on. It's fun. You write what you like to read, yeah? Reading horror can be a roller coaster if it's done right. I know a lot like to say that that safety bar's down, too, so there's no real threat. But I think there is. Art can rewire you—it's supposed to. Art, and horror specifically, can open a door in your head and your heart and your life that you didn't even know you had. You can come out of this or that horror story different than you were. Maybe better, maybe not. That's scary, to me. But danger is what's always right around the edge of "fun," just a mis-step away. It's what makes the fun: the chance of getting hurt. The more real that chance is, the more fun's in the offing. It's why there's often blood involved with good times.

What are you most excited about in the horror genre today?

All the new voices, that maybe haven't had a chance to be heard before. New DNA is what keeps a genre vital, and horror's getting a good infusion of that new DNA, lately. As a result, the genre's vital and even vigorous, right now. I like it. Feels like things are happening.

What are you most looking forward to seeing in the horror genre in the future?

Different forms it can take. Fiction can be delivered in so, so many ways, and horror can take advantage of that. It can dress itself up as other things, and so get its scare in around the side, when it's not really expected. Or, with different forms and techniques, it can keep one part of the mind occupied enough that it can smuggle a dark egg or two across while the reader's distracted. And those dark eggs, they hatch around three in the morning. That's when things get very interesting.

STEPHEN GRAHAM JONES IS THE *NYT* BESTSELLING AUTHOR OF SOME THIRTY novels and collections, and there's some novellas and comic books in there as well. Most recent are *The Angel of Indian Lake* and the ongoing *Earthdivers*. Up before too long are *I Was a Teenage Slasher*, *True Believers*, and *The Buffalo Hunter Hunter*. Stephen lives and teaches in Boulder, Colorado.

ALMA KATSU

Why do you write horror?

The world is a frightening place, full of terrors we don't understand. Fiction is a great way to explore our fears. It allows you to wade in as deep as you want without someone shaming you or trying to get you to deny it exists or otherwise trying to stop you. Horror is about facing your fears: it's empowering.

What are you most excited about in the horror genre today?

I'm encouraged by the broadening of what's considered 'horror'. It's definitely not a one-size-fits-all genre. I'm also encouraged by the broadening of the audience. It seems more people are willing to let it be publicly known that they love horror (seeing more accounts on social media celebrating horror, for instance, and not just at Halloween). More publishers are opening imprints for horror, more stores are adding horror sections.

What are you most looking forward to seeing in the horror genre in the future?

I'm looking forward to ground-breaking work from authors, whether they're debuts or old hands. Stories that take risks are going to advance the art form.

ALMA KATSU is the award-winning author of eight books, including historical horror novels *The Hunger*, *The Deep*, and *The Fervor*. *The Wehrwolf* won the 2023 Bram Stoker Award® for long fiction.

TODD KEISLING

Why do you write horror?

I'm going to quote something I wrote for Becky Spratford's blog last year: Horror's always been there, one of the few things in my life that's welcomed me with open arms and without judgment. It's where the outsider thrives, the weird are praised, and the weak become strong. It's the place where a weird little kid dons a black cape from Halloween and goes hunting vampires in his grandmother's backyard. Where the oddball child dresses up as a grim reaper to attend his church's Halloween party. It's the happiness this teen feels when all his friends scream and laugh at the flying eyeball scene in Evil Dead 2. It's the pride and honor that overwhelms this man when others enjoy the horror he's created. What began in the bedroom of my granny's house continues in the dusty attic of my cold, dead heart. Horror is my mask, my coping mechanism, my comfort. But mostly, Horror is my home.

What are you most excited about in the horror genre today?

New and diverse names pushing the boundaries of the genre, challenging long-established notions of what "horror" can or should be. New readers, too. Seems like more and more folks are turning to horror for their escape and discovering all the various subgenres and niches found therein.

What are you most looking forward to seeing in the horror genre in the future?

New perspectives! I think we're in the midst of a sea change, and I'm eager to see where the current leads.

TODD KEISLING is a two-time Bram Stoker Award® finalist and award-winning designer. His books include *Devil's Creek, Cold, Black & Infinite, Scanlines,* and many more. A pair of his earlier works were recipients of the University of Kentucky's Oswald Research & Creativity Prize for Creative Writing (2002 and 2005), and his second novel, *The Liminal Man,* was an Indie Book Award finalist in Horror & Suspense (2013). He lives in Pennsylvania with his family.

RED LAGOE

Why do you write horror?

Horror allows us to explore the darker emotions of humanity that are often considered taboo to discuss. Through horror, we can plunge beneath our skins, stir around the viscera of trauma, grief, despair, disgust, and fear, exhuming ghosts we didn't know we had. And we come out dripping with blood and sinew, but also with a better understanding of what it means to be human.

What are you most excited about in the horror genre today?

It has been exciting to watch the variety of the horror experience expand. An increasing number of bookstores are making room on their shelves for authors other than King and Koontz, they're embracing indie titles, new voices, and unique subgenres. Horror can be so many things—quiet, dreadful, terrifying, funny, disgusting, mind-bending, and more—and there's truly something for everyone.

What are you most looking forward to seeing in the horror genre in the future?

I look forward to the continued expansion of the genre. New voices bring to the table new ideas and never-imagined stories, and—ultimately—they bring in new horror readers.

RED LAGOE grew up on 80s horror and carried her paranoia of slashers and sewer creatures into adulthood, becoming a horror writer and artist. She is the author of *In Excess of Dark and Impulses of a Necrotic Heart*, and the editor of *Nightmare Sky: Stories of Astronomical Horror*. When Red is not spewing her most depraved thoughts onto the page, she can be found under an open sky with a telescope, dabbling in amateur astronomy.

ERIC LaROCCA

Why do you write horror?

I write horror because I fervently believe that it is the most honest and truthful creative thing I can do while existing on this earth as a living thing—to write about the cruelty, the brutality of mankind, to expose the terrors, the undiluted suffering of humanity. Horror does not seek to comfort its audience. It does not aim to please the consumer with fanciful ideas and notions of hope or light. Of course, some works of horror can certainly be hopeful or imbued with the promise of a better tomorrow.

However, the horror I usually prefer is bleak, unforgiving, and decidedly ruthless. I think there's so much truth to be found in horror and, more importantly, it's one of the few genres that allows the creator the space to explore the complexities of the human condition—our suffering, our hardship, our most pain-filled moments.

What are you most excited about in the horror genre today?

Of course, there are many elements of modern horror to be excited about. For the instance, the success of independent publishers, the diversity of spotlighted authors from marginalized communities, etc. I think I'm most excited about the recognition and outpouring of respect for queer voices in horror fiction. When I was a teenager browsing the shelves at bookstores, I was so intimidated, I felt so disenfranchised and worried that my queerness would essentially prevent me from participating in a genre I loved so dearly. I saw very little LGBTQ+ representation and it troubled me greatly. As I survey the current landscape of horror fiction, I'm filled with so much hope and satisfaction. It feels as though the queer kids have finally arrived at the table…

What are you most looking forward to seeing in the horror genre in the future?

I'm sincerely looking forward to more writers from marginalized and underappreciated communities achieving success and basking in the warm glow of appreciation. I hope to see the horror genre become a melting pot where others who are different are welcomed with open arms. I'm also very interested to see tropes and cliches be inverted and challenged by newer, more dynamic literary voices. Moreover, I'd love to see big publishers take risks and accept newer voices who are creating vibrant, exciting fiction.

ERIC LAROCCA (he/they) is the Bram Stoker Award®-nominated and Splatterpunk Award-winning author of several works of horror and dark fiction, including the viral sensation, *Things Have Gotten Worse Since We Last Spoke*. A lover of luxury fashion and an admirer of European musical theatre, Eric can often be found roaming the streets of his home city, Boston, MA, for inspiration. For more information, please visit ericlarocca.com.

VICTOR LAVALLE

Why do you write horror?

The simplest answer is that I write horror because I grew up with horror. It speaks to me now as it spoke to me then. But what did it say? What attracted a child to the scary, spooky things? I know I have all sorts of deeper psychological ideas about this, but the truly honest answer is that I always found the scary stuff fun. Questions of the unknown and the unknowable remain profoundly interesting to me but above all else I just find horror a blast. Whatever you can imagine, you can do. Unlike nearly any other genre there are no rules. Not really. Horror can take place anywhere and to anyone, it can be rich with physical pain or it can be deeply unsettling, getting under your skin without even breaking the skin. What a malleable, marvelous ability. There's really no other genre, or style, quite like it.

What are you most excited about in the horror genre today?

What am I excited about? Look at how much of it there is! I love the depth and breadth of the genre as it chugs its way across the threshold of the 21st century. Every subset of the genre feels like its thriving—splatter, occult, psychological and political and on and on and on. Prose, poetry, comics, film and tv, horror is everywhere. It's always been there, of course, but the rise to prominence of the small presses in the last decade or so, has been truly spectacular. My hope is that there is enough of a core audience that we can keep the small presses alive well into the future. You can't trust the commercial presses because they must, simply because of their scale, follow the larger public trends. But the smaller presses can be bold and intelligent and nimble. Long may they thrive.

What are you most looking forward to seeing in the horror genre in the future?

I love seeing horror when its blended well with other genres. You could make the argument that horror can only work if its blended with another genre because on its own—as has been said many times—horror is only a feeling. So I look forward to seeing the ways horror can get mixed together in ways I would never guess. Military romance horror? Yes, please! Historical horror told only in verse? Hell, yeah! Bring all of it to me, I want it.

VICTOR LAVALLE is the author of five novels, two novellas, a short story collection, and two original graphic novels. His novel, *The Changeling*, has been adapted for Apple TV+. He has adapted his novel, *The Devil in Silver*, for AMC TV and will begin shooting in 2024. He has been the recipient of numerous awards, including the Bram Stoker Award®, the World Fantasy Award, and the Shirley Jackson Award. He teaches at Columbia University and lives in the Bronx with his wife and two kids.

TIM LEBBON

Why do you write horror?

This is something I'm asked a lot, and something I've thought about a lot ... and the only answer I've come up with that makes any sort of sense is a saying my grandmother used to say: It's the way my mum put my hat on. Anything I write — supernatural stories, fantasy, thrillers, screenplays, even bloody shopping lists — tends towards the dark side, and that's just the way it is. I don't analyse why too much because I'm afraid of what I'll find. And I'm afraid that if I think about what I'm writing too much, and why, then something will see and sense my interest and ... who knows what might happen then? I think I'm pretty laid back in real life. I don't want to discover what I'd be like if I didn't write horror.

What are you most excited about in the horror genre today?

The genre feels more fresh and damn vital than it has in years. I've been writing a long time, and whatever's happening with the big publishers, there's always been that passion evident in the indie presses. But now it's exploded outward in a way we haven't seen in a long time, and the celebration of all aspects of horror writing, and so many diverse voices producing brilliant work and making such an impact, makes the genre we love the place to be right now. And it's about time.

What are you most looking forward to seeing in the horror genre in the future?

Lots more books by my favourite writers, and lots more books from new writers who will become favourites. I so wish I could keep up with all the new writers coming onto the scene ... but the fact there are too many to keep up with is a great thing.

TIM LEBBON is a *New York Times*-bestselling writer from South Wales, with over forty novels and hundreds of novellas and short stories published. His latest novel is *Among The Living* from Titan. He has won a World Fantasy Award and four British Fantasy Awards, as well as Bram Stoker, Scribe and Dragon Awards. He's recently worked on a computer game, a major Audible audio drama, and he's co-writing his first comic for Dark Horse. His work has been adapted for screen as *The Silence and Pay the Ghost*. Tim is currently developing more projects for the page and screen.

Izzy Lee

Why do you write horror?

This is a cliché at this point, but writing horror is truly cheaper than therapy. Plus, it keeps me out of jail. This world is an upsetting place, particularly since the end of 2016, and it just doesn't seem to stop. Horror has always been a comforting realm into which I can escape, process all the fucked up things happen, and release the horrors I feel back into the universe via alchemy. I need it, breathe it, love it, and have since I was kindergarten age. I wouldn't be me without it, and the horror community is filled with incredible badasses who have been through so much pain, yet have the kindest, welcoming hearts.

What are you most excited about in the horror genre today?

What's thrilling about horror today is that we finally get to see other points of view. Not to begrudge any talented, straight white man, I'm happy for you, but man, it's so refreshing to see other stories in film and television. We don't nearly have enough in those mediums, but there's now hope. And in literature? We are blessed to have so many stories and outlooks! Give me a universe of spices, every flavor of the blackest rainbows in horror! It's a crazy-exciting time in horror lit.

What are you most looking forward to seeing in the horror genre in the future?

More films and shows from women, nonbinary friends, and people of color. It's hard for everyone, but it's still far harder, ridiculously so, to get those works from the "non-default" made, from initial pitch meetings to completed works out in the world. You'd think it wasn't 2024, but it is. I also love the trend of gothic horror that's come back in books, as well as coastal horror! I grew up on Poe and the Vincent Price/Roger Corman/AIP films, which were so lurid and delicious. Let's get even more folklore horror from other cultures, too!

One of A.V. Club's 10 female filmmakers to hire, Izzy Lee is a director and author on the rise. Lee shadowed Adam Egypt Mortimer on the SpectreVision film Archenemy and is in post on her own feature, *House of Ashes*. Several of her short stories have found publication, including "The Beginning" in *Dark Matter Ink's Haunted Reels* anthology, curated by David Lawson, Jr. Released on 2/13/24, *I Can See Your Lies* is her first book, also from Dark Matter Ink. See what she's up to at nihilnoctem.com.

Juan Martinez

Why do you write horror?

Horror was what got me through some of the scariest times in my own life, when I was misdiagnosed with duchenne muscular dystrophy as a teenager: I spent a long year deep into Peter Straub.

What are you most excited about in the horror genre today?

I love that everyone's invited to the party right now—-that's how it feels, anyway, that so many new voices are coming in from every corner of our shared experience.

What are you most looking forward to seeing in the horror genre in the future?

I'm working on something a bit of folk-horror that leans into the comic, but I'm just excited about more funny horror books. Or just sneaky-funny bits in flat-out frightening novels. More of that, please.

Juan Martinez is the author of *Extended Stay* and *Best Worst American*. He lives near Chicago and is an associate professor at Northwestern University.

Rena Mason

Why do you write horror?

Short answer, escapism through self-entertainment. The longer answer is that once I breathe a little thought into characters, they live with me and bother me until I flesh them out and finish their story. And because I complete stories in my mind before writing or typing any words, they're forced to traverse everything in my head on their way out. I've always had an affinity for the horror genre. It's diverting of everyday troubles in my opinion. For example, maybe I'm having a bad day at work, but at least I'm not being chased by an axe murderer in a bunny mask. No other genre, in my opinion, elicits the range of emotions quite like horror, so I find it a great tool to say what I want to say through common fears and how we overcome them, or don't, and how that might affect us.

What are you most excited about in the horror genre today?

The horror genre on the forefront of so many forms and mediums, in an array of platforms, and from a multitude of diverse backgrounds is a dream come true. Childhood and teenager me didn't think it possible, and I couldn't be happier. I never thought I'd ever watch Thai horror movies with English subtitles, much less have one make it onto the Preliminary Ballot of the Bram Stoker Awards® in 2021— Banjong Pisanthanakun's, THE MEDIUM. The thirst for and production of more horror genre work from voices not our own is absolutely wonderful. Keep it coming!

What are you most looking forward to seeing in the horror genre in the future?

More horror and its subgenres from voices in every corner of the world, involving history, myths, legends, religious beliefs, various socioeconomic backgrounds, all of it in the years ahead. The horror genre in fantastical worlds, and everything else we haven't read or seen about recently or yet. More of the horror genre in science, space/not Earth-based (speculative fiction), please. And more weird horror, too!

RENA MASON is a Bram Stoker Award®-winning horror and dark speculative fiction author of *The Evolutionist* and "The Devil's Throat" as well as a 2014 Stage 32 /The Blood List Search for New Blood Screenwriting Contest Quarter-Finalist. She was nominated in 2023 for the Shirley Jackson and World Fantasy Awards for co-editing *Other Terrors: An Inclusive Anthology* for the HWA Presents series. An R.N. and avid scuba diver, she travels the world and incorporates the experiences into her stories. She currently resides in the Pacific Northwest. For more information visit her website: www.RenaMason.Ink

GUS MORENO

Why do you write horror?

A year ago I would have said I write horror because it gives me a lane to focus my work, but I'm not sure whether that's true anymore. Thinking of horror as a category became very stifling. It's much better for me to think in terms of its possibilities. Unlike other genres, horror isn't strictly defined by tropes. Horror is an emotion, and in that sense, any story has the potential to ebb into horror. That's my favorite thing about the genre. You have the freedom to go anywhere you want.

What are you most excited about in the horror genre today?

I'm excited by the genre's continual march into the mainstream. There's so much quality horror on shelves than ever before. I'm also excited by the proliferation of stories from people of various backgrounds. Before, a horror fan could say they had international sensibilities because they read manga / watched Japanese horror, but more people are getting their stories out there, and they're adding new wrinkles to what the genre can do, and how it relates to a universal human experience.

What are you most looking forward to seeing in the horror genre in the future?

I'm really interested to see how horror adapts to the coming technologies of VR or augmented reality. There's already a plethora of horror games that could be played in those mediums, but it's still early days. Once artists have a chance to get accustomed with the technology and grow with it, then we'll really see innovation storytelling wise, and I'm eager to see where that'll take us.

GUS MORENO is the author of *This Thing Between Us*. His stories have appeared in *Aurealis*, *PseudoPod*, *Bluestem Magazine*, *LitroNy*, the *Burnt Tongues* anthology, and a bunch of other places that are totally not defunct. Some of his favorite books are *American Psycho*, *Battle Royale*, and *Under the Skin*. Some of his favorite writers are Margaret Atwood, Lucia Berlin, and Amy Hempel. He likes denim jackets, professional wrestling, neighborhood pizza, and anything by The xx. He lives in the suburbs with his wife and dogs, but never think that he's not from Chicago.

PREMEE MOHAMED

Why do you write horror?

I used to say, "I don't write horror! I just want to scare the characters, not the readers!" This should have been a clue that I don't write like many writers, or read like many readers, but I didn't get it at the time. Now I get it: I write horror because it's an ongoing test of my craft; it's a way to see if I can evoke emotions across the entire spectrum; it's a text-based reality show where I have to prepare a gourmet meal using tools that constantly turn on their users. Will it be unease today? Disgust? Loss of bodily autonomy? Unresponsive institutions? I want to see the comfortable reader made uncomfortable, the safe reader made to feel unsafe, and to confront the truth of life: we are living in a world of horrors. We should write about them.

What are you most excited about in the horror genre today?

I'm constantly surprised and intrigued by horror appearing in different forms and genres, finding new ways to connect to the emotions (and glands and sphincters) of horror fans. When I was growing up it never would have occurred to me that one day we could have horror podcasts, interactive fiction, immersive games (tabletop and otherwise), all different types of horror in all different formats from all over the world. I learn about new ones all the time.

What are you most looking forward to seeing in the horror genre in the future?

I'm looking forward to more participation from non-Western horror creators, not just in writing or film but in every type of horror (podcasts, games, music, theatre, everything!). There's such a groundswell of curiosity and creativity about horror from so many cultures and backgrounds that I have no familiarity with—I would love to see that grow, be respected, and supported.

PREMEE MOHAMED is a Nebula, World Fantasy, and Aurora award-winning Indo-Caribbean scientist and speculative fiction author based in Edmonton, Alberta. She has also been a finalist for the Hugo, Ignyte, Locus, British Fantasy, and Crawford awards. Currently, she is the Edmonton Public Library writer-in-residence and an Assistant Editor at the short fiction audio venue Escape Pod. She is the author of the 'Beneath the Rising' series of novels as well as several novellas. Her short fiction has appeared in many venues and she can be found on her website at www.premeemohamed.com.

LISA MORTON

Why do you write horror?

I think I've always been attracted to not just the intense emotions of horror, but the primal morality of it – ultimate good vs. ultimate evil. I also like the fact that the good and the evil in horror are often reversed – the monster (an outsider figure) is the good so the monster slayer becomes the evil. Plus horror often seems like the sanest reaction to the world!

What are you most excited about in the horror genre today?

I love where horror is at right now, full of exciting new voices who are trying different things and spinning the genre off in some astonishing directions as well as reinvigorating some of the oldest, most classic tropes. As a writer who had been around for decades (did I just say that?!), I find it inspires me to discover and try new things in my own work.

What are you most looking forward to seeing in the horror genre in the future?

I hope this current cycle of horror doesn't experience the reactionary backlash that often hits fresh directions in art, especially during such a divisive moment in history. I'd like to see the genre continue to grow and expand and experiment and welcome those writers who will continue to lead it into the future.

Lisa Morton is a screenwriter, author of non-fiction books, and prose writer whose work was described by the American Library Association's *Readers' Advisory Guide to Horror* as "consistently dark, unsettling, and frightening." She is a six-time winner of the Bram Stoker Award®, the author of four novels and 200 short stories, and a world-class Halloween and paranormal expert. Her recent releases include *Calling the Spirits: A History of Seances* and *The Art of the Zombie Movie*; she also hosts the popular weekly "Ghost Report" podcast. Lisa lives in Los Angeles and online at www.lisamorton.com.

Emma E. Murray

Why do you write horror?

I have always been fascinated by the darker parts of humanity. The fear, obsession, grief, and anger inside us all, so that inevitably brought me into the horror sphere where fiction explores those themes in depth. In addition, I've found that I can process my own fears and trauma through fiction, and that catharsis often carries over for my readers who read these painful or frightening stories and are able to probe the darkest parts of their own psyche and past in a safe way.

What are you most excited about in the horror genre today?

I'm so excited to see marginalized authors finding their voice in horror. Reading women writers, BIPOC writers, and LGBTQ writers, all telling stories through the lens of their unique experiences and cultures, is incredible. These voices reinvigorate the genre and bring forth brand new horrors for readers who are sick of the same white/cis/straight/male stories.

What are you most looking forward to seeing in the horror genre in the future?

I love the more experimental, surreal, and strange concepts, formats, and storytelling I'm seeing more and more in horror, both in film and literature. I look forward to authors pushing those boundaries even farther and revealing new, grotesque, mesmerizing experiences in the future. Show me those fresh ideas and things I'd never come up with in a million years!

Emma E. Murray's work has appeared in anthologies like *Obsolescence* and *Ooze: Little Bursts of Body Horror* as well as magazines such as *Cosmic Horror Monthly* and *Vastarien*. Her novelette, *When the Devil*, as well as her debut novel, *Crushing Snails*, will be available Summer 2024. Her second novel, *Shoot Me in the Face on a Beautiful Day*, will be out in 2025. To read more, you can visit her website EmmaEMurray.com

LEE MURRAY

Why do you write horror?

This question is often asked of horror writers, and it elicits all the traditional responses about taking the battle to the monsters that terrorise us, daring to challenge the status quo, and finding catharsis, compassion, and connection in the denouement. Things like being entertained while also being enlightened, and the opportunities horror provides for innovation and subversion. The way that horror addresses deeply serious subjects yet is also lively and fun. How it transcends genres and ages and cultures. I should probably mention all those important reasons. Mostly though, it's because horror feels like home to me—perhaps because horror welcomes the weird, and I am a little bit weird.

What are you most excited about in the horror genre today?

So many things! For today, I'll list three: diversity, community, and poetry.

What are you most looking forward to seeing in the horror genre in the future?

As co-chair (with Dave Jeffery) of the HWA's Wellness Committee, I'm looking forward to our horror writing community leading the way in destigmatising mental illness in literature, portraying mentally ill characters with depth, nuance, and understanding, and in ways that promote compassion. I'm not talking about draining all the blood from our horror narratives—not at all; bring on the blood!—but instead creating the kind of powerful, authentic representations that offer insights to provoke real and lasting change. The committee is only in its third year and there is a lot of work yet to do, but I'm confident that our horror community will rise to the challenge. I can't wait to read that work!

LEE MURRAY is a multi-award-winning author-editor, essayist, screenwriter, and poet from Aotearoa-New Zealand. A *USA Today* Bestselling author, Shirley Jackson and five-time Bram Stoker Award® winner, she is a New Zealand Prime Minister's Award-winner for Literary Achievement in Fiction. Lee lives in the sunny Bay of Plenty with her well-behaved family and a naughty dog.

CANDACE NOLA

Why do you write horror?

Writing allows me to tell the stories that I want to tell, in a way that only I can. Horror appeals to me because it's one of the few genres that can illustrate the entirety of the human experience, from love and creation, death and fear, and everything in-between.

What are you most excited about in the horror genre today?

All the new voices being showcased, there are so many more voices being heard today than ever before, from all walks of life. It's incredible to see and gives the reader the ability to read fresh stories with diverse perspectives while allowing them to learn about other cultures and lifestyles.

What are you most looking forward to seeing in the horror genre in the future?

I most look forward to this continued progression of acceptance, inclusion, and diversity for all. There are as many stories as there are people, and they all deserve to be heard. I often tell the newer authors that I mentor when they struggle with self-doubt and insecurity that there is a reader for every story, and I believe fully that.

CANDACE NOLA is a multiple award-winning author, editor, and publisher. She writes poetry, horror, dark fantasy, and extreme horror content. Books include *Breach, Beyond the Breach, Hank Flynn, Bishop, Earth vs The Lava Spiders, The Unicorn Killer, Unmasked, The Vet,* and *Desperate Wishes.* Her short stories can be found in many anthologies within the horror community, such as *American Cannibal* and *The Perfectly Fine Neighborhood.* She is the creator of *UncomfortablyDark.com,* a horror community platform which focuses primarily on promoting indie horror authors and small presses with weekly book reviews, interviews, and special features.

Robert P. Ottone

Why do you write horror?

I write horror as a therapeutic exercise that I started after my dad passed away. Lately, I've been finding myself wanting to explore more than horror, but in the end, horror is where the heart is.

What are you most excited about in the horror genre today?

I'm most excited by the variety of voices we get to enjoy, whether it's on large presses or small. It's exciting to see different perspectives and takes on the genre we all love.

What are you most looking forward to seeing in the horror genre in the future?

I'd like to see people pushing narrative and form further. Get weirder. Go darker.

Robert P. Ottone is the Bram Stoker Award®-winning author of THE TRIANGLE and is also the best-selling author of CURSE OF THE COB MAN, THE SLEEPY HOLLOW GANG, THE VILE THING WE CREATED and NOCTURNAL CREATURES. His short fiction has been collected in WRAPPED IN PLASTIC AND OTHER SWEET NOTHINGS as well as HER INFERNAL NAME & OTHER NIGHTMARES. He holds two master's degrees in Education, as well as an MFA in Children's Literature. A bagel-loving fabulist of spooky absurdity, Ottone enjoys cigars, cocktails and time with his wife.

Hailey Piper

Why do you write horror?

I write horror because I'm a weirdo, and horror is where I've always felt like I could be most myself. It is the genre of healing, and catharsis, and a place for outcasts. I love monsters, and I love understanding what they are, and becoming them for a time, and dredging up my own personal demons and facing them down with the monstrosity of the work. We can be such lovely bloody creatures, and horror lets us do it.

What are you most excited about in the horror genre today?

The unhinged. I enjoy seeing how brazen many writers are getting these days, willing to break free of comfort zones. Taking odd concepts and treating them as the most important thing you'll ever read. It's wild, and I love it.

What are you most looking forward to seeing in the horror genre in the future?

I'm going to carry on from my previous answer—more personal strangeness. There's only one of each of us, which means each person is uniquely equipped to express the bizarre nature deep inside them. If you don't, who will? I'm looking forward to more authors getting bravely weird.

HAILEY PIPER is the -winning author of *Queen of Teeth*, *A Light Most Hateful*, *The Worm and His Kings* series, and other books of dark fiction. She is an active member of the Horror Writers Association, with over 100 short stories appearing in *Weird Tales*, *Pseudopod*, *Cosmic Horror Monthly*, and other publications. Her non-fiction appears in *Writer's Digest*, *Library Journal*, *CrimeReads*, and elsewhere. She lives with her wife in Maryland, where their cosmic rituals are secret. Find Hailey at www.haileypiper.com.

John Palisano

Why do you write horror?

Writing horror is in my blood. So, I must! For some reason, almost everything I come up with has horror elements. Some of us are just predisposed to feel our most genuine amongst dark things. My self-diagnosis is that I'm scared to death of death. It's the worst thing, right? Exploring these stories acts as a kind of reckoning with the inevitable and provides just the tiniest bit of comfort.

What are you most excited about in the horror genre today?

One of the most intriguing situations in the horror genre at the moment is the mainstreaming of not only horror, but of so many new and diverse voices occupying those spaces. It was unimaginable only several years ago to see such inroads, especially on large stages and theater screens. And horror is leading the charge.

What are you most looking forward to seeing in the horror genre in the future?

Horror has always evolved and reflected with the times. As we are experiencing such a volatile time in history on so many levels, I'm excited to read and see how the genre will react through its stories and the discussions they'll inspire.

John Palisano's writing has appeared in venues such as *Cemetery Dance*, *Fangoria*, *Weird Tales, Space & Time*, and *McFarland Press*. He's been quoted in *Vanity Fair*, the *Los Angeles Times*, and *The Writer*. He's been awarded the Bram Stoker Award®, the Yog Soggoth award and more. Visit: www.johnpalisano.com

CHRIS PANATIER

Why do you write horror?

I'm always refining this answer as I learn more about myself. I think writing horror is like holding up a mirror to humanity. In some cases it's hyperbolic, in others, there's no way we can capture the true terror humans are capable of. Whatever those limits are, I think it's an exercise in empathy for me to explore them and maybe share what I discover with others. Oh, and I love violent comeuppance.

What are you most excited about in the horror genre today?

Horror is so self-aware lately. Since the genre is defined (at least in the mainstream) by tropes, horror authors are working overtime to question them, reinvent them, and cast them in new light. I like that horror writers aren't just writing for general readers, we're also writing for each other. The best thing is seeing one author say, "Hey look what this other author did! Wow!"

What are you most looking forward to seeing in the horror genre in the future?

I'd say clowns, but there's an anthology coming soon on that. I have been enjoying the entanglement of horror and science fiction in both books and media. Sci-fi has a dark side that is super conducive to horror and I like it when an author embraces both.

CHRIS PANATIER lives in Dallas, Texas, with his wife, daughter, and a fluctuating herd of animals resembling dogs (one is almost certainly a goat). He writes short stories and novels, and draws book covers and album art for metal bands.

MICHAEL J. SEIDLINGER

Why do you write horror?

I was the kid that scared easily. The dilophosaurus from Jurassic Park. The Dead Pool stage in Mortal Kombat II. Standing up in front of English class to deliver a book report or presentation. I was scared of it all. I think it was after the original Blair Witch Project got under my skin, something snapped inside my brain. Instead of running away I became determined to go towards the fear. I needed to understand the darkness so that I could be liberated from it.

What are you most excited about in the horror genre today?

You have to love how fickle the publishing industry is, right? One minute they're shunning a book because it's something that their P&Ls and prevailing trends mark as undesirable for their lists, and then they're all about it, a quick turn in hopes that nobody noticed. But we noticed. It's great to see horror getting more shelf space, more everything. What's most exciting though is seeing how many readers are also turning towards horror instead of turning away in fear.

What are you most looking forward to seeing in the horror genre in the future?

Continued diversification of the genre to the point where it's no longer about putting the stories into specific containers and more so about being so overwhelmed and excited by all the great books coming out that horror can no longer be contained at all; it becomes life itself, to be examined and understood on the page.

MICHAEL J. SEIDLINGER is the Filipino-American author of *The Body Harvest*, *Anybody Home?*, *Tekken 5* (Boss Fight Books), and other books. He has written for, among others, *Wired*, *Buzzfeed*, *Polygon*, *The Believer*, and *Publishers Weekly*. He teaches at Portland

State University and has led workshops at Catapult, Kettle Pond Writer's Conference, and Sarah Lawrence. He is represented by Lane Heymont at The Tobias Literary Agency.

ZOJE STAGE

Why do you write horror?

Somehow my brain evolved with a fascination for the dark side of human behavior: I grew up being more interested in villains than heroes, and trying to understand how the Holocaust could happen. Since then, I've come to believe that "monsters" are something that potentially reside within each of us, and a lot of my work has explored the good-evil duality inherent in human beings. The world is full of horror because we make it that way—for instance, it isn't a mystery as to why so many Americans die from gun violence: it's a direct result of choosing to value weapons over human life. As a sensitive, creative person, writing dark stories is a coping mechanism, a process so necessary that I would go insane without it.

What are you most excited about in the horror genre today?

I love seeing how more authors are using horror as a conduit to examine the flaws of society and the darker aspects of common human experiences. Horror as social commentary is brilliant, IMO.

What are you most looking forward to seeing in the horror genre in the future?

Total female domination. (Maybe there will be a future where we have to have a Men in Horror Month?)

ZOJE STAGE is the *USA Today* and internationally bestselling author of the psychological thrillers *Baby Teeth* and *Getaway*, and the psychological horror novels *Wonderland* and *Mothered*. Her books have been named "best of the year" by *Forbes Magazine*, *Library Journal*, *PopSugar*, *LitReactor*, Barnes & Noble, *Book Riot*, and more. *Dear Hanna*—the follow-up to her international sensation *Baby Teeth*—will be available Aug. 2024. She lives in Pittsburgh with her cats be available Aug. 2024. She lives in Pittsburgh with her cats.

Richard Thomas

Why do you write horror?

For me it's not about the gore, the violence, or even about scaring people. To me it's about the human experience, the emotions we feel, and how our lives can change at any given moment. As a young Boy Scout I saw a man plummet to his death off the St. Louis Arch, and that image stays with me to this day. So much blood—a sheen as wide as the leg of the arch. I've seen strange things over the years, some hard to explain. When I tell a story it's tapping into the uncanny, the new-weird, the unknown, and unknowable. I like to write psychological horror, but it definitely has a vibe—that space between neo-noir, the transgressive, cosmic, weird, and hopeful. I want it to be worth the trip, and those moments of peace, contemplation, and growth are just as important as the terror and bleakness of a unsettling story told well. It's a maximalist immersion, across body, mind, and soul.

What are you most excited about in the horror genre today?

To me it's the hybrid work that has a heart based in horror, but crosses over into the weird, the fantastic, the wondrous, and grotesque. I see so many original voices, and that's what excites me. My experiences with Gamut (past and present) have allowed me to read a range of stories by men and women, BIPOC authors, LGBTQ+ voices, global perspectives, rooted in culture, experience, and history. I find that fascinating. Dark fantasy is very close to horror, and bleak science fiction is a kissing cousin as well. So whether it's Alma Katsu, AC Wise, CJ Leede, Steve Toase, Brian Evenson, Stephen Graham Jones, or Victor LaValle, we're in a golden age of horror that gives us such range, so many unique POVs. I'm open to everything from A24 Films to Black Mirror to Yellowjackets. It all works.

What are you most looking forward to seeing in the horror genre in the future?

I mean, aside from one of my stories on the big screen, what I'm most looking forward to is the continued expansion of horror, the ways that we've shaken off the stigma, the criticism, the reductive nature of critics who deem it less, second-rate, low-brow. People have always sought out thrills, and the rollercoaster ride of a Bird Box or Annihilation or Come Closer will always entrance. There are new presses and magazines launching all the time. Support the ones that you love, and we'll have more opportunities for everyone. I love what I'm seeing now, but what's around the corner? Man, who knows that will look like? That's the thing about horror—when it's something you know, you get the silver bullets, the wooden stake, the container of salt. But when it's new, unknown, and different you don't know the rules, so it's harder to protect yourself. And that's terrifying.

RICHARD THOMAS is the award-winning author of nine books: four novels *Incarnate, Breaker, Disintegration,* and Transubstantiate; four collections—*Spontaneous Human Combustion, Tribulations, Staring Into the Abyss,* and *Herniated Roots*; and one novella of *The Soul Standard.* He has been nominated for the Bram Stoker (twice), Shirley Jackson, Thriller, and Audie awards. His over 175 stories in print include *The Best Horror of the Year* (Volume Eleven), *Cemetery*

Dance (twice), *Behold!: Oddities, Curiosities and Undefinable Wonders* (winner), *The Hideous Book of Hidden Horrors* (Shirley Jackson Award winner), *Lightspeed, Weird Fiction Review, The Seven Deadliest, Gutted: Beautiful Horror Stories, Qualia Nous* (#1&2), *Chiral Mad* (#2-4), *PRISMS,* and *Shivers VI.* Visit www.whatdoesnotkillme.com for more information.

WENDY N. WAGNER

Why do you write horror?

I write horror to look into the dark spot of my mind's eye, a place that can torment me and wither my spirit—but when I use it in fiction, I find I can bend it to my will. It's so restorative and good for me. Plus thinking up all this gross and nasty stuff is a hell of a lot of fun!

What are you most excited about in the horror genre today?

I love the diversity of writers and subgenres right now! When I first started writing horror in the early aughts, the genre was really overwhelmed with zombie stuff, but now there's really a subgenre for everyone to enjoy. Even horror nonfiction is flourishing! Horror is an absolute smorgasbord of delights right now.

What are you most looking forward to seeing in the horror genre in the future?

Mostly, I'm just hoping this growth and diversification can continue, so we have even more writers bringing even more fascinating voices and experiences to the field. I'd like the world to see that horror is truly for everyone.

WENDY N. WAGNER is a Shirley Jackson award-nominated writer and Hugo award-winning editor of short fiction. Her work includes the forthcoming novel *The Creek Girl* (2025, Tor Nightfire), the gothic novella *The Secret Skin*, the horror novel *The Deer Kings*, and more than seventy short stories, poems, and essays. She serves as the editor-in-chief of *Nightmare Magazine* and lives in Oregon.

DIANA RODRIGUEZ WALLACH

Why do you write horror?

I loved YA horror growing up. I was a child of the '90s, and I always cite Christopher Pike as my biggest influence. His books, along with R.L. Stine and Stephen King, hooked me on the horror genre. Small Town Monsters (The Conjuring meets the cult NXIVM) is my seventh published novel, but my first horror. And I feel it's my first attempt to write the type of book I would have read as a teen.

What are you most excited about in the horror genre today?

I'm excited to see so many women writing horror. There are a breadth of movies and novels depicting what scares men, or what men think frighten women. But not too many women I know are frightened of a Michael Myers slasher in the bushes. Both of my current YA horror novels, Small Town Monsters and Hatchet Girls, could be considered possession horror, but I think female authors (like myself) are bending the trope to show what really scares us—it's not a not a fear of demons, but a fear of losing control of our bodies. I'm excited to see how horror continues to look through a female lens.

What are you most looking forward to seeing in the horror genre in the future?

It's a cliché that in horror movies and books, the marginalized character is often killed off. It's hard to think of many final girls who aren't white. So when I decided to write YA horror, Hatchet Girls (Lizzie Borden meets Supernatural) will be my second in this genre, I wanted to include my Puerto Rican roots and make my multicultural characters the center of the story. Looking to the future, I hope the horror genre continues to expand to include more female, BIPOC, and LGBTQ+ main characters.

DIANA RODRIGUEZ WALLACH is a multi-published author of young adult novels, most recently YA horror novels. Her next book, THE SILENCED, described as Girl Interrupted meets Poltergeist, comes out in Fall 2025 through Random House/Delacorte. In October 2023, she released HATCHET GIRLS, a modern twist on Lizzie Borden, and in 2021, she published SMALL TOWN MONSTERS, named one of the "13 Scariest Books of 2021" by Kirkus Reviews (both Random House). Additionally, Diana is the author of a trilogy of YA spy thrillers (Entangled), startng with Proof of Lies. She has penned YA contemporary Latina novels, a YA short-story collection, and is featured in several anthologies. She lives in the Philadelphia area. Visit: www.dianarodriguezwallach.com and TikTok: @ dianarodriguezwallach

CHRISTA WOJCIECHOWSKI

Why do you write horror?

Funny thing, I never intended to write horror. It surfaced through my fiction organically. I feel it's the unconscious trying to make sense of disorder and change, to make accept and understand the dark realities we face, and a way to process trauma. Writing horror is a means of self-discovery and has given me a way to learn things about myself I would've never been able to face otherwise. I like to pass that on to my readers, that's it's worth peering in the darkness to find the gifts inside.

What are you most excited about in the horror genre today?

I love to read voices from new perspectives and different cultures. Though most human fears are universal, it's interesting to view them through the lenses of writers who've had completely different lives and were shaped by different experiences, societal expectations, and beliefs. I also like the nuances in style and voice. We now have wider access to diverse voices in the digital age and publications that actively unearth talent beyond established names.

What are you most looking forward to seeing in the horror genre in the future?

Humans are facing a time of exponential change. Technology is exploding and there are many possibilities as well as implications. I am excited to see how writers explore the future with the latest discoveries humanity is making. What of our own creations and discoveries are we afraid of? How will we navigate this future? How will it affect us mentally and physically? I like horror with great emotional and psychological depth, horror that is cathartic in some way. We're all in this world together, and stories will help us makes sense of it as we all evolve personally and as a collective.

CHRISTA WOJCIECHOWSKI is an American dark fiction writer who lives in Panama. She is the author of *The Sculptor Series*, *The SICK Series* (Raven Tale), *Popsicle* (Crystal Lake) numerous short stories, and the founder of the Writers Mastermind virtual writing community. Christa works as a fiction editor at *Gamut Magazine* and is an active member of the Horror Writers Association. She loves to play classical piano (badly) and sip gin and soda. When she's not reading or writing, she can be found rambling through the Panamanian wilderness with her mastiff, Jack Daniels. Learn more at christawojo.com.

MERCEDES M. YARDLEY

Why do you write horror?

There's something so deliciously thrilling about fear. Horror makes me feel in a way that no other genre does. It works my brain and heightens my senses. I can put my hand over my heart and literally feel it beat harder. I need that rush in my life. Horror also lets us experience and work out our fears in a safe environment, and that leads to us being healthier, more adaptive people. It increases our resiliency.

What are you most excited about in the horror genre today?

I love that horror is championing different points of view and marginalized voices. Publishers and editors are actively seeking new and diverse work, readers are reading more widely, and I appreciate the activism I see within the genre. We're taking each other seriously and standing up for issues that are of the utmost importance. This not only leads to better horror, but to a better world.

What are you most looking forward to seeing in the horror genre in the future?

I'm looking forward to the continuation of this renaissance of horror. It's becoming more mainstream. We're becoming more familiar with different subgrenres in horror and more adept at picking them out. There was a time when most readers, and not necessary horror readers, thought that horror came in one flavor: slasher. Now they're familiarizing themselves with paranormal horror, quiet horror, splatterpunk, gothic, psychological…oh my goodness, the list goes on and on! I'd love there to be less gatekeeping in horror, and I think we're on our way there. It's exciting. Long live the horror revolution!

MERCEDES M. YARDLEY is a dark fantasist who wears poisonous flowers in her hair. She is the author of *Darling*, the Stabby Award-winning Apocalyptic *Montessa* and *Nuclear Lulu: A Tale of Atomic Love*, *Pretty Little Dead Girls*, *Love is a Crematorium*, and *Nameless*. She won the for her stories *Little Dead Red* and "Fracture." Mercedes lives and works in Las Vegas. You can find her at mercedesmyardley. com

MENTOR OF THE YEAR AWARD

*T*he recipient of the Mentor of the Year Award is Lisa Wood. The HWA's Mentor Program is available to all members of the organization. This popular program pairs newer writers with established professionals for an intensive four-month-long partnership. For new writers, the Program offers mentees a personal, one-on-one experience with a seasoned writer, tailor-made to help them grow in their writing and better market their work. For experienced writers, it is an opportunity to pay forward the assistance and encouragement other writers gave them when they were starting out. In addition, there is the added benefit of growing as a writer oneself through the act of teaching others. In short, the Program benefits all who participate, regardless of their roles.

Established in 2014, the Mentor of the Year Award recognizes one mentor in the Program who has done an outstanding job of helping new writers. The award is chosen by the current manager of the Program.

Congratulations to Lisa!

L. Marie Wood is the recipient of the Golden Stake Award for her novel, *The Promise Keeper*, a MICO Award-winning screenwriter, a two-time Bram Stoker Award® Finalist, a Rhysling nominated poet, and an accomplished essayist. Wood has won over 50 national and international screenplay and film awards. She has penned short fiction that has been published in groundbreaking works, including the anthologies *Sycorax's Daughters* and *Slay: Stories of the Vampire Noire*. She is also part of the 2022 Bookfest Book Award winning poetry anthology, *Under Her Skin*. Her nonfiction has been published in *Nightmare Magazine* and academic textbooks such as the cross-curricular, *Conjuring Worlds: An Afrofuturist Textbook*. Her papers are archived as part of University of Pittsburgh's Horror Studies Collection. Wood is the Vice President of the Horror Writers Association, the founder of the Speculative Fiction Academy, an English and Creative Writing professor, a horror scholar with a Ph.D. in Creative Writing and an MFA in Speculative Fiction, and a frequent contributor to the conversation around the evolution of genre fiction. Learn more about L. Marie Wood at www.lmariewood.com.

THE KAREN LANSDALE SILVER HAMMER AWARD

The recipient of the Karen Lansdale Silver Hammer Award is Lila Denning.

In 2022, the Horror Writers Association renamed the Silver Hammer Award to the Karen Lansdale Silver Hammer Award in honor of the tremendous amount of work Karen did starting the HWA.

Our physical award has also been updated. Instead of a hammer, a new stylized sculpture has been designed and cast by the same company that mints our statues. We look forward to sharing the new design at StokerCon2023.

The HWA periodically gives the Karen Lansdale Silver Hammer Award to an HWA volunteer who has done a truly massive amount of work for the organization, often unsung and behind the scenes. It was instituted in 1996 and is decided by a vote of HWA's Board of Trustees. The award is so named because it represents the careful, steady, continuous work of building HWA's "house"—the many institutional systems that keep the organization functioning on a day-to-day basis.

Congratulations to Lila!

LILA DENNING is the acquisitions coordinator for the seven libraries of the St. Petersburg (FL) Library System. Lila has worked in circulation and reference and has done programming for children, teens, and adults. Beyond her current role in her library, she trains librarians nationwide on passive reader advisory. Her long, rambling road to the library included stops as a manager of a comic bookstore, a manager at Barnes and Noble, and a stint at a brokerage firm, among other adventures. In addition to her MLIS, Lila has an MA in Religious Studies with a focus on Holocaust Studies.

THE RICHARD LAYMON PRESIDENT'S AWARD

*T*he recipient of the Richard Laymon President's Award for Service is Brian W. Matthews.

The Richard Laymon President's Award for Service was instituted in 2001 and is named in honor of Richard Laymon, who died in 2001 while serving as HWA's President. As its name implies, it is given by HWA's sitting President.

The award is presented to a volunteer who has served the HWA in an especially exemplary manner and has shown extraordinary dedication to the organization.

Congratulations to Brian!

BRIAN W. MATTHEWS is the author of several books, including the popular *Forever Man* series. He's also authored numerous short stories, the most recent of which have appeared in *Weird Tales* and *Space & Time* magazines. He has been a member of the Horror Writers Association since 2012 and has served as a trustee of the organization since 2020. Among his duties as a trustee, Brian has co-chaired three StokerCon® conventions, acts as the Bram Stoker Awards® Show Coordinator, and organizes the Pitch Sessions for StokerCon. He has previously been awarded the Silver Hammer Award, now renamed the Karen Lansdale Silver Hammer Award. Brian holds a graduate degree in clinical psychology and worked for twenty years as a therapist, primarily for children and adolescents. He currents works as a financial planner. He lives with his wife, Sue, in southeast Michigan.

THE SPECIALTY PRESS AWARD

THUNDERSTORM BOOKS

*T*he HWA Specialty Press Award is presented periodically to a specialty publisher whose work has substantially contributed to the horror genre, whose publications display general excellence, and whose dealings with writers have been fair and exemplary.

The award was instituted in 1997, largely due to the efforts of long-time HWA member and specialty press aficionado Peter Crowther.

Congratulations to Thunderstorm Books!

PAUL GOBLIRSCH established Thunderstorm Books in 2008. Specializing in collectible signed limited edition hardcover books, our goal is to showcase authors' works in beautiful limited editions. From both new, up-and-coming authors to veterans of the genre, we publish some of the best in the field including: Brian Keene, Joe Lansdale, Christopher Golden, Philip Fracassi, Tyler Jones, Ross Jeffery, Chad Lutzke, Cynthia Pelayo, Jeff Strand, Hailey Piper, Paul Tremblay, Edward Lee, Kealan Patrick Burke, Jonathan Janz, Samantha Kolesnik, Gabino Iglesias, Adam Cesare, Kristopher Triana, Richard Chizmar, Gwendolyn Kiste, Wrath James White, and Ronald Kelly.

STOKERCON LIBRARIANS' DAY 2024

By Konrad Stump, HWA Library Committee Co-Chair

Since its inaugural outing on the Queen Mary during StokerCon 2017, Librarians' Day has brought the library and horror worlds together annually for an entire day of continuing education and engagement to encourage the expansion of horror offerings in libraries and to foster connections between authors and libraries across the country. As the Librarians' Day team prepares to host our 8th annual event, the growth stemming from the endeavors of Librarians' Day founder Becky Spratford is evident in the network of library professionals securing more horror titles for their collections, working with authors on speaking events and writing workshops, and offering innovative and thrilling public programming.

Summer Scares, the HWA's summer reading initiative, which is led by a committee of library professionals with decades of experience in advocating for adult, young adult, and middle grade fiction, continues to grow as it enters its sixth year. Yaika Sabat, Manager of Reader Services at NoveList, joined the selection committee, and NoveList became an official Summer Scares partner alongside Book Riot, Booklist, and United for Libraries. Books in the Freezer, headed by Stephanie Gagnon, became our official Summer Scares podcast partner. And, we've teamed up with iRead, a summer reading program that is used by libraries in the United States and across the globe by the Department of Defense for libraries on military bases, to get more libraries connecting their patrons with Summer Scares titles and authors.

The HWA Library Committee recently established a Library Advisory Council made up of library professionals who work in public and academic libraries, as well as organizations that provide services and resources to libraries. Besides myself and Yaika Sabat, the council consist of Maria Fonseca-Gonzalez, NoveList Librarian; Jessikah Chautin, Community Engagement Specialist at Syosset (NY) Public Library; Meghan Bouffard, Information Services Librarian at Sargent Memorial Library in Boxborough, MA; Carina Stopenski, Teen Librarian at Carnegie Library of Pittsburgh - Woods Run; Jocelyn Codner, Reference & Outreach Librarian at Chatham University in Pittsburgh, PA; and Rebecca Leannah, Adult Services Supervisor at Racine (WI) Public Library. We are working toward building and nourishing a network of library professionals to get more communities connected with the horror genre and create opportunities for library professionals to share the great work they are doing in their communities.

StokerCon attendees will have the opportunity to hear from many of our Summer Scares Committee and Library Advisory Council members during Librarians' Day in San Diego, and we cannot wait for you to join us for this fun-filled and informative day of programming graciously sponsored by LibraryReads, NoveList, and the University of Pittsburgh Library Systems. After we get to know our library professionals over coffee and bites, the day will kick into high gear with an interactive brainstorming session to generate ideas for engaging library patrons with the horror genre. Then, you'll hear from library professionals who have done just that, whether through book clubs and book reviews or public programs and author events, sharing everything from how to develop an idea and gain support to documenting the process and sharing successes. The morning will round out as library professionals share the buzz surrounding new and upcoming titles, and we've worked with authors and publishers to arrange some stellar free books and swag for attendees.

HWA Volunteer Coordinator Lila Denning will get the afternoon sessions going by moderating a discussion with StokerCon 2024 Guests of Honor about what horror means to them and why readers of all ages enjoy a good scare. Ben Rubin, Horror Studies Collection Coordinator at University of Pittsburgh Library Systems will follow this up with a discussion about the rising popularity of folklore and fairy tales in modern horror with Yaika Sabat and authors Gwendolyn Kiste, Lee Murray, and Cina Pelayo. Yaika Sabat will cap off the day with a session all about Summer Scares featuring 2024's spokesperson Clay McLeod Chapman, selected authors Rachel Harrison and Justina Ireland, and podcast partner Stephanie Gagnon.

Librarians' Day is a fantastic networking opportunity for authors to connect with library professionals. Please join us for a full day of thrilling discussion and frightful fun as we celebrate our love of horror.

THE HWA BRINGS HORROR TO ACADEMIC LIBRARIES

By Jocelyn Codner, Reference & Outreach Librarian, Chatham University

*I*t's easy to imagine horror-themed public library programming for children, teens, and adults, but it's not as common to consider what programming like Summer Scares or collaborations with the Horror Writers Association would look like in a university setting. In my role as Reference & Outreach Librarian at the Jennie King Mellon Library (JKM) at Chatham University in Pittsburgh, PA, I've had the pleasure of building programming for busy emerging adults and introducing them to the incredible world of horror literature. I was able to draw on the amazing resources of the Horror Writers Association, the Summer Scares program, my fellow HWA Pittsburgh chapter members, and departments at Chatham to feature horror on campus.

The horror programming at the JKM ranges from book displays and collection development to author visits and events that meet the goals of the university and take advantage of beneficial collaborations. Some challenges faced were a) a non-existent budget for events, b) steep competition for students' time and attention, and c) only one dedicated library staff member to manage all details pertaining to events and programming.

JOCELYN CODNER

COLLECTION DEVELOPMENT AND READERS' ADVISORY

The Summer Scares programming guide is a valuable tool for all librarians and booksellers. The selection committee does their due diligence every year to make choices that showcase not only the quality of the genre but the breadth as well. This guide helps me expand my horror offerings in my collection and is great to reference during readers' advisory interactions. The titles featured offer so much variety that there truly is something for everyone, even busy college students and academics.

BRINGING THE HWA TO CAMPUS

The JKM combined forces with the HWA's Pittsburgh chapter and various Chatham departments to present an evening packed full of local horrors. Authors Michael Arnzen, Sara Tantlinger, Nelson Pyles, and Douglas Gwilym gave wonderful readings of their work. We screened a short student film (created with materials from the Chatham University Archives) that explored the hauntings on Chatham's campus. And students shared their own paranormal experiences with one another, open-mic style. Chatham University has a history of hauntings, and students take pride in their ghostly encounters.

SUMMER SCARES AS PROGRAM SUPPORT

Summer Scares offers inspiration, opportunity, and support to librarians looking to expand their programming options. The JKM's successful Scare the Stress Away: Spooky Crafts and Meditations event series was inspired by a Summer Scares programming suggestion in the annual programming guide. These themed events feature a craft inspired by a Summer Scares book pick and are well attended by students. They offer a fun way to relax and take a break while also introducing them to horror literature. Through Summer Scares, the JKM was also able to virtually host NYT Bestselling author Libba Bray for an author talk, something that would not have been possible otherwise.

Alumni Programming

Being in Pittsburgh, Chatham was able to take advantage of the Horror Studies Collection at the University of Pittsburgh archives, managed by HWA member Ben Rubin. We facilitated a visit to the Horror Studies Collection for alumni in Chatham's Film & Digital Technology and Communications departments. This trip was a lovely way to serve our alums, support the mission of the Horror Studies Collection, and build relationships through the Horror Writers Association.

Collaborate with Your Alma Mater's Library

Authors, you may have already considered how to create relationships with local public libraries to give readings, run programs, or help host events. You may have had conversations with librarians about how to get your book on their shelves (every library has a policy for this). But have you thought about reaching out to your high school or college library to make those same connections?

Often, school libraries will be interested in acquiring the published work of their alumni. They might also be interested in partnering with you on an event for Halloween or Summer Scares, or maybe even in offering a workshop on writing or publishing. While every library has a slightly different policy, it's always worth reaching out to your old librarians or teachers to see what kind of potential there might be for collaboration.

Thank You, Horror Community!

Horror has served as a valuable emotional and intellectual outlet for Chatham's students and opened many doors for my library. Thank you to the Summer Scares program and the Horror Writers Association for helping to create such a rich community.

THE RISING POPULARITY OF FOLKLORE AND FAIRY TALES IN MODERN HORROR

By Yaika Sabat, Manager of Reader Services at NoveList

*I*t's beautiful to witness Librarians' Day at StokerCon. The mix of library workers, authors, and all-around horror lovers creates a buzz of excitement for the panels. You get to witness library workers so dedicated to learning what more they can do with the horror genre that they've come to StokerCon. As a member of the HWA Library Advisory Council, it's so rewarding to see members of the library world embracing a genre that, while often misunderstood, is so beloved by its readers, myself included. A lot of people don't realize that if you've registered for StokerCon, you can come to Librarians' Day without any extra steps; it's open to all StokerCon attendees. There are, of course, panels aimed at library folk, like Brains! Brains! Brainstorming Ways to Engage Your Community, How to Feature Horror at Your Library, and Summer Scares: A Thrilling Reading Program. However, other panels explore the different facets of the genre or highlight great upcoming books, like Buzzing About Horror Books, What Horror Means to Me, and The Rising Popularity of Folklore and Fairy Tales in Modern Horror.

If you've read any of the original Grimm Fairy Tales, the idea that they work well with horror comes as no surprise. The same can be said if you sit down to read folklore from across the world. Violence, death, children in danger – these were hardly the tales you've seen in animated family movies. Fairy tales and folklore, like horror, give their audience a glimpse into the current issues within a society. You can trace the slight variations through a story's history to what happened at specific times. You'll see shifts in the established folklore and fairy tales as they journey through different regions and ages. Horror has always done the same. Examine how zombie or vampire stories changed depending on the decade, and you'll see the real world reflected on the pages or screen. The presence of fairy tales and folklore in horror is not new, but it's recently had a resurgence.

I work for NoveList, a division of EBSCO Information Services. NoveList is best known for our databases that help you find read-alikes for your favorite books and explore new reading options; you can usually access NoveList through your local public library. If you're not sure if your library has it, ask! Library staff are always happy to chat about resources. There are so many ways you can search in NoveList databases, such as by genre, subject, and elements of a book (like tone, writing style, and character), as well as by searching reviews of the book. I wanted to get a sense of just how much of an increase there's been in the last few years in fairy tale and folklore-influenced horror. So, I started searching in NoveList Plus, looking for horror books with "fairy tale" and "folklore" mentioned in reviews or as a keyword, and by searching for a combination of the genres horror and "fairy tale and folklore-inspired fiction."

I found that, in the last five years, there have been twice as many published books that meet that criteria than in the previous five years. I'll admit, these were not exhaustive searches and while NoveList has thousands of books in the database, it does not have every book ever published, but it gave me an idea of how much this trend has grown. It also inspired me to make a curated Recommended Reads booklist highlighting these titles in NoveList. If you have access to NoveList through your library, you'll find plenty of great horror lists by clicking "Horror" under Recommended Reads.

To take a deeper dive into the rise of folklore and fairy tales in horror, join Ben Rubin as he leads a discussion with me and a group of authors who all have outstanding examples of this trend, Cynthia Pelayo, Gwendolyn Kiste, and Lee Murray. We'll discuss how this trend can attract new readers, highlight diversity through the use of various cultural traditions, and examine it from the perspective of authors, readers, and librarians. I can't wait and hope everyone attending will leave with a better understanding of (and excited to read) fairy tale and folklore-infused horror.

STOKERCON 2024
SAN DIEGO

THE MAGIC, AND MAGICK, IN POETRY

By Angela Yuriko Smith

*I*t's a well-known truth, poetry is magic… and magick. The practice of magic and the art of poetry have been deeply connected from the beginning of history, sharing a belief in the transformative power of words. This connection highlights the human desire to understand and influence the world through language, and to connect with realms beyond the visible. Poetry, in its most elevated form, continues to be an act of magic, enchanting us with its rhythms, stirring us with its metaphors, and reminding us of the profound mystery at the heart of existence.

In the beginning, the spoken word was more than just a means of communication; it was a powerful tool believed to influence the cosmos. Ancient civilizations, including the Egyptians, Sumerians, and Greeks, understood the profound impact of words. They crafted spells, incantations, and prayers with meticulous care, believing that the right combination of sounds, rhythms, and intonations could manifest desires, protect against harm, and communicate with the divine. These incantations were the precursors to poetry, blending the artistry of language with the intentionality of magic.

The practice of magic, particularly through the use of incantations and spells, relied heavily on the poetic qualities of language. Rhythm, rhyme, repetition, and meter were not mere stylistic choices but essential components that contributed to the efficacy of the magical act. The rhythmic quality of spells, much like poetry, helped in memorization and in creating a trance-like state, both for the practitioner and the audience, facilitating a deeper connection with the spiritual realm. This melding of form and function illustrates the intrinsic link between the aesthetic qualities of poetry and the operational aspects of magic.

In The Catalpa Bow: A Study of Shamanistic Practices in Japan by Carmen Blacker, the author questions Nakayama Tarō about the language of the gods. "Nakayama points out, we can detect in the god's speech the metre which from the earliest times has been fundamental to Japanese poetry, a metre of alternating seven and five syllables… Japanese poetry began as the utterances of a shaman in a trance. Its metre and poetic devices are not the work of man, but revealed from a divine source." It thrills me to think that in Japan, poetry began as utterances of magic in a 5-7-5 meter—haiku.

Throughout the Middle Ages and into the Renaissance, the connection between magic and poetry was further cemented by the works of mystics, alchemists, and philosophers. They explored the hidden correspondences between the human soul, the natural world, and the divine. Poetry during this time was suffused with alchemical symbols and mystical themes, reflecting a world imbued with magic and mystery. The notion that words could influence the material and spiritual realms persisted, with poetry serving as a revered means of accessing higher truths and hidden knowledge.

Poetry has long been a vehicle for expressing the ineffable, for touching the sublime, and for articulating a connection to the mysteries of existence that lie beyond the rational mind. The metaphors and symbols used in poetry echo the symbolic language of magic, where objects, words, and actions carry significance beyond their literal meaning. Poets, like magicians, weave together words to alter perceptions, evoke emotions, and conjure images, effectively creating a reality that transcends the mundane. This capacity to transform and enchant is at the heart of both magic and poetry.

Today, the overt connection between magic and poetry is hardly diminished. Even as scientific understanding pushes the magical worldview to the margins, the magical essence of poetry remains. Contemporary poets continue to tap into the transformative power of words to explore themes of identity, existence, and the unconscious mind. The words we utter now still influence our cosmos.

ANGELA YURIKO SMITH is a third-generation Ryukyuan-American, award-winning poet, author, and publisher with 20+ years in newspapers. Publisher of *Space and Time* magazine (est. 1966), two-time Bram Stoker Award® Winner, and an HWA Mentor of the Year, she shares Authortunities, a free weekly calendar of author opportunities at authortunities.substack.com.

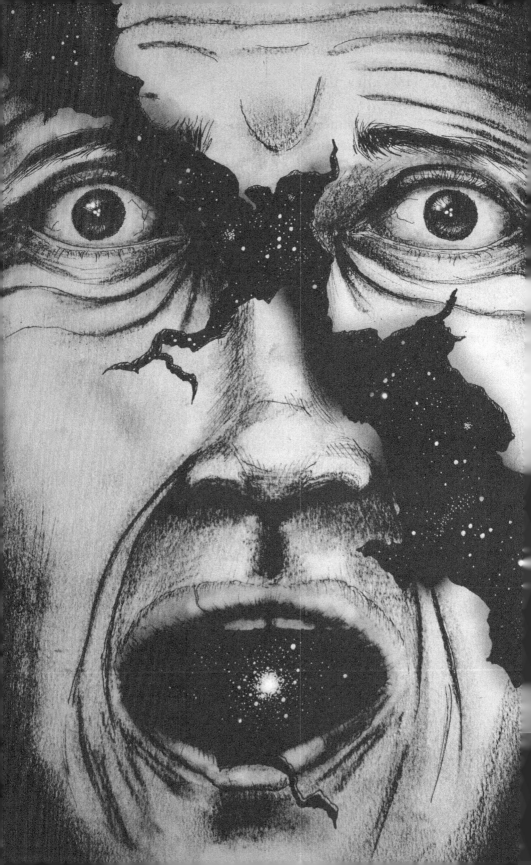

THE FINAL FRAME HORROR SHORT FILM COMPETITION

*I*n conjunction with our annual horror convention, StokerCon, the Horror Writers Association is proud to host the 9th Annual FINAL FRAME Horror Short Film Competition.

Each year, between ten to fifteen short-short films (13 minutes and under) are showcased as part of the StokerCon Horror Writers Convention. The coveted StokerCon Final Frame Award and cash prize will be awarded to one film and filmmaker, the best film shown at our event as decided upon by a panel of industry judges. We also present a variety of prizes to first runner-up, second runner-up, best writing in a short film, and the audience award.

Competition judges for 2024 include:

TANANARIVE DUE is an award-winning author who teaches Black Horror and Afrofuturism at UCLA. A leading voice in Black speculative fiction for more than 20 years, Due has won an American Book Award, an NAACP Image Award, and a British Fantasy Award, and her writing has been included in best-of-the-year anthologies. Her books include *The Reformatory* (a *New York*

Times Notable Book), *The Wishing Pool and Other Stories, Ghost Summer: Stories, My Soul to Keep,* and *The Good House.* She and her late mother, civil rights activist Patricia Stephens Due, co-authored *Freedom in the Family: A Mother-Daughter Memoir of the Fight for Civil Rights.* She was an executive producer on Shudder's groundbreaking documentary H*orror Noire: A History of Black Horror.* She and her husband/collaborator, Steven Barnes, wrote "A Small Town" for Season 2 of Jordan Peele's "The Twilight Zone" on Paramount Plus, and two segments of Shudder's anthology film *Horror Noire.*

PHILIP FRACASSI is the author of the story collections *Beneath a Pale Sky* (a finalist for the) and *Behold the Void* (named "Best Collection of the Year" by *This Is Horror*). His novels include *A Child Alone with Strangers, Gothic,* and *Boys in the Valley.* His upcoming books include the story collection, *No One is Safe* and the novels *Sarafina* and *The Third Rule of Time Travel.* Philip lives in Los Angeles and is represented by Elizabeth Copps at Copps Literary Services. For more information, visit his website at www.pfracassi.com.

JAMAL HODGE is a multi-award-winning filmmaker and writer whose films have been seen at Sundance, Cannes, Tribeca, Chelsea, and The Hip Hop Film Festival, among others. Jamal has been a segment director on the hit PBS doc-series Southern Storytellers (2023), and is the director of the upcoming series *Madness & Writers The Untold Truth,* Maybe? (2024). He is a Producer on the Animated feature film 'Pierre The Pigeon Hawk' (starring Will.I.Am, Jennifer Hudson, Snoop Dog, and Whoopi Goldberg). As a writer, Hodge is an active member of the HWA and The SFPA, being nominated for a 2021 & 2022 Rhysling Award. His work is featured in *Quail Nous 2, CHIRAL MAD 5, Unioverse: Stories of The Reconvergence,* and T*he Year's Best African Speculative Fiction 2022.* Jamal's debut poetry collection, *The Dark Between The Twilight,* is out now.

One of A.V. Club's 10 female filmmakers to hire, Izzy Lee is a director and author on the rise. Lee shadowed Adam Egypt Mortimer on the SpectreVision film Archenemy and is in post on her own feature, House of Ashes. Several of her short stories have found publication, including The Beginning in Dark Matter Ink's Haunted Reels anthology, curated by David Lawson, Jr. Released on 2/13/24, I Can See Your Lies is her first book, also from Dark Matter Ink. See what she's up to at nihilnoctem.com.

Lisa Morton is a screenwriter, author of non-fiction books, and prose writer whose work was described by the American Library Association's Readers' Advisory Guide to Horror as "consistently dark, unsettling, and frightening." She is a six-time winner of the Bram Stoker Award®, the author of four novels and 200 short stories, and a world-class Halloween and paranormal expert. Her recent releases include "Calling the Spirits: A History of Seances and The Art of the Zombie Movie"; she also hosts the popular weekly "Ghost Report" podcast. Lisa lives in Los Angeles and online at www. lisamorton.com

Rob Savage initially gained attention at the age of 19 when he wrote, directed, produced, and edited the low-budget romantic drama film Strings (2012), he later became more widely known for his work in horror films and has since co-written and directed lockdown horror hit Host (2020), co-written and directed Dashcam (2021), and directed Stephen King adaptation The Boogeyman (2023).

CURRENT HWA CHAPTERS

*Chapter descriptions by respective chapters,
compiled by Chapter Program Managers*

Do you live in an area where a number of HWA members reside, and you've all talked about forming a local chapter? That's great, and HWA encourages local chapters, which provide important face-to-face and online interaction as well as a wide range of possible local activities—everything from speaking at high schools to organizing book signings to hosting booths at book fairs.

As an HWA member, you can participate in more than one chapter and do not need to live in the geographical area covered by the chapter. However, you can only vote in your primary chapter's biannual election of chapter leaders. Complete the affiliation in your member profile to indicate your primary chapter.

Every interaction at a chapter meeting and online is governed by our Anti-Harassment Policy at https://horror.org/hwa-anti-harassment-policy/

The HWA Chapter Program Managers are available to help support US and International chapters as they form and grow. They may be reached at chapters@horror.org.

Contact information for existing chapters is available on the horror.org site under Chapters, and additional materials are available there in the Members Only section below the chapter list.

Here are the twenty-three current US chapters and four International chapters:

US CHAPTERS

CHAPTER: ATLANTA

Geographical area: All of GA, plus we welcome anyone from the surrounding Southeastern states who would like to join us. We have several members from TN, for example.

Chapter Co-Chairs: Gini Koch and Alex Hofelich

Secretary: Briana Morgan

Description: Started in 2018 by Gini Koch and the late Peter Salomon, the Atlanta chapter focuses on encouraging beginners to full-time writers alike. We are a welcoming, inclusive community that loves to write about scary things. In addition to writing programs at all meetings given by chapter members, we also do community service in and around the greater Atlanta metro area. First two meetings don't require HWA membership, so you can get to know us and all about the many ways HWA can help your writing career!

CHAPTER: CHICAGOLAND

Geographical area: Northeastern Illinois and Northwest Indiana

Chapter Co-Chairs: Shawnna Deresch and Christopher Hawkins
Secretary: Jen Mierisch

Description: The Chicagoland chapter is a group of amazing writers and artists from all over the Chicago area. Our membership includes writers at every level of experience, from best-selling authors to writers who are just starting out. In addition to our regular meetings, we work with local bookstores, libraries, and conventions to provide readings, signings, and panels that help our writers find new readers for their work. Since we relaunched the chapter three years ago, we've been growing quickly, but we always have room for more.

CHAPTER: COLORADO

Geographical area: Colorado State

Chapter Co-Chairs: A.E. Santana and Jeamus Wilkes

Secretary: Angela Sylvaine

Description: The HWA Colorado Chapter is committed to diversity and inclusion, which we strive to manifest through various means. This includes supporting and highlighting authors from underrepresented communities, ensuring our activities are accessible through online and in-person gatherings, and carefully considering the feedback from our members regarding what they would like to see in our community.

CHAPTER: CONNECTICUT

Geographical area: Connecticut and the surrounding region

Chapter Co-Chairs: David T. Griffith and Michele L. Bullock
Secretary: John Opalenik

Description: HWA-CT is a diverse chapter of seasoned professionals, newcomers, and writers of all levels. We are actively involved in local and regional events in coordination with libraries, bookstores, conventions and more, and exploring school programs to introduce children to the world of genre fiction and the opportunities it can afford. Our Discord channel serves as a central hub where members can congregate, workshop, post open calls, share event opportunities, and support each other. Monthly meetings are conducted by video call, and we host informal gatherings a few times a year so everyone can get to know each other in person.

CURRENT HWA CHAPTERS

CHAPTER: FLORIDA – SOUTHWEST

Geographical area: The I-75 corridor between Naples and Tampa

Chapter Co-Chairs: Douglas Ford

Secretary: Matthew Masucci

Description: With a membership that ranges from writers at the very beginning of their careers to *New York Times* best-selling novelists, our chapter functions as a welcoming community and a mainstay at Florida events and cons, such as Spookala and Spooky Empire. With monthly meetings, as well as occasional movie nights and seminars, we bond through a shared love for craft and our favorite genre. We prioritize celebrating the successes of our members and keeping each other inspired. A special shout-out to the Phantom History House B&B for serving as the location for our Tampa meetings!

CHAPTER: INLAND NORTH STATES

Geographical area: Idaho, Montana, Wyoming, North Dakota, South Dakota

Chapter Co-Chairs: Josh Hanson and Christi Nogle

Secretary: Gwen Nix

Description: The Inland Northern States is a brand-new chapter designed to give a home to a whole constellation of low-population states. We're just getting started, but we have lots of plans for creating a community for some of the HWA's most isolated members.

CHAPTER: LAS VEGAS

Geographical area: Nevada

Chapter Co-Chairs: Jeff DePew

Secretary: Mercedes Yardley

Description: The Las Vegas Chapter has quite a handful of talented authors who attend the bi-monthly meetings. We are a group that strives to encourage one another to succeed by discussing ways to write and story ideas while also critiquing each other's work!

CHAPTER: LOS ANGELES

Chapter Co-chairs: Kevin Wetmore and Joanna Parypinski

Secretary: TBA

Description: HWA LA has an active and robust membership. At our meetings, we often have a guest speaker, such as HWA President John Lawson, Librarian Goddess Becky Spratford, or Horror University Chancellor Jim Chambers. Eric Guignard shares a monthly short story market report. We close with our Round Robin, in which members share their latest news, a demonstration of how exciting and dynamic our chapter members are. We also sponsor tables at events like Midsummer Scream, the Los Angeles Times Festival of Books, and the City of San Fernando Book Fair. The chapter is currently developing a database of local horror writers for use by local libraries and schools.

CHAPTER: MARYLAND

Geographical area: Maryland

Chapter Co-Chairs: Jennifer Barnes and Stephanie Pearre
Secretary: Vaughn A. Jackson

Description: The Maryland Chapter recently celebrated its one-year anniversary. In that time, we've participated in a showing of the Blair Witch Project in its hometown, Burkittsville. We've had fantastic guest speakers, including library expert Becky Spratford, author Tim Waggoner, agent Cherry Weiner, Victoria Nations as a representative of the membership committee, as well as editors Mike Allen and Lesley Conner. Like true Marylanders we feasted on crabs.

We participated in several readings and tabled at multiple events. Our chapter was strongly represented at StokerCon in Pittsburgh, and we had the most epic white elephant gift exchange ever.

Chapter: Missouri/Kansas City

Geographical area: Primarily MO and KS, but we also have members from Iowa, Arkansas, Texas, Oklahoma, and Indiana.

Chapter Co-Chairs: Amanda Worthington

Secretary: Tommy B. Smith

Description: Horror in the Heartland provides a sense of community to horror writers in Missouri and adjacent states without a chapter. Recent efforts have included incorporating presentations from chapter members on writerly topics into our meetings and making inroads into rural pockets where writers of the macabre may find it difficult to find the support needed for industry success. We meet virtually but plan to supplement our meetings with in-person meet-ups. The chapter will have a presence at Authorcon IV in St. Louis and will also be sponsoring Between the Page's annual short story contest in Springfield, Missouri.

Chapter: New York

Geographical area: New York, plus many members in New Jersey

Chapter Co-Chairs: James Chambers and Carol Gyzander

Secretary: Chris Ryan

Description: The NY Chapter is more than ten years old and is going strong, with many longtime members plus new members joining frequently—both experienced and new writers. We have monthly online meetings with both a business agenda and social time, a newsletter with event and market listings, several critique groups, some in-person readings, and book-related events such as the Brooklyn Book Festival. We host the online Galactic Terrors reading series with chapter members and outside guests. Come take a bite of the Big Apple, whether in the NYC area or upstate orchards!

CHAPTER: NORTH CAROLINA

Geographical area: North Carolina

Chapter Co-Chairs: P.M. Raymond and Sirius

Secretary: Tori Fredrick

Description: If you call North Carolina home, come join the newly formed HWA NC Chapter! We've been pretty damn dynamic so far, with several guest appearances during our Zoom chapter meetings (including HWA president John Edward Lawson and Jonathan Maberry), an in-person reading at a local bookstore with 100+ attendees, and several in-person gatherings. So, yay for where we've been, but the good news is that we are just now hitting our stride, and the timing is perfect for YOU to join us and help create the group we are forming together. We promise that our initiation ritual is almost completely bloodless!

CHAPTER: OHIO

Geographical area: Ohio

Chapter Co-Chairs: Rami Ungar

Secretary: Neil Sater

Description: Ohio isn't just scary because we're a swing state. Ohio has more haunted locations than any other state, as well as legends such as the Loveland Frogman and the melon heads. Is it any wonder we have so many horror writers here, including some Bram Stoker winners? It's a great breeding ground for horror, and we're happy to be here.

CHAPTER: OREGON – HORROREGONIANS

Chapter Co-Chairs: Sarah Walker, J.B. Kish, and Elle Mitchell

Secretary: Frances Lu-Pai Ippolito

Website/Discord: Alan Lastufka

Description: The Horroregonians have been busy! In 2023, we ran several author events with the Portland Book Festival, HP Lovecraft Film Festival, and local bookstores. With the help of the amazing Alan Lastufka (Shortwave Publishing), you can find us at oregonhorror. com and on Discord, where our members lead writing sprints and writing challenges/prompts, plan events, and share successes and challenges. For 2024, we have many plans in the works, including a local horror author event that is scheduled with Beaverton City Library in October. At our monthly meetings, speakers present on craft, publishing, and marketing. Our Zoom meetings are on the third Sunday of every month from 5-6 pm PT.

CHAPTER: PENNSYLVANIA

Geographical area: Generally Eastern PA, but we welcome anyone, especially from the tristate area.

Chapter Co-Chairs: Kenneth W. Cain and Amanda Headlee

Secretary: Jacque Day Pallone

Description: We usually meet on our own Discord server but try to get together in person at least once a quarter, including a potluck feast. We also try to attend local events when possible and even have some field trips planned.

CHAPTER: PITTSBURGH

Geographical area: Western Pennsylvania

Chapter Co-Chairs: Ben Rubin and Frank Oreto

Secretary: Douglas Gwilym

Description: The Pittsburgh Chapter members include a diverse group of writers, librarians, and academics. In the city that brought us the zombie and now houses the HWA archives and the horror studies collection, it is a perfect place for all things horror. Our members are active with literary events in the city, including readings, book releases, and more. Always looking for more to join us in our ghastly endeavors!

CHAPTER: SAN DIEGO

Geographical area: San Diego

Chapter Co-Chairs: KC Grifant and Sarah Faxon

Secretary: Dennis K. Crosby

Description: We are honored to be the host of this year's Stokercon! Our chapter was co-founded in 2016 by KC Grifant. Since then, we've had a vibrant and supportive community of horror creators and fans—ranging from early-career writers to *New York Times* bestselling authors—join the chapter. We meet at the independent bookstore Mysterious Galaxy, and we frequently host readings and signings at various local bookstores and libraries. Our members regularly participate in literary and horror events such as Midsummer Scream, San Diego Comic Con, WonderCon, the San Diego Festival of Books, and many more.

CHAPTER: SAN FRANCISCO BAY AREA

Geographical area: San Francisco Bay Area + 50 miles, as far north as Petaluma and south to Monterey

Chapter Co-Chairs: Ken Heuler and Francesca Maria

Secretary: Ben Monroe

Description: The SF Bay Area HWA chapter is a supportive group of horror writers that meets monthly, discusses all things that go bump in the night, has lectures from our academic members, and participates in regular events like the Bay Area BookFest, LitCrawl, Summer Scares and more. Our members range from Bram Stoker nominees to novices learning how to stretch and expand their dark musings. All are welcome to join our merry band of misfits.

CHAPTER: SEATTLE

Geographical area: Washington State

Chapter Co-Chairs: Brianna Malotke and Josef Wilke

Secretary: Naching T. Kassa

Description: The Seattle chapter is open to anyone in the PNW who wants to join us! We meet every other month in person with a virtual option. We've worked with indie publishers for workshops for our members, and we've recently had social outings to attend book releases and signings. We're attending Crypticon Seattle and have a huge Spring Into Horror event with Barnes & Noble coming up in May.

CHAPTER: UTAH

Geographical area: Utah and surrounding areas

Chapter Co-Chairs: Cody Langille and Charlene Harmon

Secretary: Joshua P. Sorensen

Description: Our chapter is the go-to ambassador for all things horror writing in Utah. We've allied with the League of Utah Writers and are an established presence in the community, offering get-togethers, ghost hunts, specialized presentations, and publishing opportunities.

CHAPTER: VIRGINIA

Geographical area: Virginia

Chapter Co-Chairs: D. Alexander Ward

Secretary: Joe Maddrey

Description: In the past year, the good folks of the Virginia chapter of the HWA (who gather once a month in an always well-attended virtual meeting) have hosted three (3) beta reader workshops and have maintained chapter tables at four (4) in-state conventions. Also, nineteen (19) chapter members had stories published in Death Knell Press's recent Virginia-themed horror anthology, Dark Corners of the Old Dominion. We are always looking toward the future of Horror, and from the state of Virginia, the future looks amazing!

Chapter: West Virginia

Geographical area: West Virginia

Chapter Co-Chairs: Bridgett Nelson

Secretary: TBA

Description: "County roads, take me home..." To the monsters, legendary ghosts, and creepy "hollers" found in our state. Members participate in various bookstore events and local conventions.

Chapter: Wisconsin

Geographical area: Entire State of Wisconsin

Chapter Co-Chairs: Sarah Read and Dave Rank

Secretary: Margie Sponholz

Description: Linking more than 35 like-minded writers from across the state who spend way too much time staring into shadows. With quarterly meetings both online and in person, an annual writing retreat, and resources to help members advance their work. Attend book festivals and writing conferences.

CURRENT HWA CHAPTERS

INTERNATIONAL CHAPTERS

CHAPTER: ATLANTIC CANADA

Geographical area: Nova Scotia, Newfoundland & New Brunswick

Chapter Co-Chairs: Heddy Johannesen and Mike Hickey

Secretary: Tiffany Morris

Description: The HWA Atlantic Canada chapter comprises the Atlantic regions (Newfoundland, Nova Scotia, New Brunswick, and PEI). We offer opportunities for authors to showcase and celebrate their works. We are a fledgling Atlantic chapter that enables authors to engage in professional development and networking. The HWA Atlantic is open to new members & new opportunities.

CHAPTER: GREATER VANCOUVER, BRITISH COLUMBIA, CANADA

Geographical area: British Columbia, Canada

Chapter Co-Chairs: Janine Cross and Philip Harris

Secretary: Janine Cross

Description: We welcome all members of every level of the HWA in British Columbia to create a welcoming, inclusive, and accessible professional community of authors, poets, editors, publishers, artists, filmmakers, and other dark arts creatives. We host monthly Zoom meetings, email updates, a Facebook page, Book Swap & Beer get-togethers, and an online blog. We've hosted Bram Stoker Award®-winning guest speakers such as Tim Waggoner, screenwriter and actor Jamie Flanagan of *Midnight Mass* fame, Angela Yuriko Smith, *New York Times* Bestselling author Kendare Blake, Gwendolyn Kiste, Eric LaRocca, Hailey Piper, and L. Marie Wood (just to mention a few!). Come check us out!

Chapter: LATAM

Geographical area: Mexico, Central America, and South America

Chapter Co-Chairs: Hamant Singh and Victor Nava

Secretary: Sandra Becerril

Description: The aim of this chapter is to create a community of Latin America-based horror writers to share work that resonates with others. We are a friendly bilingual group that wants to promote the voices that come from this part of the world.

Chapter: Ontario, Canada

Geographical area: Ontario & Quebec, Canada

Chapter Co-Chairs: Monica S. Kuebler and Julianne Snow

Secretary: Melody E. McIntyre

Description: The Ontario Chapter of the Horror Writers Association is dedicated to building community and supporting genre writers at every stage of their writing career through a combination of bi-monthly meetings, our Discord channel, and engaging events, both online and off. We have hosted readings featuring chapter members at Toronto's Little Ghosts Books and have provided panel discussions and readings for Fan Expo Canada. Through our Twitch channel (twitch.tv/HWAOntario), our chapter has hosted several seasonal events, including Halloween and Christmas ghost story readings, as well as informative sessions on selling short fiction, etc. We welcome all horror authors based in Ontario and Quebec. Join us!

THANK YOU TO OUR VOLUNTEERS!

Ashley Santana, James Jensen, Kevin David Anderson, TJ Kang, Rachel Brune, Frances Lu-Pai Ippolito, Dianna Sinovic, David Agranoff, Q. L. Pearce, Doug Fruehling, Sarah Read, Chad Stroup, Kathrin Rohrmeier, Cory Oakes, Scott Sigler, Tiffany Michelle Brown, Allie Yohn, Max Kennel, Jon Cohn, Brian Asman, Brent Kelly, Kate Jonez, Kerri-Leigh Grady, Eric Guignard, and more!

ABOUT THE ILLUSTRATORS

CASSIE DALEY is a writer and illustrator living in Northern California. Her nonfiction has been published by Unnerving Magazine, and her short fiction has appeared in several horror anthologies. Her first YA horror novella, BRUTAL HEARTS, was published in 2022. She is also the creator ROSIE PAINTS WITH GHOSTS, the first book in an illustrated horror series for kids. You can find Cassie on Instagram and Twitter as @ctrlaltcassie, and you can find her portfolio and more at ctrlaltcassie.com.

RED LAGOE grew up on 80s horror and carried her paranoia of slashers and sewer creatures into adulthood, becoming a horror writer and artist. She is the author of *In Excess of Dark and Impulses of a Necrotic Heart*, and the editor of *Nightmare Sky: Stories of Astronomical Horror*. When Red is not spewing her most depraved thoughts onto the page, she can be found under an open sky with a telescope, dabbling in amateur astronomy.

A freelance cover artist and co-owner of Rooster Republic Press and Strangehouse Books, DON NOBLE has a decade of experience in bringing books to life. He is a lifelong horror fan, and his work is a love letter to the genre. Feel free to reach out for covers, logos, ads, and anything design-related that a book launch might need. www. roosterrepublicpress.com/

CHRIS PANATIER lives in Dallas, Texas, with his wife, daughter, and a fluctuating herd of animals resembling dogs (one is almost certainly a goat). He writes short stories and novels, and draws book covers and album art for metal bands.

ABOUT THE DESIGNER

TODD KEISLING is a two-time Bram Stoker Award® finalist and award-winning designer. His books include *Devil's Creek, Cold, Black & Infinite, Scanlines,* and many more. A pair of his earlier works were recipients of the University of Kentucky's Oswald Research & Creativity Prize for Creative Writing (2002 and 2005), and his second novel, *The Liminal Man*, was an Indie Book Award finalist in Horror & Suspense (2013). He lives in Pennsylvania with his family.

ABOUT THE EDITOR

CYNTHIA PELAYO is a Bram Stoker Award® winning and International Latino Book Award winning author and poet.

Pelayo writes fairy tales that blend genre and explore concepts of grief, mourning, and cycles of violence. She is the author of *Loteria, Santa Muerte, The Missing, Poems of My Night, Into the Forest and All the Way Through, Children of Chicago, Crime Scene, The Shoemaker's Magician*, as well as dozens of standalone short stories and poems.

Loteria, which was her MFA in Writing thesis at The School of the Art Institute of Chicago, was re-released to praise with *Esquire* calling it one of the 'Best Horror Books of 2023.' *Santa Muerte* and *The Missing*, her young adult horror novels were each nominated for International Latino Book Awards. *Poems of My Night* was nominated for an Elgin Award. *Into the Forest and All the Way Through* was nominated for an Elgin Award and was also nominated for a Bram Stoker Award® for Superior Achievement in a Poetry Collection. *Children of Chicago* was nominated for a Bram Stoker Award® in Superior Achievement in a Novel and won an International Latino Book Award for Best Mystery. *Crime Scene* won the Bram Stoker Award® for Superior Achievement in a Poetry Collection. *The Shoemaker's Magician* was released to praise with *Library Journal* awarding it a starred review.

Her latest release, *Forgotten Sisters*, from Thomas and Mercer is an adaptation of Hans Christian Andersen's "The Little Mermaid."

Her works have been reviewed in *The New York Times, Chicago Tribune, LA Review of Books,* and more.

She is represented by Lane Heymont at Tobias Literary.

SOUVENIR BOOK SPONSORS

The Horror Writers Association is grateful to its many sponsors.
We appreciate their generosity.

DRAGONS' ROOST PRESS

GEORGE A. ROMERO FOUNDATION

RUNNING WILD PRESS

THE UNIVERSITY OF PITTSBURGH

NOVELIST

ZOETIC PRESS

TOR/NIGHTFIRE

EMBERLETTER PRESS

HOUSE OF GAMUT

Nightfire & Tor Teen Congratulate Our 2023 Bram Stoker Award Finalists!

SUPERIOR ACHIEVEMENT IN A NOVEL

Chuck Tingle

Photo Credit: Sam Rand

SUPERIOR ACHIEVEMENT IN A FIRST NOVEL

Johnny Compton

Photo Credit: Louis Scott / Scott Photography

SUPERIOR ACHIEVEMENT IN LONG FICTION

Cassandra Khaw

Photo Credit: author

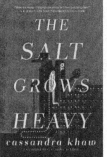

SUPERIOR ACHIEVEMENT IN A FIRST NOVEL

CJ Leede

Photo Credit: Sydney Angel Photography

SUPERIOR ACHIEVEMENT IN A YOUNG ADULT NOVEL

Kristen Simmons

Photo Credit: Anne Gregoire Photography

NIGHTFIRE

@tornightfire
@tornightfire

TOR TEEN

@torteen
@torteen

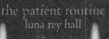
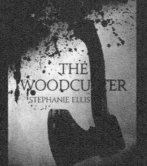
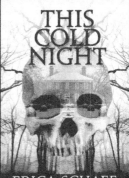

SIGNATURES

SIGNATURES

SIGNATURES

SIGNATURES

SIGNATURES

SIGNATURES

Made in the USA
Monee, IL
18 May 2024

58442739R00198